Read what people are already saying about

WHAT WE DIDN'T SAY

'A touching, even-handed and thoroughly engaging tale of love, jealousy and fatherhood'

Jim Crace, multi-award-winning author of *Harvest*

'At first it's a bitter-sweet love story, then it turns dark and harsh, then it's sour-sweet again, and you have to keep turning the page to find out where this intricate, irresistible novel is going to take you next'

Ferdinand Mount

'I love a book that evokes a strong emotional reaction and makes you think about the nuances of human behaviour and *What We Didn't Say* certainly did this for me. A wonderful debut novel by Rory Dunlop . . . A book I highly recommend'

Bloomin' Brilliant Books

'I think there is much in this poignant read which readers will be able to relate to. A book that shows the importance of honesty and communication'

Portobello Book Blog

'Deeply moving, insightful, and captivating . . . This is a poignant novel that reminds us that life is short and precious, and that   loved'

Than Books

WHAT WE *didn't* SAY

Rory Dunlop studied Classics at Oxford and worked as a teacher and journalist before being called to the Bar. He spent a year in Strasbourg, writing judgments for the European Court of Human Rights, failing to learn French and falling in love with Lika. They now have two daughters and live in London. He's written a text book on immigration law and several book reviews for the *Spectator* and, very occasionally, people read his tweets.

WHAT WE *didn't* SAY

RORY DUNLOP

twenty7

First published in Great Britain in 2016 by Twenty7 Books

This paperback edition published in 2016 by
Twenty7 Books
80–81 Wimpole St, London W1G 9RE
www.twenty7books.co.uk

This is a work of fiction. Names, places, events and
incidents are either the products of the author's imagination
or used fictitiously. Any resemblance to actual persons,
living or dead, or actual events is purely coincidental.

A CIP catalogue record for this book is
available from the British Library.

Paperback ISBN: 978–1–7857–7042–5
Also available as an ebook

10 9 8 7 6 5 4 3 2 1

Designed by Nicky Barneby @ Barneby Ltd
Printed and bound by Clays Ltd, St Ives Plc

Twenty7 Books is an imprint of Bonnier Zaffre,
a Bonnier Publishing company
www.bonnierzaffre.co.uk
www.bonnierpublishing.co.uk

To Lika, Mary, Connie, Mum and Dad

Here he was walking across London to say to Clarissa in so many words that he loved her. Which one never does say, he thought. Partly one's lazy; partly one's shy ...

In came Richard, holding out flowers ... roses, red and white roses. (But he could not bring himself to say he loved her; not in so many words.)

But how lovely, she said, taking his flowers ...

He must be off, he said, getting up. But he stood for a moment as if he were about to say something; and she wondered what? Why? There were the roses.

'Some Committee?' she asked, as he opened the door.

'Armenians,' he said; or perhaps it was, 'Albanians.'

Mrs Dalloway by Virginia Woolf

Dear Michael,

I've put these papers together because I want you to understand some things about your dad and me. I'm sorry we haven't explained them before but we thought it should wait until you were eighteen. The easiest way is just to leave you to read what I've printed off – some emails, your dad's diary (with my corrections) and our letters to you.

You may wonder, as you start to read, why you need to know about the ups and downs of our marriage before you were born, but keep going and you'll understand.

Don't worry – this won't be your only present!

Lots of love,
Mum

Part 1

From: Laura Ferguson
Sent: 3 March 2011 16:06
To: Jack Randall
Subject: Call me!

Jack,

I know how it must have looked but it wasn't like that, I swear. I'm sorry if I said the wrong thing but I hadn't seen you in two years and then you just turned up with no warning. I was too shocked to think straight. Please give me a chance to explain. I'll call you again this afternoon.

Laura

From: Laura Ferguson
Sent: 3 March 2011 19:54
To: Jack Randall
Subject: Re: Call me!

I've called and texted so many times it's becoming ridiculous.
Can we just talk please? It's so easy to mistake the tone of
emails, don't you think? Even if you're angry with me, it would
be reassuring to hear your voice.

L

From: Laura Ferguson
Sent: 4 March 2011 02.23
To: Jack Randall
Subject: Re: Call me!

Jack,

I'm getting fed up with this. I don't need any more stress at the moment. I was worried enough, even before. If you want to have a conversation, as adults, then fine, call me, but I'm not going to beg anymore. This is the last email I'm going to send.

Goodbye,
Laura

From: Laura Ferguson
Sent: 4 March 2011 06.45
To: Jack Randall
Subject: Re: Call me!

Oh, Jack, you haven't done anything stupid, have you? You know how much I worry about you. Even if you hate me, just tell me you're OK. L

📎 The Strasbourg Diaries

Dear Laura,

I don't hate you and I've not 'done anything stupid',
whatever that may mean. I just didn't want to speak to
you. I'm sure you could have explained that happy little
scene I walked in on, and I'm sure it would have all made
perfect sense, but I'm tired of being the fool. I'm not calling
you a liar. I dare say most of what you tell me is true but
it's never the whole story, is it?

I don't want my last message to you to be bitter. I still love
you and I'll always want the best for you. I'm attaching
something I've been writing – I called it The Strasbourg
Diaries but, in truth, it's more about our break-up than my
life since then. I wrote it for myself – as a way of coming
to terms with the last couple of years – but I'd like you to
read it because, even after twenty years together, there's so
much we never said.

I'll write again one day, but not soon. When I came back
to London to see you, I was so full of hope and excitement.
Give me some time to adjust.

Your husband,
Jack

📎 The [Edited] Strasbourg Diaries [Part 1]

Dearest Jack,

I've been reading your diary and I don't know whether to laugh or cry – you misunderstood so much! I haven't reached the end yet – I got a bit too tired and emotional – but I've been adding some comments and corrections as I go. Please read them. I want you to see our break-up as it really was – just a series of misunderstandings and miscommunications. Maybe it's too late for us to undo the last two years but there's no reason we can't see each other, as friends if nothing else. I miss you, Jack, and I think you miss me too. So give me a call.

Laura

The [Edited] Strasbourg Diaries [Part 1]

I

I'm living, for now, in Strasbourg – a city of kitsch, cloying beauty; of Hansel and Gretel houses; of souvenir clutter and rusted postcard carousels; of sluggish canals and idle swans. When the sun is out, there's enough warmth to feel like spring. As evening settles though, and the shadow lines creep up the walls, the temperature plummets and the noise and tourists drain from the echoing flower-boxed streets. At night all is quiet and bone-piercingly cold. Nothing but cobblestoned loneliness and shivering sky.

I live in a block of flats above a shopping centre in Place des Halles. I haven't met any of my neighbours, save for the burly middle-aged man in the flat next door. I see him every now and then on the way to or from the lift, always in a suit and always accompanied by a pug, which prances proudly beside him, like a gangster's moll. I often tell 'Mr Pug', in my stilted O-level French, that his dog is beautiful but, in truth, when I see the poor creature's crushed little face, or hear its pathetic, snuffling attempts to breathe, I feel a mixture of pity and revulsion. Every time

I compliment his dog, Mr Pug smiles at me, in a knowing sort of way, as if to acknowledge a fellow connoisseur.

My flat is modern and functional; every inch of space is used. The electric blinds in the bedroom and sitting room can be made, with creaking, shrieking reluctance, to reveal the stiletto tower of the cathedral high above the terracotta rubble of roofs. Sometimes I lie in bed for hours, smoking cigarettes and staring out at that view, meditating over the past, the present and (when I dare) the future.

I've fantasised, many times, of returning home, but I'm not ready. My career is ruined and my reputation destroyed, but that's not what holds me back. I can't face seeing Laura with another man. It's better to be in a different country where there's no chance of bumping into her or anyone who knows her. I handled everything terribly, of course, but it's difficult to see what else I could have done. I suppose I could have just ignored it. Pretended I hadn't noticed. Or given her my blessing. Have the open relationship she always wanted. But I don't think I could live like that, always waiting for the next humiliation, stifling the anger and hiding the pain. Sitting at home alone, wondering when she'll get back and whether I should ask where she's been. I'd rather know she's not coming.

[Jack, you silly man, I never wanted an open relationship! I was faithful to you for over twenty years. I never had even the slightest interest in anyone else.

I think I know where this comes from. It's that story I told you about Julian, isn't it? How he let his wife go home with that other man, when he saw them flirting at a party? I didn't tell you that because I wanted you to do the same! It was just gossip. If you knew Julian, you'd have understood why it amused me so much. He looks so Establishment. He wears a Savile Row suit to work every day – there's never a crease in his shirts or a shadow of stubble on his face. And his wife is this shy little creature in pearls and cashmere who speaks so quietly you can barely hear her. I never got more than two words out of her at the office party. You couldn't imagine a less likely pair of swingers.

So if there was admiration in my voice (which I don't believe there was), it was only because I like it when people surprise me. You forget that, unlike you, I never thought sex was that big a deal. That's probably why I don't get jealous like you do. If, while we've been apart, you've found yourself in bed once or twice with that ex of yours (what's her name – the one with the eyes too close together, like a baboon?), it wouldn't bother me.]

2

It's 4 p.m. and I'm sitting outdoors at a round metal table in Place du Marché Gayot.

I discovered this square by accident when I was trying to get away from the crowds outside the cathedral. I walked down Rue des Frères and happened to glance to my right. Through the open windows of a café, I glimpsed a courtyard I'd never seen before. I retraced my steps and found a break in the stone walls that flanked the road.

A man-sized rock sits, unexplained, in the middle of the cobbled square. On all sides there are old wooden houses with zigzags of timber cut into their faces. Trees and parasols are scattered here and there, among the cafés and restaurants, giving a balance of light and shade. Nothing is quite straight – the flimsy metal chairs are pitched at odd angles by the rolling floor, and the tables wobble when you move your drink.

My café is the last one to have the sun and, for that reason, it's always the most popular in the afternoon. My waitress has a pallid complexion and two twists of curly black hair over her ears. When she served me yesterday, I noticed a tattoo on the inside of her arm – Chinese letters running down to a bluish wrist. It's hard to tell whether she recognises me. I've been here most days for a month, so she ought to, but maybe her mind is on other things – although we've spoken many times, she's never looked into my eyes.

A constant buzz of chatter echoes around the houses, like the noise in a theatre when a play is about to begin.

So far, I've resisted going over it. I bubble-wrap the past with little circular sentences like 'What's done is done' or 'It is what it is'. I know as well as anyone I'm lying to myself – that grief is more damaging if it's unmourned. I've seen so many patients use the same defence, with the same effect.

If this were therapy, I'd start with my mother but I'm done with that. There's nothing I could write that I haven't talked about and analysed already and I don't have the strength to push that churn anymore. I don't believe in blaming everything on parents. The idea of criticising Mum for my faults, when she gave me more love and attention than most people get from two parents, is unthinkable. If that's a defence, then it's one I'll never topple. It's a supporting wall of my personality. No, if there's anyone to blame, it's me, and Laura, and Zac Ford of course.

    [And Claudia. Mostly Claudia. In fact, almost entirely Claudia.]

It's hard, now, to recall how my life used to be. It's like being woken from a dream – I can feel an absence but I can't picture what's missing. I spent thousands of days with Laura and yet I can only bring to mind a handful.

I remember the first time I saw her – the black-haired undergraduate, breathless from the stairs, in a glow of her own beauty, smiling at some secret joke; the yellow pad of paper clutched to her chest; her Bambi-legged skip across my room. All through that first tutorial she smiled, and when she'd gone the mystery of her smile stayed.

[Do you not remember why I was smiling? Let me describe that first tutorial.

I've signed up for a course on Freud and literary criticism (without knowing or caring much about either) and I'm late. Caroline (I think you remember her!) is at the top of the stairs, batting her eyelids and thrusting her cleavage at Neil, who's dressed like a drug dealer, in baggy jeans and a baseball cap, even though we all know he went to Westminster.

Two tall, red-haired girls come out the door, staring into each other's eyes and laughing.

'Come in,' says this confident, authoritative voice. There's an odd burr to the accent, like a southerner pretending to be Mancunian.

At the other end of an ancient table is this extraordinary-looking man. Handsome, in a way, but the first thing I notice is the reddy-brown hair floating above his head like an Afro. His shirt is creased and the edge of his collar is frayed. His face is fine and angular, like a cat, and he has the palest, softest, bluest eyes I've ever seen.

'Sit down. Sit down.' There's something about the flickers of his mouth, or the light in his eyes, that makes it look as if he were about to tell a joke. He tosses us each a book and we flap to catch them as they slide off the table. 'This,' he says, 'is the Penguin translation of *Oedipus Tyrannus* by Robert Fagles. I've bought you each a copy. Now turn to page one, the stage direction at the top. Has any of you read it in the original?'

'No,' says Caroline in a sad, breathy little voice. By now, she's forgotten all about Neil and turned her chair to face this flirty tutor, tipping her breasts forward to give him a better view.

'Lucky you,' says the tutor. 'I had to spend a year learning ancient Greek just to read this bloody thing in the original. Anyway, one thing I learned, probably the only thing, is that there are no stage directions in Greek tragedy. So what we find here, at the top of page one, has been made up by Robert Fagles. Read it,' he says, looking at me and curbing a smile.

'*The doors open. Oedipus comes forward, majestic but for a telltale limp* . . .' I look up, smiling awkwardly because I haven't got the joke.

'What old Bob Fagles has done, you see, is he's thought to himself, *What do I know about this Oedipus bloke? A. He was a king. B. He had a swollen foot.* So Bob's put two and two together. The only thing is I don't think Bob's done much directing. It's not all that easy to act this one out. Have a look.'

So Mr Flirty hops out of his chair, lifts up his chin and puffs out his chest. He bows and makes his way slowly across the room, waving royally, nodding haughtily and having a quick peak at Caroline's boobs, all the time dragging his foot like a zombie. By the time Mr Flirty reaches the other end of the room, Neil is on the floor he's laughing so hard. Even Caroline, after a confused hesitation, allows herself a few high-pitched giggles.

By the end of that first lesson, I was in love with this funny, flirty man and his phony accent. He wasn't like the moody, silent boys I'd been out with before, who'd punch anyone that dared laugh at them. I worked so hard to win this man's approval, to turn those lovely soft blue eyes away from Caroline's breasts for just a few moments.

Poor Jack! It was the wrong student that turned up at your door at the end of term, wasn't it?]

But that's so long ago it wasn't really Laura, just a half-formed idea of a girl who grew up to be Laura. I was more in love with her then but I loved her more later, when I knew her, or thought I did. The years of days that connect Laura the girl to Laura the woman are out of reach. A great white mass of fear and regret pins me down and bats away my attempts to grasp for memories.

I want to understand where it went wrong, but my thoughts fall away, like a dying rocket. An invisible shield of resistance is protecting some truth I don't want to acknowledge. Perhaps I'm ashamed of how I won Laura – the older tutor and the fatherless pupil.

[I was not fatherless! Dad may have left home but I still saw him, sometimes. He came to almost all my birthday parties. And you're only eight years older than me! Do you really believe in this psychobabble? I don't. I'll tell you something. Do you know what my favourite memory is? It's from our first holiday together – in New York.

I'll admit, when we left London, I was still in your thrall. I had a job by then and you were the student, or at least the trainee psychotherapist, but somehow I still looked up to you as if you were my tutor, treasuring your every laconic remark and puzzling over each frowny silence. And when we stepped out of JFK, into the wall of warm air and honking cars, it was you I looked to first, thinking you'd know what to do. I even remember what you said, as we held hands on the ripped leather seats in the back of the cab, locked in the traffic over Queensboro Bridge. You said the city seen from the bridge was 'the city seen for the first time, in its first wild promise of all the mystery and the beauty in the world'. I was so in awe of you – I thought you'd just made that up, until you told me it was F. Scott Fitzgerald. But do you remember the next day? I'll remind you.

It's Central Park in the sharp of autumn. The rocks sparkling, the leaves maroon. I suggest a bike ride. You, the confident, wise old father figure, hesitate for a moment. *What's wrong?* I wonder. *Have I said something stupid? Can we not rent bikes?*

'I thought I saw some bikes for rent near the ice rink,' I say.

'But we don't want to go back there, do we?' you say, frowning.

'Come on,' I say timidly. 'It'll be fun.'

'OK,' you say, all manly and determined.

I can't understand why you look so grave as the bearded bike man in his bobble hat shows us how the lock and the stand work. You look handsome and young in your shiny red helmet, pursing your lips when I pay for two hours.

'So, it's just a normal bike?' you say. 'No unusual features? You just pedal as normal?'

The poor bike man is very confused by your questions. And then you take a deep breath and push hard on one pedal. Such a sweet, serious face as you turn in a slow, descending arc! When your shoulder finally hits the floor, you're still gripping tight onto the handlebars, as if you'd hoped, till the last instant, that they might stop you falling.

When you looked up at me, with your sheepish expression and wonky red helmet, you were a different person. I realised I'd misunderstood a lot of things about you. When you'd been so quiet with my undergraduate friends, it wasn't because you were too clever and mature for our conversations, it was because you felt shy and out of place. Your voice was always so calm and authoritative that you'd tricked me into thinking that you were always right and always in control. I didn't love you any the less when I realised you weren't. You could say that it was the moment when I began to love the real you rather than the idol I'd imagined.

So if ever I saw you as a father figure, that idea shattered on the New York pavement over fifteen years ago. And a good thing too. Far from wanting you to replace my father, I wanted you to be the opposite – Dad was good to me but he made Mum miserable with his philandering and his boozing.]

It can't have been just transference. Laura loved me long after I stopped being her tutor. She used to say all the time how lucky we were and how happy she was. Only three years ago, on the way to our anniversary dinner, she made me sit on the pavement under a street lamp and look her in the eye, while she told me how much she loved me. I found it weird at the time. I said I loved her too of course, but my mind was full of other things, like how long she'd want me to sit there, and whether we'd lose our reservation, and what we'd say if someone we knew walked past, and whether there'd be a mark on my trousers when I stood up. I remember it fondly now though and perhaps that was the point. Because, when someone tells you they love you nearly every day, it stops being memorable. I know she wanted me to be more expressive but my love for her was too obvious to need voicing, let alone repetition. It's like walking up a mountain. The view is less enjoyable if you have to stop every few minutes to talk about it.

[I made you sit down and look at me because, when you have something like we had, it's too easy to take it for granted. A relationship is not like a view because two people, standing side by side, may see it very differently. I wanted your reassurance that you loved me as much as I loved you. You used to say I was insecure because I wasn't sure of my parents' love (which isn't true, by the way) so why didn't you make me sure of yours?]

Sure we argued, as every couple argues, about trivial things like how often we went out and where we'd go on holiday, but Laura's bad moods never lasted long. And even if our holidays weren't in Mexico or Thailand, she found something about them to make her happy and that made me happy. For Laura's spirits were a kite to which I held the string – most of the time she flew above me, lifting me with her, but every now and then she'd drop to the floor and then I'd rush to detangle any crossed strings, and run and drag and jump until she was up in the air again.

[Why did you have to stay on the ground? And those arguments weren't trivial to me. If we do get back together (and I'm not saying we will or even that I want to), easyJet must no longer define the limits of our world.]

No, no. She loved me all right. At least until Zac Ford appeared. Maybe it wasn't *all* his fault – maybe he didn't set out to destroy my marriage and my career, but if Laura had never met him; if he hadn't come to my book launch; if he hadn't barged his way up the stairs into my world – with his radioactive tan, and his puffed-up muscles, and his manscara-ed eyelashes, all macho effeminacy like some post-modern Bond villain ...

What was he doing there anyway? His name wasn't on the Excel spreadsheets that Christine and I shuttled anxiously back and forth. Health and safety limited the room above the Princess Victoria to thirty people. Friends (colour-coded green), ex-colleagues (red) and family (yellow) made up sixty. For weeks we chased replies, called up substitutes, checked commitments till, with persistence, discussion and diplomacy, we had a confirmed list of thirty.

We were half an hour into the party and only ten guests were there.

'I'm dreading the speech,' I said.

'It'll be fine,' Laura said, 'you're a brilliant public speaker when you want to be. Just pretend the audience is made up of pretty undergraduates with big cleavages.'

'Very funny,' I said. 'It's not so much the public speaking I'm worried about; it's more the fact there is no public to speak to.'

'Don't worry. I'll write an article about it and make it sound like you packed out the Albert Hall.'

'No, don't do that,' I said. 'Everyone knows you're my wife.'

'So?'

'So, it'll look bad. For your journalistic integrity.'

'Journalistic integrity? Are you joking? The only reason most of us still work for that magazine is the freebies we get when we plug things.'

Christine came over to stand beside us. She looked worryingly thin – there was no curve to her upper arm and I could see the triangle of her shoulder blade. I wondered if she might be punishing herself for being single. We'd first met at university and in all the time I'd known her she'd only had one relationship. The mystery of why such an intelligent and attractive woman could not find anyone was often debated in her absence and never discussed in her presence.

[Only by you. The rest of us could see the obvious – that she was in love with you. Among my friends, she was known as Camilla Parker Bowles.]

'Hi Christine,' I said. 'I was just talking to Laura about the speech.'

'Oh good,' she said, 'I was going to suggest we make a start.'

'Now?'

'Yes, it's a good idea, generally, to make the speech at

the beginning of the party,' Christine said, 'before people
start to leave.'

'Let's wait,' I said, 'for the people who're coming late.'

'Mmm ... OK,' she said with an anxious look. 'But not
too long.'

Where was the best place to speak from? Whichever way I
turned, there were people behind me and gaps in front.

'Maybe Christine's right,' Laura said, 'and you should
kick things off.'

'Well, maybe, but Adam's not here and ...'

'If you wait for Adam, you'll be here till closing
time ...'

'He'll be here ... Who's that?' I said, as the stairs
creaked beneath us. The back of Ford's head appeared,
his hair pulled back in stripes, like brushstrokes. He was
zipped into a scarlet leather jacket that fell somewhere
between biker and poseur. At the top of the stairs he
paused and looked smugly around the room as if it
conformed to his low expectations. He stopped when he
saw Laura. 'Who is that?' I repeated.

'OK,' Laura said, as if she hadn't heard me. 'Good luck!'
She kissed me leavingly.

I was watching Laura head towards the stairs when I
felt a tap on my shoulder, and turned round.'Adam,' I said,
'you made it!'

'Of course!' He'd obviously tried to dress up but the
stitching on the shoulder of his jacket was splitting and,
by attempting to shave, he'd made things worse, leaving a
patch of stubble under his lip and some spots of blood on
his neck. 'I got here ten minutes ago. Your friend Christine
collared me. She, um ... she told me that you need to start
the speeches soon.'

21

Adam was looking down at his feet, embarrassed to tell me what to do, even as a messenger.

'I know that,' I said, 'but more people are coming.' He nodded and I was worried my tone had been too sharp. I wanted to tell him how touched I was he'd made it – I knew he'd had panic attacks in smaller groups than this. 'Thanks for making the effort.'

'What, you mean this?' Adam said, looking down at his frayed tie. 'Sorry. I couldn't find a new one.'

'That's not what I . . .' The stairs creaked again and I looked down to see Andrea frozen mid-step, like a musical statue.

She winced and caught my eye. 'Sorry, Jack, I have to get back for bath time. It's the most difficult part of the day. Luca will kill me if I'm late. Laura's promised she'll send me a copy.'

'All right, Christine,' I said, 'I'm ready.'

Christine had the microphone in her hand.

'Thank you all,' she said. Most voices continued. Christine coughed. 'Thank you . . . thank you very much for coming. It's my great pleasure and privilege to welcome you here and to introduce the author. But before I say a few words about him I'll just mention that I have copies of *Freud and Holmes* with me, over there by the stand, and there's a twenty-five per cent discount if you buy today. It has to be cash though as I haven't brought the card machine. Anyway, Jack has been a friend of mine since university so I'm biased but it's not just me, everyone at Wildebore and Fisher feels so lucky to be involved in publishing this book. It's very rare, trust me, to find an author who combines such intelligence, warmth and insight. And the book's not bad either.' Christine laughed.

'Anyway,' she continued, 'without further ado, I give you Jack Randall.'

Confused applause.

'Thank you,' I said, taking the microphone, crouching and unfolding my speech one-handed on my knee, 'so much . . .' The microphone was too loud so I switched it off. 'For coming. Can you still hear me?' Silence. 'I'm taking that as a yes. Anyway, I wanted to say I'm really touched and grateful you could make it. I thought I might talk to you, just for twenty minutes or so, about the central thesis of my book – how I see Freud more as a literary detective than a scientist. But then I thought, actually, the best way to thank you for coming is by NOT talking to you about the central thesis of my book.' A smattering of laughter. 'The friends among you will have heard it many times and the rest of you won't buy the book if I tell you the best bits.' One laugh. Some shuffling of feet. I looked up. The man in red leather was stood next to Laura, whispering in her ear. She smiled and nodded, without turning to him.

'So,' I said, skipping the next two paragraphs, 'I'll just get straight to the thank-yous. First, to Christine, my publisher, for having faith in the project. God knows, it's taken faith. I wondered, at first, why no one else had thought of writing this book. After seven redrafts and two years out of my practice, I realised that lots of other people had thought of writing this book, they'd just had the good sense not to do it.' Laura's chuckle covered the silence. Red Leather didn't smile. I put the speech back into my pocket. 'And secondly, to my wife, Laura, without whose love and support this book would have been finished in half the time.' Laura's bright eyes smiled at me. 'Sorry, that's a P. G. Wodehouse joke. In truth, Laura, I couldn't have done it without you. Freud said that work and love are all that matters. I'm a lucky man to have both.' Laura blew a kiss.

My heart beating fast, I handed the microphone to Christine. Thank God that's over, I thought.

Christine passed the microphone back and whispered, 'Signing.'

'What? Oh right, sorry, I meant to add that if you'd like, I'd be happy to sign your copy. I'll be in the leather armchair over there in the corner.'

I didn't want to think about the gaps in the room so I looked straight ahead at the beaming, ruddy-cheeked bald man in a tweed jacket who stood directly in front of me, clapping heartily. Who was he? He wasn't on the list, was he?

'You were brilliant,' Laura said, kissing my neck.

'No, I wasn't,' I said. 'I was awful.'

[You really were brilliant. I remember lots of people laughing, not just me. You were so funny and sweet and self-deprecating. You have this beguiling, shy confidence when you're up on stage. If your book had been marketed properly, and there had been more people at the launch, I'm sure it would have been a success. Not that it wasn't a success. But you know what I mean.]

'Please,' I said, 'make someone come to have their book signed. Pay them. Threaten them. I don't care. I just don't want to spend all evening sitting in that chair on my own. It would be too awkward.'

'Ha,' Laura said. 'Don't worry. They'll be queuing up.'

'I don't think there's enough people to make a queue.'

I nestled into the black-buttoned wingback and checked my phone. No one came so I got up in search of a drink. With a bottle of unscrewed white in one hand and two glasses in the other I looked down at the armchair. Was it more awkward to stand near it, waiting to sit, or to sit down while I waited. It looked weird to stand alone near a chair and not sit in it. And yet, what if no one came? It would look weird and fidgety if I sat down and got up a third time. Did I have to stay near the armchair? It's not as if it would be hard to find me. Could I not just walk around, talking to people? Or would it look like I was pressuring them?

Laura came towards me with the old man from the front row, who was still beaming.

'Great speech,' he said, handing me a copy of my book.

'Thanks,' I said. I sat down, creased the book open at the front page and looked up. He was waiting for me. Oh Christ, I thought, I do know him. But who is he? A don? A friend of Laura's parents?

'Good to see you,' I said. 'It's been a long time.'

'It has,' he said.

'Too long,' I said.

'Yes.'

'When was it last?'

'I don't know,' he said, 'but it must have been a few years.' There was a pause, as I tried to catch Laura's eye. 'I'd love a dedication,' he continued.

'Oh yes, of course,' I said, widening my eyes at Laura and jerking my head to the old man. 'A dedication. 'Who shall I make it out to?' I said.

'Just to me,' he said.

'What would you like me to write?' I asked.

'Whatever you want,' he said. 'You choose.'

I pretended to think. When he looked down, I stared at Laura and jabbed a finger at my name on the title page. She smothered a laugh. Should I ask him how he spells his name? What if he's called Ben?

'Hmm,' I said, 'my first dedication.'

Laura stepped behind him and mimed something with a clenched fist and an open mouth. I frowned. She did it again and pointed at her fist. I shrugged. Carelessly and a little afraid, I made a scribble that I hoped would pass for bad handwriting.

'Thank you,' he said, pausing his good humour as he squinted at the page. 'What does it say?'

'It says "Good job!"'

'Huh,' he said, still not leaving, as if unsure whether to ask for something else. 'Well, thanks.'

'Who the hell was that?' I whispered when he'd gone.

'Michael Towne, my godfather,' Laura said.

'Michael? Why were you miming a blow job?'

Laura burst out laughing. 'That wasn't a blow job, you idiot, that was a microphone! A mike. As in Dear Mike.'

'This is going to be a nightmare,' I groaned. 'Can you please stand in front of me and introduce yourself to everyone so I can hear their names?'

'OK.'

'Hello,' Laura said, curtseying camply to a bemused Adam, 'I'm Laura, the author's wife. What's your name?'

'Not Adam!' I said. 'People I might not remember!'

The wine tasted weak and the glasses were small so I kept pouring myself more. I had short conversations, always searching for a joke or a way out with each person who approached. Red Leather never came. He was always at the other side of the room and he never seemed to be looking my way.

At last it was just Laura and me. She went to the loo and I sat back in the armchair and closed my eyes to rest.

'Jack, Jack, it's time to go.'

I opened my eyes again. The chairs were on the tables and the light was too bright.

In the taxi, I slid in and out of sleep, mixing memories and dreams. The man in red leather was leaning over me, staring, as if into a grave.

'Who was that guy?' I asked.

'Huh?'

'The guy you were talking to at the party?'

'Which guy?' Laura said.

'The young one in the red leather jacket. I didn't invite him.'

'Oh, Zac Ford,' she said. 'He's an artist. I told him all about you. He has a friend who needs to see a therapist so I recommended you.'

'But why was he there? Who invited him?'

Laura mumbled something that sounded like 'dunno'. I was too tired to ask more.

Claudia, the young woman who came to see me, was not so much Zac's 'friend' as his girlfriend, or at least one of them. I should, of course, have referred her to a colleague – as I usually would with a friend of a friend – but I took her on because I was short of patients and income. I knew it was a mistake, although I had no idea how bad. My motives were not entirely selfish – Claudia did have serious problems and I wanted to help.

> [No doubt, no doubt. But are you sure you've identified *all* your motives in taking on a sex-obsessed model as your patient?]

Most of my patients could be divided into one of two categories: threatened men and bored women. The threatened man was typically someone with a high-powered job who felt ashamed of having to see a therapist. He'd be

forever trying to establish his superiority over me –
turning up late, for example, just to show he had more
important things to do. And if I made a suggestion or drew
a connection he hadn't thought of, he'd say something like
'I'm not sure I buy that.' Always the language of money.
He'd ask me to repeat myself or say I wasn't making
myself clear. He'd remind me how much he was paying me
and question whether he was getting value for it. It was
hard winning his trust. It was even harder to hold off the
countertransference and make myself care about someone
who made me feel envious and inferior.

The bored woman was equally difficult. Typically, she
had a relatively minor problem (insomnia, claustrophobia,
anxiety, etc.), which years of therapy had failed to cure.
When you probed, you'd find a gap in her life. She'd
given up her career to look after children that were now
at school. Her husband was away at work a lot, or had
left her. What she wanted was not a cure but a counsellor
– a person to whom she could complain, without guilt,
about the neglectful husband or the ungrateful children.
There was never any change or even desire to change, just
stagnating resentment, and it was hard to know what to do
other than to sit and listen and watch the clock.

Claudia was different. She was a beautiful woman in her
early twenties [mid-thirties] who was so malnourished she'd
stopping having periods. Her arms were bone thin and
there was a pinched look in her face as if she were always
pouting. She needed help urgently.

She talked about Ford in every session. In good moods
he was her saviour – the gorgeous and talented man
that had stood by her, in her hour of need. She spoke,
with jagged lust, of what he looked like topless in jeans.
Other times, Ford was cold and vain and cruel, a phony

playboy who'd tricked her and forced her into an abortion she didn't want to have. Each time she mentioned him, it made me uncomfortable – my mood would drop and I'd find myself clenching my jaw or shifting in my seat. Partly it was guilt. I should never have taken Claudia on. The therapy was polluted from the start. How could I be objective about Ford when he was the one who'd recommended me and he was the one who paid my bills? But the negative emotions I felt, each time she mentioned Ford, were too raw to be mere guilt. It was as if I were jealous of him for reasons I didn't dare probe. When Claudia stopped coming, it was a relief. I thought I'd never have to think of Ford again. I was wrong.

It was a Saturday over a year after I'd last heard from Claudia. Laura was twisting and rolling in our bed and I was lying still, enjoying the alarmless peace. Years of marriage had synchronised our body clocks but I was a slower riser so I'd often pretend to be asleep.

[Is this a joke? I always woke up before you. You didn't notice because you were asleep.]

'Are you awake?' Laura said. I ignored her. 'Are you awake?' she said louder.

'I am now,' I said.

'Sorry,' she said. 'I can't sleep.'

'That's because you're talking.'

Laura laughed. My eyes still closed, I listened to her snorting chuckle and it made me feel alive and happy.

'What do you want to do today?' Laura said.

'Be with you.'

'Come on,' she said, 'what else?'

'Have a massage.'

'No way.'

'What about if I make pancakes?'

'All right. Five minutes.'

I turned onto my front and Laura pushed her thumbs gently into my back. She was a poor masseuse but I liked being the focus of her attention. The pushes became even gentler and then stopped on one side.

'Are you looking at your phone?' I said, twisting my head.

'Shall we go to the cinema?' she said.

'I'm taking injury time for this.'

'How about *The Death of Mr. Lazarescu*?'

'Well,' I said, 'we could spend the nicest day of the year so far sitting in a dark room watching a movie about death in communist Romania.'

'All right,' she said, 'what do you want to do?'

'I'll answer that question when my injury time is over.'

'Ha.' She pushed her palms into the flat of my back a few times and jumped off. 'Done! So?'

'What about we go for a walk in the park and feed the ducks?' I said.

'We did that last weekend,' she said.

'I know and it was nice.'

'It was nice but it can't be our thing,' she said. 'It's a hobby for old people with plastic bags.'

Everything was right that morning – the tiles were cool but not cold underfoot, the whisk didn't spill, the batter had no lumps, and each of the pancakes turned with a flick and landed inside the pan. There are consolations, I thought to myself, to not having children. We could have these lazy weekend mornings and do whatever we wanted. Our friends would have been awake for hours by now, tired and irritable, fighting over whose turn it was to change the nappies, being nagged into yet another trip to the playground. I wondered whether to say this to Laura. It was a dangerous subject.

When I came back into the room, with the proud stack of pancakes, Laura was staring at her iPhone, clawing at it with the nail of one finger. I put the plate on the bedside table.

She turned lazily. 'Thank you, sweetheart,' she said as I got under the duvet.

'My pleasure,' I said. 'There's just one thing you can do for me in return.'

'Oh yes?' she said, smiling with her eyes.

She yelped as I tried to warm my foot on the inside of her thigh.

'Come on!' I said, as she pushed me away. 'I always let you.'

I leaned my head on her chest and kissed her neck. She dipped her chin into me. I put my hand on her hip.

'What about the pancakes?' she said.

'Oh fuck the pancakes.'

'Tell me something nice,' she said, her eyes flashing.

As I was rising onto my elbow, her phone buzzed. She turned from me to pick it up. She sucked in her breath.

'Guess what?' she said.

'What?' I said, trying to pretend I wasn't annoyed.

'We've been invited to a party!'

'Oh really,' I said, leaning towards her. Before I could kiss her, she turned away to tap at the phone.

'Don't you want to know whose party?' she said.

'Tell me.'

'Zac Ford! Isn't that cool?'

'Zac Ford?' I pulled my arm from underneath her and sat up. 'Why are we being invited to his party?'

'Does it matter? It's the opening of his new exhibition.'

'When?'

'Thursday night. Apparently, there's going to be a performance at the gallery.'

'Hmm ...'

'You don't seem very enthusiastic,' she said, frowning.

'No, no, I am. It's just ... Thursday ...'

'I checked,' she said, brightening. 'We're both free that night.'

'It would have been great,' I said gently, 'but I really don't think we can go, what with Claudia having been my patient and ...'

Laura looked at me watchfully. 'You told me Claudia didn't turn up.'

'No, she did for a bit. She was my patient for three months before she stopped coming. And that was less than a year ago. We can't go to a social event where I might meet a former patient. She might feel like she has to tell me why she stopped coming. She might even want to come back. It's just ... it's far too awkward.'

The phone buzzed again and Laura smiled. 'Claudia's not coming,' she said.

'How do you know?' I asked.

'Zac just told me.'

'Can you just talk me through this?' I said. 'So Zac Ford, a man you've met only once before, at my book launch over a year ago, where he turned up for no reason, has just texted you, out of the blue, to say please come to my party, I've just split up with my girlfriend?'

'She was never his girlfriend,' Laura said.

'How do you know that?'

'Oh, someone told me. Whatever. It doesn't matter. The point is I knew you'd worry about Claudia being there so I asked Zac if she was coming and he said no.'

'Really?

'Really.'

'Hmm.'

'So we're going?' she asked.

'I don't know,' I said. 'I mean, the doctor did say I shouldn't over-exert myself. So, maybe we should give this one a miss. Go next time.'

'But that was over two years ago,' she said.

> [I never would have said this and it hurts that you think I did. I was always more anxious about your health than you were. Do you not remember? I had to beg you to have that operation. You kept saying there was no rush, it was only prostate cancer, it might take twenty years before it was dangerous, there were side effects, we should keep trying, etc. I couldn't sleep I was worrying so much. I'd never have brushed aside Dr Kumar's advice.]

'It's only been eighteen months,' I said, 'and that's not that long after a big operation.'

'OK, sweetheart. Fair enough,' she said. 'I'll go and you just stay at home.'

'What?'

'You can order a takeaway, watch football, drink beer, go to bed when you like. Get Adam round. You'll have fun. You've never really liked parties anyway.'

'You mean you're going without me?' I said.

'Why not?' she said. 'I'll be fine. Or are you saying you don't trust me?' Her expression was stern.

I was stunned. There had been a time, not so long before, when Laura and I did everything together. We might argue about what that should be but, whatever it was, we'd be together. She'd even cried when I didn't go to her office party.

> [I didn't cry because you didn't come to my office party. I cried because I was tired and cold and perhaps a little drunk

and you were so late picking me up the doorman made me
wait outside. Also, I didn't understand why, just for once,
Adam couldn't sort himself out. I felt bad later on, when I
was in the back of the car with Adam's mum and you'd gone
to fetch him from the hospital. Did I ever tell you what she
said? After you got out, we were silent for a few seconds.
I thought she might have forgotten me but then she turned
and said, 'He's like a doctor, isn't he? So reassuring.']

'I'm not saying I don't trust you,' I said. 'I'm just
saying ... Never mind. I'll probably be more in the mood
on Thursday.'

'So, we're going?' Her girlish good humour had
returned.

'OK,' I said. She squealed and kissed me on the cheek. I
hesitated, worried it would spoil her mood, before asking,
'Did you give him your telephone number at my book
launch?'

'Who?' she said, looking down at her phone.

'Ford.'

'Oh come on, Jack.' She turned to me. 'You know
you don't have to be jealous. We only talked for five
minutes. I told you, all I talked to him about was how
brilliant you were and how you were the best therapist in
London.' I said nothing and she continued in a softer voice.
'Sweetheart, it will be fun. It's so long since we went out
together.'

'We went out on Sunday.'

'That was the pub quiz. That doesn't count.'

[You make me sound like a Belieber! All girlish squeals
at the thought of Zac Ford's party. I was thirty-nine, not
thirteen! I didn't want to go to Zac's party because he was
good-looking or famous. I just wanted to go to a party, any
party. Don't forget I met you when I was at university. You

spent most of your twenties single – sleeping around with baboon-face and all those earnest short-haired women. I spent my twenties with you. Which I loved, of course, but I also missed out on things. I don't mean casual sex, which I don't care about. I mean, I never had a time of my life where I was free, to do whatever I wanted, whenever I wanted, without having to explain myself to anyone.

Don't get me wrong. It's not that I wasn't happy with our life – I was. I didn't mind the pub quiz, even if it wasn't my ideal night out, and I do really like Adam, even if he is stuck in a never-ending eighties adolescence. I just wanted to see other people. And I don't mean 'see' as in 'sleep with'. I just wanted to broaden my world.

I felt lonely sometimes when it was just you and me. I told you this once but I hurt your feelings. Let me explain it better. You used to say that our relationships with our parents determine our character. The happiest memories of my childhood are the earliest, when Dad still lived with us. He'd bring home people every night: writers, publishers, journalists, pub storytellers, random school friends he'd bumped into in the street. Andrea and I would sit on his lap, listening without understanding to the laughter and the shouting. That's what I missed. I didn't mean I wasn't happy with you. I just meant that being with you was not like being with other people because you weren't other people. You were a part of me.]

3

I was not in the mood to rush to Zac Ford's party. I let Laura clatter on ahead of me in her busy high heels. She couldn't go too far as I had the map.

She stopped, turned to me and scowled. 'Why are you walking so slowly?' she said.

'Why are you walking so fast?' I replied calmly, taking my time to catch up.

'You know I hate being late,' she said.

'Well, you're the one who spent forty minutes getting ready,' I pointed out.

'You didn't warn me we were getting late.'

'Why is that my job?' I asked.

'You have a watch,' she said.

'I gave you a watch too,' I said.

'That was ten years ago.'

'You never wore it.'

'Watches don't suit me.' She walked ahead, before stopping and turning again. 'You never wore that Paul Smith jacket I bought you.'

'What's that got to do with anything?' I said, half amused.

> [I still get annoyed when I think of that jacket. You could have been so handsome in it. It took me so long to find it and you never wore it. You didn't even pretend to be excited when you opened it. The next time I saw it, it was in the bag of clothes you were taking to Oxfam. I was so hurt!]

'Give me back my phone,' she snapped.

'In a second,' I said. 'I think we're nearly there.'

'That's what you said ten minutes ago. Aren't men supposed to be good at directions? Isn't that what you're always telling me?' Her eyes glittered. I recognised the smile – it said, 'I've just landed a blow on you. If you strike back, I'll hit you harder.'

I rolled my eyes and looked down. The circle on the map was lagging behind us but, if I was right, we should now be on Montclare Street. There were no numbers on the doors, so it was hard to gauge which direction 21 might be. I noticed a tall, skinny girl dressed entirely in black standing in an open doorway.

Before I could say anything Laura cut in. 'There it is.' She pointed to where I'd been looking and we crossed the road. 'Lucky you had me with you, eh?' she said.

I snorted, but not so loud that she could hear.

The tall girl passed a silver pen several times up and down a list of names on a clipboard, as if she didn't realise they were in alphabetical order, then waved us in.

'The performance is about to begin,' she said. 'In the basement. You'd better hurry.'

We entered an enormous room with a concrete floor and glass walls on two sides, like the corner of a fish tank. There were thirty or forty people inside, all lit by the

37

demonic rays of the setting sun. I was the only person in the room wearing a suit.

A queue had formed in the stairs that led down to the basement. It was hard to tell whether they were trying to go up or down or neither. Near the top of the stairs was a plastic bucket overflowing with bottles and ice. The beer was a Japanese brand I'd never heard of.

'Have you noticed,' I said, handing a beer to Laura, 'that all the other men in this room have either got a beard or a skirt or both? Was there a dress code? Beards and trannies?'

'Very funny,' Laura said in an unamused voice. I double-checked and she was frowning. Usually I could dissolve her bad moods with a joke. It was only at the peak of her anger I couldn't make her laugh.

The queue wasn't moving. As I collected a second beer Laura hissed, 'Are you coming?' She was halfway down the stairs.

In the middle of the basement were ten or fifteen actors frozen as if in the middle of a bar fight, fists resting against cheeks, tables balanced on heads. The guests surrounded them, silent as if they were watching a play. For several seconds no one moved. A fat man with a large camera round his neck walked through the middle taking close-ups of the actors.

'I think I've seen these guys before in Covent Garden,' I whispered to Laura. 'One of them was Charlie Chaplin.'

'Shh!' said Laura. She still wasn't smiling.

I couldn't understand it. She was always irritated when we were late but that should have worn off by now. She was no more a fan of contemporary art than I was. Yet here she was staring intently at the human statues, pretending not to notice me.

[I wasn't pretending not to notice you; I was just concentrating. The human statues were actually moving very slowly. Apparently, that was the point – the piece was called *Barfly* and it was supposed to show how a fly would see a bar-room fight. You're probably right, it probably was all bullshit, but at the time I was trying to keep an open mind.]

I waited a bit longer but nothing happened so I went upstairs for another beer. A man in a three-piece linen suit with a trilby hat was standing next to the beers.

'You're wearing a suit!' I said. He looked confused. 'I thought I was the only one.'

I opened a bottle of beer and we introduced ourselves. He was called Timmy. I asked if he was a collector, and he said he dabbled. I asked if he'd bought any of Zac's work and he looked at me coyly, as if I'd said something indiscreet.

'Timmy!' A bearded man with hairy legs and bright red shorts leaned across me to kiss Timmy twice on the cheeks.

They chatted and I loitered by the side, unsure whether I should stay or go. I looked around the room and there was no obvious person to talk to, so I interrupted.

'You both know more about contemporary art than me. Can you explain something? How does performance art work economically? I mean, with painting I get it. Someone buys the painting and hangs it on their wall. But that thing with all the actors downstairs. How does anyone buy it? And if they don't buy it, how does the artist make a living out of it?'

'You mean money? You're asking how they make money?' Timmy asked.

'Well, yes. I am.'

'I couldn't tell you.' Timmy frowned. 'Not my field. I believe there are ways.'

39

I saw Laura at the other end of the room, in a semicircle of people staring at a small square canvas with red splotches on it. Ford was in the middle. He was wearing torn designer jeans and a tight grey T-shirt that showed up every contour of his pecs. (Bodybuilding is a classic sign of insecurity – a shell to hide behind.) He'd grown a thick beard since last I saw him (another barrier). I crossed the room until I was just behind Laura. She didn't turn. Ford's eyes darted around like a nervous fly as he talked. His words flashed past my brain and I couldn't make out what he was saying. I was studying the back of Laura's cheek, trying to figure out if she was cross with me. I kissed her on the neck and she stiffened. Why was she so angry with me?

[I wasn't angry; I was just focussing on Zac. He was talking about how he'd made the pigment in exactly the same way that a fifteenth-century painter would have made it. He matched the colour perfectly with a portrait by Botticelli and then squeezed the paint through small skin-like pores onto the canvas so it looked like blood. This is what we have to do with art, he was saying – we have to be violent with it. Now that we have cameras and TVs, Renaissance art is pointless. We have to crush and destroy it to create something new.

Maybe I was a bit irritated. Your body language, when we arrived, was like a sulky teenager who's been dragged to their cousin's wedding. Even when you were stood behind me, I could picture your grumpy face. It made me feel guilty and that annoyed me as it wasn't my fault. I'd warned you not to come.

I know, I know. I should have been more sympathetic. My poor anti-socialite. A Zac Ford party must have been as terrifying to you as getting on a bicycle! I feel quite touched

now, when I think of you there, standing apart from the
trendy crowd in your grey suit, too proud to complain and
too shy to mingle.]

I replayed the conversation before we'd arrived and
savoured the injustice – it was her decision to turn left out
of Whitechapel; I was the one who'd got us back on the
right track and yet she blamed me for us getting lost. It was
completely irrational.

[Of course I don't care about this now but it was
definitely you that took a wrong turn.]

Ford paused and I looked at him.

'And then,' he said, 'I stop . . .'

There was a silence. We waited for him to continue. He
said nothing. Time passed.

'Why do you stop?' The man who asked this was
standing apart from the rest of the group, wearing an
Adidas T-shirt and a mustard yellow skirt over his jeans.
He looked surly, as if he were annoyed that he had to ask.

'I stop,' Ford said, 'because there's nothing more to say.
The white blends into the walls and disappears into silence.
Come,' he continued after a long pause, 'I want to show
you something else.' He led us to a collage of poorly cut
paper. You could just about make out that the paper had
once been a painting of a child.

'Sometimes,' he said, 'you hear people say, about
contemporary art, that a child could have made this. And
I think to myself if only . . . if only . . . Because if you're an
artist, that's what you try to find – the freedom of the child.
It's so hard, when you're an adult, to free yourself. Most
adults just copy, you know . . . The only time in our lives
that we have the full power of originality is when we're
children. You know I work a lot with children. I mean,
most days I'm in Great Ormond Street or the Evelina or

the Royal Alexandra. And people always say that it's very kind of me, but really it's not. Because I get so much out of it. Children have so much to teach us. So this work here, for example, it started with me painting a little boy, five years old, called Marcus. Such a brave, bright boy. When I finished, I gave Marcus the painting and I said, "Cut it, cut it any way you want," and he cut it with these cute little children's scissors with rounded ends. And then, when we had maybe twenty or thirty pieces, I said to him, "I want you to glue those pieces together so it looks like how you feel." And the interesting thing was he didn't try and put the pieces back together like a jigsaw. He put them in an order that no adult would have followed.' One of Zac's sockless loafered feet jiggled as he spoke. 'So I made a series of these portraits and I'm selling them now in an auction and all the money's going to Great Ormond Street.'

'Wow, that's great,' Laura said in a husky voice that she reserves for those who don't know her.

[I've never said 'wow' in my life.]

'No,' Ford said, flicking his hand as if he were brushing away a mosquito, 'seriously. What I do is nothing compared to those guys at Great Ormond Street.' I looked around for an eye to catch but all the other faces were serious. 'And the kids there,' he continued, 'are so amazing. Children reflect the society they live in and here in the West that means children are often so materialistic. They watch Nickelodeon and they see a hundred adverts an hour for toys and they think that's what they want, and the parents buy them this plastic crap they don't even play with – little cash tills to prepare them for a life of supermarkets and credit cards. But then you meet the children at Great Ormond Street and it's so refreshing because they look on life so differently. They don't want things; they want

to create. Paper. Scissors. Paint. That's what they want.'
He paused. 'I'd say children are my greatest inspiration.
They're right up there with Picasso and Gandhi and John
Lennon and Basquiat ...'

'Have you heard that guy talk?' I couldn't listen any more
so I'd walked off to get another beer. There was a stunning
girl of about nineteen next to the beer bucket. She was
wearing nothing but a black silk bra under a pin-striped
jacket.

> [This was 'Chaz' Fortescue (real name, believe it or not,
> Chastity). 'Stunning' is not how I'd have described her,
> although she did have that kind of blow-up-sex-doll look you
> seem to be drawn to – like Caroline, your old favourite.]

'You mean Zac?' she said.

'Yeah,' I said. 'I just listened to him talking about art. It
was *un*believable.'

'I know,' she said. 'It's rare you meet a true genius.' I
coughed and beer went up my nose.

When I next saw Laura, she was sitting beside Ford on a
white L-shaped couch on the first floor. The girl in the bra
was sitting on a Perspex box, staring into the mid-distance
and smoking a joint.

Ford was looking at Laura as if they were sharing a
joke. 'I like your style,' he said to her and laughed. I sat on
the sofa. Ford flicked his eyes to me and back to Laura.

'I'm Jack,' I said, holding out my hand to Ford. 'You
were at my book launch.' He looked blank. '*Freud and
Holmes: The Other Oedipus Complex*? Just over a year
ago?' My hand, which he still hadn't shaken, felt heavy.
Was it more embarrassing to leave it there or withdraw it?
'That's where you met my wife, Laura,' I said, pointing her
out with a nod.

'That's right,' Laura said. 'Don't you remember, Zac? You were in a pub and you happened to walk upstairs and stumble into Jack's book launch. And that's where you met me.' A chameleon's tail of a smile appeared and vanished from Ford's lips. He didn't say anything. Laura continued hurriedly. 'I was being so boring, just boasting about Jack and you said you knew someone who might want to see him.'

'Oh yes,' Ford said, crushing my hand, 'I remember now. I put you in touch with Claudia, right?' He let go and placed his hand on my shoulder.

'You gave her my number,' I said.

'Poor Claudia,' he said, his hand still on my shoulder as if he were consoling me. I knew what he was trying to do – 'tactile' men always start by touching the husbands – so I tried to edge away but he just gripped me tighter.

[Zac was probably trying to be friendly. When you get to know him, you realise he's extremely insecure. His father left home when he was only ten and ever since he's craved the respect of other men. He went to an all-boys school. He was big for his age but he wasn't into sport and had nothing in common with the other boys. He told me he's always found it easier to get on with women. I actually think he might be gay, or at least bisexual.]

'Don't you think Zac's work at Great Ormond Street would make for a really interesting article?' Laura asked.

'I don't know,' Ford cut in, 'I'm not into the whole self-publicity thing.'

'It won't look like you're boasting,' Laura said.

'Oh, it might,' I said.

'Not if it's written by the right person,' Laura said through a hostile smile.

Ford started talking again and I nodded without

listening. A waiter in black shorts held out a tray of spring rolls. I took one and dipped it in the orange sauce. It broke awkwardly in my mouth and a drip fell onto my lapel. Ford drawled on and I kept looking down at the stain, wondering if anyone would notice it. There was a pause and Ford said, with the rising pitch of a punchline, 'Not in this lifetime!' Everyone burst out laughing. Ford laughed loudest and, as he did so, he leaned forward and stared directly into my eyes. I felt obliged to fake a chuckle.

The waiter came back.

'No thanks,' I said, looking down at my lapel. 'I had a bit of an accident with the last one.'

'A couple more stains like that,' Ford said, 'and you might need to go to the dry-cleaner!' The others laughed, including Laura. [If I laughed, it was only out of awkwardness.] 'Or maybe it would be cheaper to buy a new suit!' They laughed again. 'Just kidding, buddy,' said Ford, who leaned forward to punch me on the shoulder. I kept up a smile, to make it seem like I didn't care, till the laughter died.

I was looking around the room, so I wouldn't have to look at Ford, when I saw someone that looked like Christine. My smile relaxed when I realised it was her.

'I've just seen someone I should say hello to,' I said, standing up. No one replied.

Christine was standing as still as a mannequin, listening to a handsome man in a tight grey T-shirt. When I touched her elbow, her eyes widened in shock before she smiled. The man she'd been speaking to disappeared in the time it took to kiss her on both cheeks.

'I'm sorry,' I said, 'I didn't mean to intrude ...'

'Don't worry,' she said. 'You didn't interrupt anything. It's been a long time, Jack. I seem to see you less and less now! Why is that?'

'I don't know,' I said. I folded my arms and held my beer bottle in front of the stained lapel. 'I'm so happy to see you.' It didn't sound right. I hadn't said it with enough enthusiasm. What I meant was I would have been happy to see her if I wasn't bridling with irritation at Ford's put-down. 'It's stupid how seldom we meet. The few of us who don't have children should stick together!' Christine said nothing and I winced. 'So,' I continued as cheerily as I could, 'are you a Zac Ford fan?'

'I was,' she said.

'What happened?'

'Oh, nothing,' she said. 'I just went off him. Have you been in touch with Marcus and Toby?'

'Not for ages,' I said, disappointed at the change of topic.

'You were such close friends at university. Do you remember ...' Christine began an anecdote I must have told her but I didn't interrupt. I enjoyed her enthusiasm and I found myself laughing at her impression of Marcus's face. We reminded each other of more stories of friends we no longer saw doing silly, funny, drunken things and I'd almost forgotten about the stain on my suit and the wound to my pride when I saw Ford and Laura rising from the couch.

'How long,' I said, looking at my watch, 'do these parties go on for?'

'I don't know.' The smile died on her lips and I felt anxious.

'It's not that I want to leave. I mean, I'm really enjoying talking to you. It's just. You know drinks parties are not my thing. Particularly not when everyone's so trendy.'

'I know what you mean.' Her attention was distracted by someone behind me. 'You see that guy over there?'

she said. I looked around the room. Ford and Laura had
gone. 'The one with the black silk shirt,' she said. 'He just
asked if I wanted a fuck. Can you believe that? We were
having a perfectly normal conversation – I told him I was a
publisher and he said he was a painter and then, when we
were getting on really well, he just stopped and said do you
want a fuck in those toilets over there?'

'Really?' I said, searching the room for Laura. 'And
what did you say?'

She frowned. 'I said no, of course!'

'Oh yes, of course,' I said. 'By the way, speaking
of would-be writers . . .' Her gaze shifted from me. 'Is
everything OK with the book? I don't want to pester; it's
just I haven't heard anything for a while.'

'Fine, fine . . . no problem . . . It's early days.' Christine
looked at her feet and then at the ceiling, tilting the last
dregs of her beer down her throat. 'I need another drink
and there's someone I must talk to over there. Do you
mind?'

I lied with a shake of my head, then scanned the room
for Laura, sifting through a jumble of images. A rosy-
cheeked man. A bowler hat. Fake eyelashes. Cockatoo hair.
Lipsticked snarl. No Laura.

'Steve Kinch.' A fat man with a camera round his neck
stepped in front of me, his face too close.

'Jack Randall.'

'I've been watching you,' he said. 'You're the new boy.
Or man I should say. And what do you do?' Ford and
Laura appeared on the staircase above Kinch's shoulder
and disappeared behind his head. 'I saw you talking to
Christine Wakeman. Are you a publisher?'

'No,' I said, stepping back. 'I wrote a book and she's
my editor.'

47

'Oh, a writer! Me too.' He smiled and somehow, without any apparent movement, he was too close again and I could smell his hot, sour breath. 'I'm freelance at the moment. Do a bit of work for Zac now and then. Press releases. That kind of thing. What's your book about?' Laura and Ford were spiralling round the metal stairs.

'Freud,' I said.

'A great painter but such a bastard.' He began a story about a neglected daughter and I stopped listening. It looked like Ford had his arm round Laura's waist. It was certainly behind her but the railings were in the way. 'What are you looking at?' Steve said, turning behind him. 'Oh, you poor man,' he said. 'You've got it bad, haven't you?' The staircase led to a door. 'I've see you doing this all night. You can't take your eyes off him, can you? Well, he's gone now. You're just going to have to let go.'

'What's up there?' I asked.

'Oh, you're not thinking of it?' he said.

'Can you just tell me? Is it another lounge or what?' I said.

'A lounge!' he said with a snorting laugh.

'What is it then?'

'It's Zac's bedroom of course.'

'Bedroom?'

'Yeah, he likes to sleep at the gallery sometimes. And sometimes,' Kinch said coyly, 'he just needs a bed . . .' I moved to my left but he followed me like a dancing partner. 'Oh you are such a spoilsport. You can't go up there,' he said.

I stepped past him and our shoulders clipped. He tried to hold my arm but I pulled free. I hurried up the clanging stairs two by two, and the room spun in and out of my sight. I paused at the top to catch my breath and lurched giddily at the handle. The catch clicked and two voices stopped. I steadied myself and pushed the door with the palm of my right hand. As it swung away from me, I froze, with my arm out in front and my fingers spread, as if to halt the scene that was opening up in front of me.

[While you were talking to Christine, Zac was taking me on a tour. He showed me several abstract paintings – brightly coloured dots or squares or lines scattered around a white canvas. He'd stand with me in silence and I wouldn't know what to say. I felt foolish saying they were pretty but that was all I could think of. Sometimes he'd give a brief explanation that hinted at more – like there were some curly lines, I remember, which were something to do with the way smell travels. Wherever we went you could sense that the people around us – however cool or glamorous they were – were excited to be near Zac. They wouldn't say anything. At most they'd catch his eye but you could feel their reaction. They would stop talking or whisper and steal glances at him and me.

'I wish I could see the originals of the portraits you did,' I said, 'before they were cut up.'

'Oh, someone might have photographs,' he said, 'but I never keep any. Do you want to know if I can paint? If I can do a good likeness? Get the hands right?' The truth was that I did but I didn't say it. 'It's so unimportant. Do you really think those people who sit at the edges of parks selling portraits of Elvis and Marilyn are good artists?'

'In a way,' I said.

He laughed. Chaz came up to us saying she was tired. She draped her head on Zac's shoulder.

'Well, go to bed, then,' said Zac. Chaz glared at Zac and then at me and walked away. 'Sorry about that,' Zac said. 'I tell you what,' he said, 'since you're so into portraiture, I'll paint a picture of you. You can do what you like with it, once it's finished, so long as I don't have to see it. But there's one condition. There has to be something original about the painting. You have to give me something you've never given anyone.'

'Like what?' I said.

'That's for you to decide,' he said. 'Come.' He pulled my elbow gently.

'Where?'

'Upstairs.'

'We're not doing the portrait now, are we?' I said.

'No,' he smiled, 'not now.']

4

I don't want to think about Zac and Laura today. Instead, I've been searching for the French edition of my book. Something troubled me, when I was trying to remember that conversation with Christine two years ago. She told me she'd sold the rights to France but when I asked her for more details she was evasive. My book's not in Librairie Kléber and the snotty man at the counter said there was no record of it on his computer. I've emailed Christine to find out what's going on.

In the internet café, I couldn't resist a look at Facebook. There was little change. Laura had a new profile picture – a photo from about fifteen [more like five] years ago. I scrolled down. There were some new photos, all with girls, and just one post – Laura had been to see some movie and wanted to clap 'like a seal' at the end. Some twat called Hubert felt the need to say, 'Not seen it yet but will do – ☺.' Why the wink? And why did this conversation have to take place in front of the whole world? And who was this Hubert?

[I met Hubert once in a Ceroc class. Andrea thought it funny to swap places so I had to dance with him. He was perfectly nice but all I could think about was the ultraviolet dandruff on his shoulder.]

Now I must return to that party. What a dreadful thought.

5

When I burst in, Ford and Laura were kneeling with their backs to me on the carpeted floor. Their elbows were touching and they were stooping over a vast mint-white bed. There was something corrupt about their posture and I cried out 'Laura!' They both turned with guilty expressions and, in the gap that opened up between them, I saw an upside-down CD, its belly striped with white powder.

[When Zac led me to the top of the stairs and opened the door, I was surprised to see a bedroom. I'd never been there before of course so there was no way I could have known. I was going to leave immediately but then he bent down to look inside the drawer of a bedside table and I waited out of curiosity. I thought it was one of his paintings he was looking for but instead he pulled out a coloured square. He unfolded it to reveal a page from a porn magazine with a pile of cocaine inside. As he marked out the lines, I was looking at the unlocked door wondering what to do. I was jumpy, not guilty, when you burst in, Jack. It's not that I wasn't pleased to see you – I was always pleased to see you – I was just on edge. And you looked so cross; it made me feel defensive. It felt like I was in trouble even though I'd done nothing wrong. I wasn't thinking about how it must have looked to you. It felt like the Allens' Christmas drinks, do you remember? When I was having a perfectly innocent conversation with that Sri Lankan guy at the bar and you elbowed your way between us and said you were my husband. He was so threatened he apologised, when all he'd done was talk to me.]

'It's only Jack,' Laura said with a sigh.

'What are you doing?' I asked.

'Nothing,' said Laura in an exasperated tone. 'We're just doing some coke. We'll be down in a minute.'

'I'll stay,' I said.

Ford asked, 'Do you want a line?'

'Oh Jack won't have any,' Laura said, in the dismissive way a child might speak of their younger brother.

[That was the opposite of what I meant. I was proud that you never took drugs. You weren't judgemental or prudish or close-minded, like some of my friends. You just had the strength of character to decide drugs weren't for you. I respected that.]

I was irritated by the presumption. I hadn't taken any drugs in over twenty years but that was mostly because of my career and no one had ever offered me cocaine before. I'd always wanted to try it. Even so, I'd have refused if it hadn't been for Laura's tone. She seemed to think I was so predictable that she could answer for me.

'Actually, I will have some,' I said.

Laura looked astonished and I felt satisfied for an instant. Ford brought a tightly curled banknote up to his nostril. I was nervous. What was I doing? I could be struck off for this. And why? To show off to my wife? Could I make an excuse? A sudden fit of sneezing?

Ford bent down and inhaled a line of powder with a fluid, circus seal bob of his head. Laura took the note, tightened it, and took two or three ungainly sniffs at the powder. She licked her finger, smudged it onto the leftover bits, and rubbed her gums as if she were brushing her teeth. I couldn't do it. It was so undignified – kneeling down on the bed where this wanker wanted to fuck my wife. I stood up.

'Are you not having any then?' Zac said in a smug tone, as if he'd known all along I'd lose my nerve.

'Sure I am.'

I coughed on the third sniff. The back of my throat felt hot and raw. I leaned back and looked around. The fear and suspicion lifted from my heart.

'Love is stronger than hate,' Zac was saying. 'It sounds banal . . . I mean, sure, love is more powerful than hate. Of course. But, if you think about – if you really think about it – it's very profound.'

Laura was frowning as if she were 'really thinking' about it and I burst out laughing. I loved her for trying. She was worldly, when it came to drugs and sex, but in her heart she was a child. I thought of our tenth anniversary. She'd wanted to go somewhere hot and exotic but when I told her I'd booked a cottage in the Highlands she'd seemed pleased. She bought walking boots, maps, even a compass we never used. I still have a photograph of her smiling on the top of a hill, one proud boot on the peak like a mountaineer, jumper tied round her waist, hair tossed by the wind. She was so excited and kept stopping to take photographs with her phone. It was like being with the best kind of child, when their enthusiasm makes everyone around them feel good. I couldn't share that enthusiasm – if you've seen one photo of a heather-clad mountain you've seen them all – but I loved that she was excited.

[I always thought you were annoyed at me for taking
so many photographs. You'd stand there, hands on hips,
waiting for me to finish. And you made that joke about how
you loved it when it was just you, me and my 700 closest
friends on Facebook. Still, I did love that trip. The north-
west of Scotland is beautiful – if it were about fifteen
degrees warmer it would be the perfect place to go for a
holiday.]

'Jack!' Laura shouted.

'Huh?' I said.

'Zac was asking why you were laughing. Did you not
hear him?'

'No.'

'What were you thinking about?'

'The Highlands,' I said.

'The Highlands?' Laura's face was pinched with
confusion.

'Love is stronger than hate,' I smiled.

Laura turned to Zac, who looked at me suspiciously.

I burst out laughing. This was not what he'd had in
mind when he'd brought Laura up here – the husband
sprawled on the floor laughing at him. My brain was hot
and I felt a surge of energy and bonhomie. I looked around
the room again. This man was no threat. He was such an
obvious phony. What kind of an artist has a plasma TV in
their bedroom?

'This is a great bedroom you've got,' I said.

'Thanks,' said Zac cagily.

'Yeah, I love the plasma TV. Is there another one in
the toilet? Cos in footballers' cribs, on MTV, they always
have one in the toilet. To watch when you're in the hot
tub. [I nearly cracked up but I saw Zac's face. His lips were
tightening, the veins on his neck stood up and his breathing

shallowed. I'd heard rumours he had a violent temper and I was scared.] You know what, I've got an idea for a new project. You could get those kids from Great Ormond Street down here to smash up your TV and then make it into a video installation. You could call it –'

Laura interrupted: 'I think it's time we went back to the party, don't you?'

We circled down, Ford, Laura, and me, stepping in time to the samba beat of blood pumping round my head. A kaleidoscope of laughing, shiny faces flashed in front of me and I smiled at no one in particular.

At the foot of the stairs, I saw Christine and was filled with joy. I rushed over. I told her how great it was to see her and hugged her. Christine seemed touched and I nearly cried with happiness. My brain throbbed and my vision blurred as if I'd been staring at the sun. Words bled from my mouth. I'd no control over what I was saying – the thoughts were articulated before I'd even become aware of them. I had a new idea for a book – *What Freud Would Have Said*: a psychoanalytic analysis of current affairs – like why George Bush really wanted to invade Iraq. Christine seemed to be excited too. Cocaine was amazing. It released so many ideas. I should do it more often, I thought. Maybe I should do it before I meet my patients.

'Christine,' I said, 'there's something I want to tell you but I'm not sure if it's appropriate.'

'What is it?' she said. She seemed to be holding her breath.

'The front cover of my book,' I said. 'I never really liked it. I didn't want to make a fuss but ...'

Christine looked annoyed.

[Poor Christine! She must have thought, for a second, that her dreams were about to come true.]

'It's too late now,' she said sternly. Of course, I thought
to myself. How ridiculous! My confidence was punctured
and the high spirits drained away. I realised I'd been talking
too much. Christine slipped away and I felt anxious. I must
have been boring her.

    [I doubt it. You could have read the phone book to
    Christine and she still would have laughed and made big
    eyes at you.]

I locked myself in a toilet on the ground floor. I had
to get a grip. There was a walk-in shower with a fold-up
seat. That would sober me up, I thought. I started taking
off my clothes. When I'd taken off my shirt and shoes, I
stopped. Wouldn't it look strange if I came out of the toilet
with wet hair? Who has a shower in the middle of a party?
I was putting my clothes back on when someone knocked
and said, 'What are you doing in there?' That was close, I
thought. If I'd had that shower, this could have been really
embarrassing. I just had to get home as soon as possible
without drawing any attention to myself. Just be normal.
No showers. Just do normal things. It should be fine as I
was really good at being normal. I never knew how good I
was at being normal.

I drank some water and felt more in control. Laura and
Ford were back on the L-shaped couch. She was leaning
into him and her hand was on his knee. They were alone.
I hurried over, crouching under trays and twisting through
gaps in the thicket of people. Laura took back her hand
and stretched her arms. I took a seat beside her and put
my arm round her neck. She leaned forward to break the
contact. She and Ford talked on but their voices had no
gaiety and I had a sense I'd interrupted something.

    [You didn't interrupt anything, I promise. Zac and I were
    just talking. I was enjoying myself. I felt young again: a

party, new people, some excitement. It was like being at
university, with my life ahead of me and nothing to limit me.
There was nothing illicit about any of it.]

'I think it's time we left, Laura,' I said.

'Why?' she replied. 'It's still so early.'

'It's past eleven. I've been working all day,' I said. 'I'm
exhausted. And I've got the appointment tomorrow. You
remember.'

'No,' she said.

'The one I told you about,' I said with a frown.

'I don't think you did,' she said.

'Didn't I?' I said. 'It must have slipped my mind but I do
have to get up early tomorrow so ...'

'OK,' she said, without getting up. I stared at her and
she looked defiantly back at me. 'Well, go on then. Off you
go. If you have to leave.'

Fine, I said to myself, I'm not going to beg. I waited
outside for a few minutes in case she changed her mind.
I typed 'please come' into my phone, but didn't send the
message.

I had a collection of half-true one-sentence criticisms
of Laura, built up over twenty years, which I kept, like
business cards, in the back of my mind for when I'm angry
with her. As I stared at the taxi door, I flipped through
them: she's selfish; she's thoughtless; she's a flirt.

[Which halves are supposed to be true? Being friendly
doesn't make me a flirt and I'm no more selfish or
thoughtless than you are.]

It was an hour before Laura came home. She didn't sit
next to me on the sofa, where I'd pictured our argument
(and reconciliation) would take place, but walked straight
past me to the desk at the far end where she turned on
her laptop. I paused, unwatched, and went to the kitchen

to pour myself a glass of water. The tap coughed and spluttered and the water was grey. I came back in, still unnoticed, and Laura was typing.

'Who are you writing to?' I asked in a flat, measured voice.

'Someone,' she said without turning to face me.

'Of course you're writing to someone,' I said, anger rising inside me. 'Who?'

'A friend,' she said. Her tone was so cold. It was as if she wasn't the person I'd known and loved for twenty years, but a headstrong stranger.

'Which friend?'

'No one special.'

She still hadn't turned to face me.

'How *dare* you ignore me!' I shouted the word 'dare' with all the volume of my anger. 'How *dare* you treat me like this!'

'Like what?' Her voice was calm and cold.

'Like I'm nothing to you. All night, you deliberately humiliated me by flirting with that horrible smug man.'

'Don't be ridiculous. You embarrassed yourself tonight and you embarrassed me.'

'You are such a ... cruel person.' I couldn't bring myself to say 'bitch'. I crouched down beside her so I could see her face. 'You couldn't keep your hands off him and you were looking at him all night like you wanted to kiss him. How do you think that makes me feel? You're my wife!'

'I hate this.' She turned away. 'I don't want to be in a marriage where I can't talk to whoever I like.'

We both fell silent at this threat.

> [It wasn't meant to be a threat. I just wanted you to understand I needed my freedom.]

'Anyway,' she continued, 'why shouldn't I talk to Zac?

You seemed to be having a pretty good time talking to Christine.'

'That's different.'

'Why?'

'Because Christine's my friend and I wasn't flirting with her ...'

'Oh really? Well, why did you say Christine would be your perfect wife?'

'I didn't say that. About three years ago, I said that it was a shame Christine was single as she'd make a wonderful wife *for someone*. Not for me. *For someone.*'

> [You did say Christine would be your perfect wife. And maybe it's true. She's probably better suited than me to being a wife.]

'Why don't you just admit that you'd prefer to be with that humourless ano?'

> [I definitely didn't say this. I like Christine. I just find it a bit strange the way she invites people round for calorie-bomb suppers and then eats none of it herself. If you want to marry her, go for it. I'll come round with a tray of brownies.]

'Christine's not humourless.'

'Oh right, so she makes you laugh, does she? Or is it just that she laughs at everything you say?'

'Look, you're straying from the point. I wasn't groping Christine and I didn't disappear into her bedroom.'

'Oh come on, Jack. You saw what that was. We were just having a line of coke.'

'God knows what that would have led to if I hadn't come in. Just tell me the truth. What is going on with you and Zac Ford? Did you really meet him for the first time at my book launch? Are you sure there isn't something you're not telling me?'

'You don't trust me. I don't believe this.'

'Don't try and make yourself the victim here. Just answer my question.'

She groaned. 'I'm not having an affair with Zac Ford.'

'That's not what I asked.'

'I just talked to him,' she said. 'For the first time in about ten years we went to a party. We drank alcohol. We talked to people. We did what every other childless couple in London does all the time. You know I miss going out and yet –' her voice wavered and her eyes shone – 'you can't even let me have one night.'

'Laura!' I said then paused. When she cried, I found it impossible to be angry with her. No tears came so I continued. 'You always do this. You know you're in the wrong but you just can't admit it so you make yourself into the victim.'

'Oh yes, I know. Of course. You're always right and I'm always wrong.'

'That's not what I'm saying.' I groaned. Laura's lips thinned. 'I'm saying right now, tonight, you hurt me. Maybe I am over-sensitive and jealous, but that's who I am. That's who you married.'

'Well, you married someone who likes to go to parties and talk to people.'

'You can do that. But just please spare a thought for my feelings. This isn't the first time. Remember when you let that guy at the bar buy you all those drinks?'

'He was just being chivalrous!'

'No, he was not just being chivalrous. He thought you were going to sleep with him. He nearly fell off his stool when I turned up. You may not realise it but you can be very flirtatious.'

'Oh for God's sake!' She sighed. 'What do you want me

to say? Do you want me to say "I'm sorry. I'll never talk to another man without your permission. Please forgive me, oh mighty husband"?'

'No!' I punched the wall with my fist, jarring my elbow. Laura didn't react. There was a triangle of loose skin on one knuckle. 'I want you to say "I love you. I don't want anyone else but you."'

'Well, I can't say it. Because right now, it wouldn't be true.'

[I've rerun this conversation so often I can't distinguish what I said from what I wish I'd said. If I did say what you have me saying, what I must have meant was that I was so angry I couldn't *feel* my love for you and so, just in that instant, I couldn't say 'I love you'. I definitely didn't mean that I was in love with Zac or that I'd stopped loving you. I was just being defensive. You were attacking me for being a flirt. Maybe I should have said something kinder and more reassuring but I can't do that when I'm angry. I just can't.]

I sank onto the sofa. Laura left the room and in a few minutes I could hear her brushing her teeth. I stared at the floor, waiting for her footsteps. The bedroom light clicked off. When I looked in, only a few minutes later, Laura looked to be asleep. I lay on the bed beside her with my nose an inch from hers. She didn't wake up so I kissed her and she groaned and rolled away.

'Sweet pea,' I said into her arched spine.

'Go away,' she said.

I couldn't sleep as the things Laura had said and the things I should have said were rebounding round my head. I didn't want to let go of the anger as then I'd be left with only the fear. Could Laura really have meant that she didn't love me anymore? Marital fights have their rules, like boxing, and you never tell the other person you don't love them. Not unless you want a divorce.

But divorce was unthinkable. We were melded together by a lifetime of unspoken memories. We couldn't be separated. Laura couldn't really want us to separate. She liked to pretend sometimes that I was holding her back – that, without me, she'd be a free spirit roaming the world with just a backpack full of contraceptives – but that was a joke, wasn't it? She'd always come back, at night, to my side of the bed. She used to say she couldn't sleep without my kiss. Until now anyway.

I could get us past this fight. I just had to remind Laura of what we'd been through together and why we could never be apart. I just had to find the right words. So, at around 3 a.m., I emailed Laura from the laptop in the living room:

Sweetheart,

I'm so sorry about tonight. It scares me when we go to bed angry with one another. You know how much I love you. You're all I have. That's why I feel threatened when other men flirt with you.

It's not that I don't trust you. I do. But my job has taught me that even loving and loyal people can sometimes be unfaithful and it's the secrets that destroy marriages more often than the infidelity. So, if there's something going on between you and Ford, now's the time to say. It feels to me like there's something you're not telling me. If my fears are groundless – if it was just a flirtation – then tell me and we can put it behind us. We need never see Ford again.

> [I wish I'd read the rest of the email. I stopped here because it was one of thirty waiting for me at work the next day. One of our freelancers had pulled out and we were one

article short with only a day to publication. I was stressed and short of time. When I got to this part about me being a flirt and how I could never see Zac again, I thought I knew what the rest of the email would say so I stopped reading.]

When you're replying, try not to use attack as a form of defence. Take the time to think about it and try to see it from my perspective. Try to understand that my jealousy is a symptom of my love. I couldn't cope without you. Do you remember when I was told about my prostate? It was you that persuaded me to have the operation. It was you that rang the doctors and found Dr Kumar and pleaded with him for an earlier date. It was you that spoke to all my patients and made me take time off work. If it hadn't been for you, I wouldn't have had the operation. I don't think I ever explained why. It's not that I wasn't frightened of dying. If anything, it was the opposite – I was too frightened to think about it. But you made me overcome that. By looking at me with that anxious expression when I said maybe; by reading me articles and quoting statistics every day; by saying you'd never leave me, whatever happened. When I saw how much you cared, it made me want to fight to stay alive. You are my reason for living. That's why I can't stand by and do nothing when I see another man trying to take you away from me.

Your loving husband,
Jack

[If only I'd read this. Oh, Jack, I'm sorry. Please forgive me. Even now I can't find the words. Please believe me. If I'd read the whole email, I'd have responded very differently.]

When I got back into bed, Laura's leg was taking up half of my side. I pushed but I couldn't budge her. Her mouth was open and she was breathing heavily. I was annoyed that it was so easy for her to sleep. I pushed her again and she moaned and pulled the duvet away. I lay still for a few minutes, worried I'd woken her. I was too anxious to sleep. What would Laura think of my email? Would she forgive me? Or say sorry? Or be angry?

I checked my watch and it was 4.30. I got up and emailed Laura again: *If you're still angry, please wait before you reply.* Then I turned to the World Wide Web. When I'd finished, the images I'd been so engrossed in became revolting and ludicrous, but after closing the browser quickly and rushing to bed, I still had enough endorphins to lull my anxieties and let me sleep.

[Looking back on it now, it's kind of funny, don't you think, that you got so upset about my just talking to another man and yet it was fine for you to watch 'Sexy Secretary Fucks Pizza Guy' on my laptop?]

6

I'm too annoyed to continue the story for the moment. I've just received this email from Christine:

Hi Jack,

It's great to hear from you. We were all beginning to worry about you. You scared us all doing a Lord Lucan like that. ☺

I'm afraid we did have to drop F&H as the sales were disappointing. It's a difficult market at the moment. I did all I could.

Best,
Christine

My heart is still racing. How could Christine 'drop' my book without telling me? And 'F&H'? No wonder the sales were so bad if she was going round calling it that, as if it were some cheap cigarette brand or discount clothes store. And who was she talking about when she said '*we* were *all* beginning to worry'? Toby? Mark? All the other old university friends who hadn't bothered to call or email since I left England? And the smiley! To be compared to a wife-beating murderer is bad enough but when that insult is capped by an automatically generated computer grin it's too much.

Flushed with anger, I drafted the following reply:

I'm surprised and disappointed to hear that you 'dropped' Freud and Holmes: The Other Oedipus Complex (as I like to call it), without telling me. Please do tell anyone that's interested that I'm fine – I haven't killed anyone and I am still contactable by email (neither of which could be said for Lord Lucan).

Malcoordinated with rage, I could hardly type. I saved the message, walked out of the café, smoked a cigarette and returned. When I reread it five minutes later, I was barely more composed. I deleted the parentheses – the first was too bitter and the second too obvious – and sent it. The vanishing envelope took with it some of the poison in my heart.

To soothe myself, I went to Amazon to read my only review: five stars from alpiggott of Hertfordshire, who said:

What a fantastic book! An eye-opener in every sense – it really transformed how I thought about psychiatry. I've read everything about Sherlock Holmes and yet this was completely new to me! I can't wait to read more.

I'm not a hundred per cent sure what he meant by saying it's an eye-opener in *every* sense but I'm touched that someone I don't know felt moved to say such nice things. It's not just me either – nine out of ten people found the review helpful. That one review makes all the years I spent trying to redraft my PhD seem worthwhile. I didn't write to be famous or win prizes or make money. I wrote because I had ideas I wanted to share and even if there's only one or two alpiggotts out there, that will do me.

Many times I've wondered who this alpiggott was – a man or a woman? Al Piggott or A. L. Piggott? I've often thought of writing to him or her – starting a correspondence about psychology, philosophy, life – but there's no email address with the review and there are too many Piggotts in Hertfordshire to call them all. I searched for other reviews by alpiggott but there were none. I googled the name and found a prolific eBay user and a paedophile on Cincinnati's most wanted list. I bought a second-hand digital camera, which I didn't want and have never used, from the former and sent him an email saying 'I wonder what Sherlock Holmes would have done with this?' He replied with a solitary question mark. It's frustrating to know that somewhere in the home counties there's a soulmate I'll never meet.

[I was your alpiggott. Not literally (although I was one of the nine who found his review helpful), but I loved everything you wrote, from the PhD to the Freud book and the perfectly grammatical, smiley-free texts and emails you used to send every day. You didn't need to go trawling round the home counties looking for a soulmate – you had me.]

On the way back from the internet café, I was drawn to a shop called Concorde. At first I wasn't sure what it was selling [oh right, yeah, sure] – it was all jazzy music and bright lighting, like a record store. On closer inspection, I could see the DVDs were pornographic but it bore no relation to the shops in Soho I'd sneaked into as an adolescent. They do sex so well, the French. There was no shame or prudery in that shop, except for from me. I tried to give the impression I was neither embarrassed, nor a regular, but my self-consciousness must have been obvious. The other customers looked comfortable, even bored, as if it were a normal shop. The woman behind the till wore cream linen trousers and a blouse with a bow. A girl of no more than eighteen with sunburnt shoulders handed her a vibrator. She turned it over in her hands and gave some advice I didn't understand. When it was my turn, she asked if I had a '*carte de fidelité*'. Is that a routine question, I wondered. She didn't ask the girl that. At least this porn habit, which even now makes me feel guilty, becomes a French kind of fidelity.

7

As I worked in private practice, most of my patients had
jobs. Our appointments were usually in the afternoon or
early evening and I was often at home in the morning with
little to do. I woke late on the day after Zac's party and
there was still no reply to my emails of the night before.
That didn't worry me too much. Laura would need a
bit of time to calm down and there were probably more
urgent things in her inbox. I was happy making breakfast.
Without Laura around I could have guilt-free scrambled
eggs, bacon and sausages. Laura hadn't bothered to rewrap
the butter and there was a teardrop of raspberry jam on
its face. The milk was out too. Being rich and pretty had
shielded Laura from some of the harsher realities of life
– like the fact that milk goes off if you don't put it in the
fridge. [I'm just not a milk drinker. That's all.] I bet – in fact I
know – that even as an undergraduate, there was someone
who'd tidy up after her. That gloomy boy with the long
hair and corduroy jackets, who'd follow her to the pub and
never say anything. I can picture him solemnly washing up

her bowl of ragu, all because she once thanked him with a peck on the cheek. [Ha, ha. Lawrence, who was very charming and not at all gloomy, did the washing up for all the girls in the house, not just me. He said he liked it.]

I cleared up Laura's breakfast and put the sausages in the oven. The inside of the kettle had a brown sludge I couldn't dislodge. The bacon was finished – the empty packet was splayed out on the floor about a foot from the bin.

I put on some toast and broke some eggs into the pan. The laptop made a noise like 'oh well' and I rushed to the living room. It was spam. I was back in time to save the eggs.

The enjoyment of my breakfast was broken by three more emails, all false alarms. By 1 p.m., Laura's lunch break, I still had no reply. Why was she taking so long? Was it to punish me? I wanted to beat my fists against the wall of her silence, to write something short and nasty to provoke a response. At least it might give a moment's relief – a release of some of the anger and frustration that was swelling my heart. But I resisted. Instead, I went for a run. After a few minutes, I began to feel my shins digging up into my knees and I gave up and limped home. There was still no message from Laura. I broke and sent her an email:

Why haven't you written yet?

Because I'm busy and you told me not to write while I was still angry came the almost immediate reply.

I emailed back: *When will you stop being angry, do you think? Roughly. Hours? Days? Weeks?*

Five minutes later, a little box appeared in the corner of the screen:

I don't know. I really can't say at the moment. Maybe I'll stop being angry with you when you stop being ...

The box faded from view and I clicked on Outlook:

I don't know. I really can't say at the moment. Maybe I'll stop being angry with you when you stop being needy and possessive and learn to give me the trust I deserve. I really don't have time for this right now. Please don't bother me with any more emails. We can talk about this when I get back.

> [You have to understand that when I wrote this, I still hadn't read the sweet things you said about me and your operation. It was frantically busy. I was rewriting an article we'd spiked months ago about the secret gardens of London and trying to make it look topical. And at the same time I was getting angry phone calls from our theatre critic, who was pissed off about the way I'd edited his review, and trying to placate a retired admiral whose name I'd used (by mistake) in an article about drag queens. My stress levels were high even without all these emergencies as there were rumours that we were going to be turned into a free magazine, which meant redundancies.]

I deleted the message, then called it up again from Deleted Items. A small voice in my head suggested that Laura might have a point but anger and pride shouted it down. I wrote something about her being vindictive and sent it before I had time to calm down. It was several hours before I could see the argument from Laura's side. Maybe I should have trusted her more. Maybe I was too possessive. An ageing man locking up his pretty younger wife. That story only ended one way. Clinginess is not attractive. I had to be stronger.

Neighbours opened and closed the front door to the building six or seven times that evening. They creaked the floorboards outside our flat and tried to impersonate

Laura's step. At last, around 7 p.m., a key pecked at our lock.

'I'm sorry, sweetheart,' I said.

Laura looked startled then mumbled, 'S'ok', without looking me in the eye and walked past. I found her in the bedroom getting changed. She pretended not to notice me.

I stifled my annoyance. 'I mean, I guess we were both in the wrong,' I said. 'I should have trusted you more and ...' She turned to glare at me. 'Anyway, the point is from now on, I'll be better.'

'So you won't mind if I meet Zac for a drink?' she said.

'Am I not invited?' I said with a half-hearted attempt to smile.

'No,' she said. 'It's for work. I want to interview him alone. If you trust me, that is ...'

'I do trust you,' I said with a shrinking heart.

In the days that followed, things were nearly normal. We put on a mediocre performance of a week in the life of Jack and Laura. The dialogue was plausible, if a little polite and humourless, but our movements were stiff and our faces expressed no emotions. Neither of us smiled much and we avoided physical contact.

The drink with Ford was fixed for Wednesday. When I came home on Tuesday evening, Laura met me at the door. She seemed happier.

[I was happier. It had been a momentous day at work. Julian called me into his office that morning and closed the door. He asked if I'd heard the rumours about his leaving. I said I'd hoped they weren't true. He said he was afraid they were. He hadn't made his mind up till the day before, when he met the owners. He'd wanted me to be the first to know. I said I was sorry and he said I shouldn't be. It might be for

74

the best for all of us. We know what we are, but not what we may be. The owners had decided to make the website the focus from now on. That was the future of magazines, apparently. We made four times more from online sales than subscriptions. They wanted someone younger to lead them into the digital age.

I said I thought they were making a big mistake. He was the best editor they'd ever had. He'd saved the magazine. I said I'd write to them, threaten resignation. He smiled and said there was no need for that.

I asked if they knew who was going to replace him. He said they were going to interview me and Siritha. I said something like, 'That's good.' He frowned and said I shouldn't count my chickens. Siritha may not be a journalist but the job's more about marketing these days.

I explained that he'd misunderstood me. I didn't expect to get the job and I wouldn't mind if Siritha did. I'd be sad to see Julian go, but proud that, at last, we had a female editor. It could be me or Siritha. It didn't matter. At this point Julian started smirking in that annoying way of his. This irritated me. I asked if he didn't believe me. I said he obviously didn't know me very well because if there was one thing I was passionate about, it was equality. In every profession, women are still held back. Women need to support each other if they're ever going to get the place in society they deserve.

The more indignant I became, the more amused he seemed to be. By the time I'd finished, he was openly laughing. He said something like 'Sure, sure' and then added that I could always get in touch with him if things didn't work out. He had a few friends in this business.

This made me anxious. Why was he suggesting things wouldn't work out? No reason, he said. Are they going to fire me too? I asked. No, he said. He'd told them I was the best writer and the best editor on the magazine. That's why they were interviewing me. He was just saying he hoped we wouldn't lose touch.

I felt depressed watching him take his prints of Pembroke College off the wall. In a few minutes a twenty-year career was reduced to two cardboard boxes. As he made his way, smiling and nodding, towards the door, we banged our desks with our fists, some of us in tears. He stopped at the door, balanced the boxes in the crook of his arm and waved goodbye. When the banging stopped, there were a few seconds of silence – a rare event in the magazine – while most of us wondered whether we'd be next. A telephone rang and it jolted me into a different train of thought. Siritha was an astute and capable woman – she'd done great things with our advertising revenues – but surely they'd want a journalist to edit a magazine with a reputation for its writing. I could be the first female editor, at only thirty-nine.

I couldn't wait to get home and tell you. I wanted you to be proud. You had helped me so much, proofreading all my first articles; it was almost like a joint career. I bought a bottle of champagne on the way home. You weren't back so I changed into a long green dress and put the champagne in the fridge. I was imagining your joy when I told you, us embracing and drinking toasts. I wanted you. My spirits were so high I knew I could lift you up with me. When you saw how happy I was, and how much I loved you, your silly jealousies would evaporate. Everything would be just like it had always been.]

'Excited about your date tomorrow?' I asked. The smile in her eyes died and she turned from me and we hardly spoke the rest of the night. That's an image I've often returned to. Even though I had every reason to be angry, I still feel guilty when I think of how I killed her smile.

We met at the door the following evening. She was wearing lipstick and eyeliner.

'Where are you meeting him?' I asked.

'Oh, just the Troubadour,' she said. 'I should be back in a couple of hours.'

'Shall I cook something?'

'If you want,' she said. As the door closed I caught the smell of the Jo Malone perfume I'd bought for her birthday.

This was not a problem, I said to myself. It's only a couple of hours. A couple of hours for a journalist to interview an artist in a bar. What could be wrong with that? Laura was sober. Without the glamorous hangers-on and the trappings of wealth and success, she'd see Ford for the pompous, conceited arse he so obviously was. In only (check watch) one hour and fifty-eight minutes, we'd be sat next to each other, laughing about what a tit Zac Ford was. This dinner was going to be a turning point.

Jamie Oliver's *Thirty-Minute Meals* and Delia's *How to Cheat at Cooking* wouldn't keep me busy long enough so I took out the Ottolenghi cookbook Andrea had given us. The pictures were amazing but most recipes had at least one ingredient I'd never heard of (sumac? mograbiah?) or required marinating overnight. At last I found something I thought Laura would like – roast pork belly, with gooseberry, ginger and elderflower relish.

I was almost whistling with happiness in the supermarket. Twenty-five minutes of the two hours had passed and I wasn't feeling jealous at all. They'd run out of thyme but no matter. I hesitated over whether to buy

champagne or cava. In the end, I bought two bottles of
Tesco Finest red wine, reduced from £15 to £7.50. I was
so busy heating ovens and chopping rosemary and ginger
that I barely noticed the hour mark. The pork took ninety
minutes to cook so I put it in the oven. I texted Laura to
ask if she knew where the blender was. Ten minutes later,
she hadn't replied so I called her. She didn't pick up the
phone so I left a voicemail in a breezy, cheery tone:

'Hi, sweetheart, I can't find the blender. Do you know
where it is? I need it for the meal I'm cooking. Give me a
call. Lots of love.'

I tried stirring the relish with a fork but I kept thinking
how much easier it would be with a blender. Laura must
have got my voicemail by now. Why hadn't she called me
back? Or had she turned her phone off? But why would
she do that? She never turned it off when she was with me.
I couldn't resist calling again a few minutes later, and it
went straight to answerphone:

'Hi, sweetheart. Me again. You don't seem to be
answering your phone. Can you give me a call back?'

Perhaps she was on another call. I called again and still
the phone rang without answer. I felt irritated now and
I made a few more calls, just for the sake of it. At last I
found the blender in the cupboard for teabags and sugar.

I called again: 'Is your phone on silent? Because you
don't seem to be picking up. Anyway, I'm just calling to say
you don't need to worry about the blender. I've found it.
Someone put it in the tea cupboard. Bit weird. Anyway, it's
eight o'clock now so I guess I'll be seeing you in about half
an hour.'

At 8.30, I'd still heard nothing from Laura. That's not a
problem, I said to myself. The pork has another half-hour
to cook anyway. I turned on the TV but found it difficult

to concentrate. There was a cookery programme with a presenter I found irritating and a historical documentary I couldn't follow, so I laid the kitchen table instead. I took out a candle but put it back again because I thought Laura might think it naff. The oven alarm sounded. Laura was half an hour late. I turned the oven down and mashed the potatoes.

I left another voicemail: 'Sweetheart, don't think I'm being a possessive husband or anything but I'm just wondering when you'll be back. You see, the dinner's ready now and it's going to go cold soon. OK, love you, bye!'

Two hours and five unanswered calls later, I was frightened and angry. I couldn't wait any longer. I had to do something so I walked to the Troubadour. I couldn't see them from the window so I went in.

Laura was leaning forward, elbows on the table, gazing into Zac's eyes and smiling. They could have been holding hands but a menu propped against a candle blocked my view. Each had a large half-empty glass of red wine. There was no sign of a notepad or tape recorder.

[I promise you, Zac and I were not holding hands. It was an interview – albeit not a very successful one – not a date. Zac refused to take me seriously and wouldn't answer any of my questions directly. When I asked him about his personal life, he laughed as if I were flirting with him. I went to the loo to escape the awkwardness and checked my phone. I was going to text you about what a nightmare I was having but I was put off by the missed calls and all that stuff about the blender. I thought it would do you good to learn that you can't expect me to be on call whenever you want. When I got back to the table, Zac had ordered another bottle of wine. It seemed rude to leave him with a full bottle so I stayed a bit longer. He asked me if I'd decided what I'd give him in exchange for the portrait. I said I'd forgotten about that, but in truth I'd made up my mind to text him after the interview was over saying I didn't have time to sit for a portrait.]

'Laura!' I said.

She turned and her face hardened. 'What are you doing here, Jack?'

'You're late and you weren't answering your phone, so I came to find you.'

'I'm sorry,' Laura said, not to me but to Ford.

'No problem,' he replied with a smirk. 'You go. I'll get the bill.'

'No,' she said, 'I insist. It's journalistic ethics. Let me at least pay half.'

'You buy it next time,' he said.

'Next time?' I asked as we walked home in silence.

'Yes,' Laura said. 'He's going to paint a portrait of me.'

'I thought this was a one-off,' I said. 'An interview.'

'It was,' she said. 'And now I'm going to have a portrait painted.'

'Why were you there so long?' I asked. 'You said you'd be back in two hours.'

'I don't have a watch,' she said. 'You know that.'

'You could have checked your phone.'

'It was on silent,' she said. 'It's rude to look at your phone when you're talking to someone. You told me that.'

'It doesn't stop you when you're with me.'

The mashed potatoes were cold and the pork belly was black but the relish looked OK.

'Here's the supper I made,' I said.

'I'm not hungry,' she replied without even looking at it.

I ate alone with a glass of wine. The pork was dry so I coated it in the sweet relish. It tasted of sadness.

80

Laura was asleep, or pretending to be, when I came into the bedroom.

> [I feel terrible now, reading this. I'm no good at diplomacy. I should have thanked you for cooking supper and told you all about my failed interview and you'd have understood there was nothing to be suspicious of. And I should never have agreed to sit for that stupid portrait. I'm sure we'd have forgiven each other and you'd never have got in touch with that psychotic, lying bitch.]

When Laura was with Zac in his studio, I could think of nothing else. I mustn't complain, I told myself, as that will only make it worse. In a couple of weeks it will all be over. I never mentioned the two hours a week Laura spent with Zac, even as the weeks became months and the painting still wasn't finished. Even when Laura wasn't with Zac, I thought about when she'd next be seeing him and what they'd done, and would do, together. I couldn't believe she was cheating on me and yet, at the same time, I thought she probably was. The betrayal was too great to be fathomable. Laura was supposed to be the one person who really cared about me. It was her love that gave my life meaning. She knew, because I'd told her many times, that it would crush me if she were unfaithful. She openly told me when she was going to see Zac for her 'portrait'. I couldn't accept that she'd be lying to me so brazenly. The image (which regularly passed through my mind) of her and Zac lying naked in bed, laughing post-coitally at my naivety, was just catastrophising.

And yet the evidence was overwhelming. When she got back from Zac's studio, she'd always shower and change her clothes. She never put her phone down, even when she was getting changed. And, looking at it objectively,

or pessimistically, or both, why wouldn't she want to
sleep with Ford? He was younger, taller, richer and more
glamorous than me. There had also been signs, even before
Ford, of Laura being restless in our marriage. She'd even
suggested a threesome once.

'With another man?' I asked.

'Why not?' she said with an irritatingly broad smile.
'That won't make you jealous, will it? I mean, you'd be
right there.'

'And that's supposed to make it better?' I said. She waited
expectantly. 'It's about the worst thing I can imagine except
... I don't know ... watching someone beat you to death.'

'How can you compare it to my being beaten to death?
I find that really insulting.' And Laura sulked, as if I were
the one who'd said something hurtful.

Most tellingly of all, in the months of the 'portrait' we
stopped having sex. Throughout our relationship, we'd
always had an equal and instinctive desire for each other, as
well matched as our body clocks or our senses of humour.
The lightest of touches, or a few well-chosen words and
I could see, in the sinuous movements of her body or the
flashing of her eyes, that Laura was turned on. After Laura
started meeting Ford every week, this changed. In bed,
she'd be too tired. Everything else, even the ten o'clock
news, took priority. Our private language had changed its
meaning: 'Tell me something nice' meant that I had to find
a way to compliment Laura that was original – something
I'd never said before in twenty years together – and so
subtle she wouldn't realise what I was doing. Almost
invariably I was caught out and she'd complain I was being
cheesy. On the rare occasions I got the balance right, I had
to keep up a stream of poetic-but-not-too poetic praise
for five or ten minutes before any physical contact was

allowed. If I moved too early or showed any obvious sign of wanting her, she'd recoil and the momentum would be lost. If I moved too late, she'd be too sleepy. I made some tentative suggestions about why she might be rejecting me, but they only enraged her and made it even less likely we'd have sex.

Pride overcame lust and I stopped playing this losing game of grandmother's footsteps. Resentment at the thought that I'd be rejected made it hard to find the right words or tone. Besides, there's only so many ways you can say 'You look beautiful' or 'I want you'. Pornography became not just a sleeping aid but a substitute for a sex life. The draw was not so much the stone-hard beauty of the women – I wanted Laura far more than any of them – but the ease of the language. I love it. I need it. I want it. In the language of porn, sentences are three words long. Subject verb object. She fucks him. They fuck her. They fuck them. Nouns take turns at either end.

Freud said lust creates more problems than other instincts, like hunger, because it's the only urge we can gratify immediately, without anyone or anything to help. As a result, we never have to think rationally about sex. To satisfy hunger we need food, which is not always available. So we train hunger to wait. And not all food satisfies – some things taste bad or make us sick. These experiences teach us to desire food we've eaten before as we know it will be safe. The sexual appetite is not trained in this way. It has the strength of the wild and it's not limited to what we've tried before. Every kind of fantasy can be fulfilled in our imagination. And these days, we don't even need an imagination. We just need broadband.

In the after-porn lows I wondered if what I'd been doing was living out Laura's fantasies, kneeling in submission, watching powerless as a succession of muscle-bound men slammed into actresses I'd chosen for their tanned skin and black hair. Maybe that's why I found it so hard to find the words to seduce Laura – maybe I was worried that, if I let myself talk too freely, I'd end up encouraging her to fuck Zac and let me watch.

[I wasn't sleeping with Zac. If our sex life did slow down that was for reasons that had nothing to do with Zac. Nor was it, contrary to your 'tentative suggestions', to punish myself for not having a child. It was simpler than that – I could feel you were angry with me. You wouldn't say it but I knew it. When you touched me, it felt mechanical and cold. That's why I wanted you to talk to me. I wanted to feel how I used to feel – to believe that it was me you wanted, not just sex; that I was irreplaceable.

I don't think the pornography helped. I don't disapprove of pornography per se. The plastic puffed-up secretaries, nurses, French maids and nuns (!) that littered my browser history (yes of course I checked) were more cheesy than sinister. These women (who look nothing like me, by the way) should be free to use their bodies however they want. What bothers me about pornography is the way it magnifies and accelerates sex. There's no conversation, no intimacy and no humanity. The foreplay is peremptory or non-existent. Pornography trains men to think there are women out there who'll get down on their knees and start sucking them off as soon as they step within a cock's reach. If our sex life diminished, that was not the cause of your watching pornography. It was the effect. You expected me to be in the mood in the time it takes to click a mouse. I felt pressured.]

I used to have patients who'd say things like: 'I don't get why he won't talk to me on Skype when he's away on business?'; or 'I found condoms in his jacket but apparently they were two years old and he'd forgotten he put them there'; or 'He gets these phone calls. I understand they're important clients but why do they have to call at midnight?' And I wanted to scream at them 'He's cheating on you!' but I didn't because I thought it was a game on their part; they knew but they wanted me to say it, so they didn't have to. But going through the same thing, I realised that it was more complicated. They believed the excuses even though they knew they weren't true.

It's like death. Even when I had cancer, I didn't believe I was going to die. It was only prostate cancer and I was only just over forty. I'd always been fit and healthy. All the statistics were on my side. What scared me was not so much the thought that I would die then, or in the year or two afterwards. That was too unlikely to be real. What scared me was the reminder that one day it would be real. One day, I will know that death is coming soon and I won't be able to put off thinking about it any longer. Because that's always been my defence – like a parent changing the channel when a sex scene begins, I divert my thoughts from death. And so it was with Laura's affair. The idea that Laura might want to leave me, or sleep with other men, had often occurred to me. The trick had always been to think of something else before my imagination gave it reality. Now, with all the evidence mounting, I couldn't ignore it.

One evening I cracked. We were sat on the couch, watching a documentary about whales neither of us was interested in, touching distance apart, not touching.

'How's your portrait going?' I asked Laura.

'Fine,' she said.

'How far's he got?'

'What do you mean?' she said testily.

'What do you think I mean?'

'I don't know,' she said. 'Why don't you try explaining?'

'How far is Ford from finishing your painting?'

'Dunno,' she said. She picked up the remote and raised the volume.

'Why not?' I asked. 'Have you not looked at it?'

She clicked her tongue, turned her head to the wall and sighed. 'Yes,' she said, 'of course I have.'

'And? What's it look like? Is it just a head? Or the whole body?'

'Um, not sure.'

'But you just said you'd looked at it.'

'At the beginning. Not recently. It's changed. He tore up the first one.'

'You're doing a second portrait?!'

'Yeah, I guess. So what?'

'Seems convenient. What kind of pose are you in?'

'Foetus?'

'What, on the floor?'

'No, on a bed.'

'You're on his bed?'

'No, I'm on *a* bed, not *his* bed. It's like a couch. Your patients lie on a couch. What's the big deal?'

[This is how I remember the conversation:

YOU: So how's the great portrait?

ME: Fine.

YOU: Has he cut it up with scissors yet?

ME: No.

YOU: Is he painting you with his faeces?

ME: No.

YOU: Your faeces?

ME (refusing to rise): No.

YOU: What are you doing in the picture?

ME: I'm curled up in a ball on a bed.

YOU: On a bed?! For fuck's sake. What is this – a porn casting?

ME: Fuck off! I'm fully clothed. I'm only on a bed because there are no spare chairs.

YOU: Right. No spare chairs but a bed. That's convenient.

ME: Actually, it's because he doesn't paint portraits anymore.

YOU: Ha! I bet he doesn't. He just gets women to come and lie on his bed till they'll sleep with him.

ME: That's ridiculous. He's a serious artist.

YOU: Give over.

I'll tell you what actually happened. A few hours a week, I'd go to that filthy studio and sit there among the paint and stale smoke. You'd have freaked out if you'd seen the mess. It was an old warehouse in a trendy area of east London. It was probably worth millions but it looked like a slum inside. Open tubes of paint spilled out on the floor. You had to tiptoe through old plates of curry and pizza just to make it into the room. There was a kitchen at one end with a wall that had been half knocked down. An electric drill lay on the kitchen surface next to a kettle. In the corner of the main room was a bed – a yellowy-brown sheet had slipped off one of its shoulders to reveal a grey mattress.

'Where's all the art?' I once asked. 'Or is this a homage to Tracey Emin?'

'Do you know Tracey?' he asked, as if I'd implied that I did.

'Not really,' I said. 'I was just referring to the bed.'

'Oh,' he said with a wolfish smile, 'you want to know about my bed.'

'I was wondering where all the art is,' I said.

'Oh, it's at the gallery,' he said. 'When I finish something, I make sure it's taken away as soon as possible. Otherwise, I find myself tinkering with it or destroying it. I need to clear the space to move on. I'm sorry there aren't any chairs – I haven't done a portrait in years – you'll have to sit on the bed.'

So I sat on the edge of his sordid bed. This became tiring after a while. That's when we agreed that I could lie down. I asked if I could read a book but he said no, I had to look at him. Only I couldn't see him most of the time. He'd look me up and down for a few seconds – I was fully dressed of course – then disappear behind the canvas for minutes at a time, leaving me to stare at the brown stains on the ceiling. To pass the time, I'd talk about whatever was on my mind. I don't know whether he was listening, or just concentrating on the painting, but he seldom replied. It was how I imagine your therapy sessions to be – his silence encouraged me to talk. I talked about us, a bit, and about work and whatever else was on my mind. Every once in a while, Zac would kneel on the bed and put his hands on me, so that I was in the right position, but it was no more erotic than a tailor adjusting a jacket. I honestly can't remember how long it took but after five or six visits, let's say, he let me have a look at the painting and it was pretty good. Looking at a picture of yourself is like listening to a recording of your voice – it's never how you imagine yourself to be. Even so, it was well crafted – a good likeness save for the nose, which was a little too big. I pointed this out and Zac had the most ridiculous tantrum. He turned his brush round and stabbed it through the canvas.

'What are you doing?' I said. Zac ignored me and continued punching holes in the canvas. 'It's not that bad. I really liked it, apart from the nose.

'I hate portraits.'

'Why? You're really good at them.'

'That's why I hate them,' he said, at last putting the brush down. 'When I was at Goldsmiths, they said I was a natural portrait painter. That fucked me off. It's like telling a jazz musician he'd make a great piano teacher.' He lay on the bed next to me. 'There's always something wrong with portraits. That's why I don't paint them anymore.'

'Why don't you just repaint the bits that are wrong?'

'I prefer to start again,' he said, rolling onto his side, so we faced each other.

'But I really liked that painting and it was nearly perfect.'

'Oh come on!' said Zac, looking at my mouth. 'Let's not pretend you're here to have your portrait painted.'

'What do you mean?'

'Every week you come here, lie on my bed and tell me your husband doesn't understand you and you need to feel free again. I think we both know why you're here.'

I was furious but before I could answer, he closed his eyes and pressed his lips on mine.

I fell off the bed, trying to get away from him. 'You've made a big mistake,' I said, quickly gathering my things.

'Have I?' he said, smirking.

So you were right about Zac's intentions but not about me. I walked out of that door, determined I'd never see him again.]

The image of Laura in Ford's bed wouldn't leave my mind. Laura had admitted it but I still couldn't believe it. I tried to imagine her in Ford's bed, fully clothed, with him at a safe distance behind a canvas, but he kept sliding in beside her and her clothes kept coming off. Unable to sleep, even after a prolonged visit to YouPorn, I went to my email account and clicked on NEW EMAIL. The computer recognised 'clau' as Claudia Alvares. For subject heading, I wrote 'How are you?' Then I typed the following message:

Dear Claudia,

I hope you're well. I'm mostly writing to check you're OK. It's been several months and I've not had any of your usual updates. I hope that's a good sign.

Also, I wondered if, by any chance, you've seen Zac Ford recently? If so, has he spoken to you about a woman called Laura Ferguson? It's nothing important – I'm just curious.

Anyway, I hope you had a good summer.

Best wishes,
Dr Jack Randall

Of course it was a bad idea but bad ideas often look like good ideas in the dark of a sleepless night.

8

Emotions and memories are dangerous when they're not articulated – they rattle around the mind, smashing up things. The logic of language puts everything in its proper place. That's one of the ways in which therapy helped me most – I got into the habit of managing my emotions by identifying and describing them. I thought when I started writing this diary that I was just continuing that habit; I was using words to put my shame and anger in proportion. However, the longer I go on, the more I think that there's another motivation – I want there to be a physical record of what actually happened. I want someone to read this.

The problem with having a reader in mind, even a theoretical one, is now I'm worried about things like introducing the characters and breaking confidences. To tell my story, I need to explain some things about Claudia that no therapist should ever reveal. It's a low risk though, as the only person I can think of giving this diary to is Adam, and he never reads more than a page of anything.

It'll just sit on a shelf next to the motivational books his mother gives him.

Claudia grew up in a family that was dominated by her father, a sculptor with a fiery temper. Her mother was a refugee from Kosovo, who'd trained to be a psychiatrist but could only find a job as a steward at football matches. Her maternal uncle, also a refugee, lived in a small bedroom in the same house and spent most of his time reading one-pound classic novels. She had a sister, Maria, around four years younger, who was prettier than her and better behaved [i.e. who wasn't a psychopathic liar]. Her father worked in a Portakabin at the bottom of their garden. She was never allowed inside but she'd watch him sometimes from the window. One such memory stood out. Her father was stood in a strange position, too close to the window. When she got nearer, she realised, with a horror and revulsion she didn't understand till later, he was holding Maria up by the waist and leaning her over the table.

As she grew older, she became close to her uncle, who used take her to the playground and read her stories about princesses and dragons. In her adolescence, she grew thinner and lost a lot of energy. Her parents took her to doctors who referred her to nutritionists. One said she was lactose intolerant, another said wheat was the problem, another advised against gluten. She was diagnosed with so many intolerances there was little left she could eat and she grew thinner still. In despair her parents took her to a therapist. Under some form of hypnosis, she 'uncovered' a hidden memory of being sexually abused by her uncle. The uncle was thrown out of the home, protesting his innocence. When he'd gone, she began eating normally again.

I'm sceptical about uncovered memories but I didn't confront her with my doubts. She was convinced she'd been abused by her uncle and, in the world of the unconscious, there's little difference between what actually happened and what we believe happened.

[Back here on Planet Earth, there's quite an important difference between what happened and what didn't. Shouldn't you have tried to get Claudia to distinguish between the two?]

When she was sixteen she'd lost her virginity to a married teacher at her school. He told Claudia he'd never leave his wife and, in response, she cut her wrists. Her parents got the truth out of her and there was a scandal. The school sacked the teacher. The teacher accused Claudia of lying [probably because she was] – said she'd been the one who'd tried to seduce him and he'd turned her down. She had to move to another school. Her next boyfriend was a semi-professional poker player, fifteen years older than her, with four children from four different women. He said he'd been tricked by each of them. He'd travel to casinos round the world and she'd torture herself with the thought of what he was up to. After that came the TV presenter who kept texting his ex-girlfriend. And so she went on, all the way up to Ford, always repeating the same mistake.

In her conscious mind she'd not made any connection between her father's preference for her sister and the men she'd chosen to go out with. She'd obviously never dared criticise her father. Instead, she found substitutes – unfaithful men about whom she could complain. I think this explained her eating disorder too – I've often found that anorexics live in families where something cannot be discussed. It's almost as if the pressure to keep their mouth shut makes them unwilling to eat.

[This is all very neat and clever but how can you be sure it's right? I'll give my interpretation of Claudia's life. Little

93

girl resents her sister for being prettier than her. Little girl makes up nasty stories to get more attention from her parents. Little girl grows up to be big lanky ostrich who still makes up stories. Ostrich tricks rich artist into sleeping with her, then makes him feel so guilty he pays for her to see a therapist. Ostrich then tries to trick therapist into sleeping with her by making up yet more stories.]

In Freud's day I'd have just said 'aha', explained my interpretation, lit a cigar and left her to get on with it. The trouble is that hardly ever works. Patients won't accept it. They need to intuit it themselves. They need to work through it.

So instead Claudia and I would analyse how she felt about therapy, or what she dreamed, or what she'd eaten. As the weeks went on, her appearance changed. She put on some weight and she'd wear make-up and short skirts. One day she said she felt uncomfortable at the way I was looking at her. I asked her why and she claimed I was looking at her legs (which I wasn't). [If not, you did well. Claudia's legs must have taken up most of the room.] I asked her why that made her uncomfortable and she said it was too sexual. I asked if she'd considered that someone might look at her legs for other reasons, perhaps because they were concerned by her weight [or because they'd never seen ostrich legs on a human being] and she said no, she hadn't.

In the weeks after that, her health continued to improve. She told me she was eating large breakfasts – bananas and yoghurt and granola every morning. [Imagine me, doctor, just out of bed, my mouth round a banana!] She asked me if her legs were looking better and laughed. Her mood brightened and she could be light-hearted and playful. She spoke about Ford less and I got the impression they might have separated.

[Claudia and Zac did not 'separate' as they were never
a couple. Zac slept with Claudia once, when he was drunk,
and when he refused to sleep with her again, she went
crazy, accusing him of getting her pregnant and abandoning
her. She threatened to go to the papers, left poison pen
letters at his gallery and his home, rang him at all hours
till he changed his number, and waited outside his flat,
accosting any woman that came out of the front door till he
called the police. She only stopped stalking Zac after she
started seeing you.]

At this point, I need to explain my working routine.
I had an office in a tower block in Acton. By stairs or
lift you could reach my landing, which was shared by
a Bangladeshi family who lived opposite. I had the
door to the right and it was protected by a PIN code,
which I only gave to patients I'd agreed to take on.
Inside, there was a toilet straight ahead, marked WC,
and a waiting room hardly bigger than a toilet to
the right.

Sessions started on the hour and finished at ten
minutes to. All patients were told that, if they arrived
early, they had to stay in the waiting room until it was
their time. This was to be measured by a large clock on
the wall of the waiting room, which I synchronised with
my own watch every day. On no account was a patient to
leave the waiting room if they heard voices outside, unless
I expressly asked them to. A right-angled corridor bent
round the waiting room and led to a heavy white almost
sound-proof door. When this was closed, patients were not
allowed in – if there was some urgent reason they needed
my attention, or if their hour had already started, they
were told to knock and wait for a response.

The room in which I worked was deliberately bare. As you came in, there was a couch facing you, with a pillow on the left so that anyone lying on it could look out of the window. In the far left corner was my chair, which had casters so I could swivel with my thoughts. In the opposite corner, but only a few feet away, was another chair, made of black leather like mine but without wheels. Against the back wall was a cupboard and the only other object in the room was a black-and-white photograph of a blossom tree from Laura on the wall facing my chair. Claudia was the only patient who'd ever mentioned it – she asked who'd given it to me. I asked why she wanted to know.

In the ten minutes between my patients, I'd wash my hands, dry them thoroughly (wet handshakes raise questions) and straighten my tie in the bathroom mirror. Every time, I'd think of what Freud said about how a therapist should look – like a person you might trust if they introduced themselves at a casino. Then I'd pause in the doorway and check that everything was in its proper position – the spare chair was in line with the wall at forty-five degrees to my own; the couch had a fresh sheet of Kleenex on the pillow; the photograph was straight; and the floor was clean.

The patient before Claudia was a woman in her early thirties I'll call Susan. Susan had been in depression for many years before she came to see me. With her life story, it wasn't hard to see why. Her mother and brother died of cancer when she was a child. Her father distanced himself from her, whenever he could, leaving her in the care of a succession of girlfriends. Susan moved in with Geoff, the first man she'd slept with, without questioning whether she loved him. They stayed together although they never married. He drank too much and when he was drunk he'd bully her. She worked as a TV sub-editor. It was her job to sit alone in a dark room watching hours of film, looking for the right places to make a cut. She took a break in the hope she'd have a child but she never did. They tried IVF but it didn't work. Geoff told her it was her fault. She went back to her old job and the people who'd been runners when she last worked there were now senior to her. They'd patronise her. Geoff would be drunk when she'd get home. She told me many times that she was going to leave him but she never did. There was always an excuse – a problem at work that meant it wasn't the right time, or a hint that he might give up drinking, or a holiday for which they'd already bought the tickets.

Although I felt pity for Susan, I couldn't feel empathy. This was my failing. Every week she'd describe, with a trilling, fake laugh, some new insult she'd suffered, either at home or at work. She seemed to delight in taking the most negative possible interpretation of other people's actions and words, and using them to confirm her own pessimism. I found myself irritated by the façade of world-weary cynicism behind which she hid. We never seemed to get anywhere because she wouldn't open up. No doubt this irritation was countertransference on my part. I have a tendency to drift into pessimism myself. I probably kept myself distant from her because I was afraid of becoming her.

[Am I being paranoid, or is there a suggestion that I'm in some way like Geoff? In fact, I was much more like Susan, at least at work. Did I ever tell you what Siritha said to me the week after Julian left?

SIRITHA: You've probably heard by now that I've been made editor. I just wanted to say –

ME (genuinely happy for her): Actually I hadn't heard but that's great news. Well done! I'm so pleased they've recruited internally. And that it's a woman.

SIRITHA (with a brief, fake smile): Thank you. I just wanted to say that I have a lot of respect for you. I don't see any reason why our relationship should change just because I'm now your boss. The fact that you applied for the same job is not going to be an issue between us, as far as I'm concerned.

ME: Technically, I didn't really apply for the job. Julian put my name forward.

SIRITHA: Really? Because I heard that you wrote to the owner saying they needed someone with experience in editing rather than marketing to edit the magazine.

After that, I made a big effort to get to the office at 9 a.m., even though it made no difference to the work I had to do. Siritha didn't notice the many times I got there on time, she only noticed the few occasions I was late. Even if it was only about ten past, she'd give me a catty look. She hired someone in her first week. Naive as I was, I didn't suspect a thing. Peter was a thin, tall man with a brown satchel and a wispy beard, who had a lot of followers on Twitter or Facebook or some sort of blog. Like a lot of internet extroverts, he was shy in real life. He said he was a fan of my work and asked me for my thoughts on a couple of articles he'd written. His style was a bit overblown – like a left-wing Jeremy Clarkson – but he was kind of funny. I gave him a few tips and he seemed genuinely grateful.]

One afternoon, I had a breakthrough with Susan. She was talking about her mother's death. Her mother was scared as she knew she was going to die. Susan stayed by her side in the hospital, smiling, holding her hand, talking to her about anything other than what was coming. Susan would run to the toilet to make sure her mother wasn't alone for long. Just once, when it seemed safe, she left the hospital to go to Starbucks. When she returned, ten minutes later, her mother was dead. 'I left my mum to die alone for a coffee.' She stopped speaking and a single tear rolled down her cheek. Her eyes welled red and more and more tears started to flow. I thought of my own mum and had to check myself from crying. I looked at my watch and it was six minutes to the hour. I told Susan, in my softest voice, that it was 'time' but she didn't show any sign of having heard me. Her mouth sank and she began to sob. Her neck rose and she cupped her shaking face. I didn't want to intrude but when it got to four minutes to, I had to repeat that it was time. She was wailing by now and, when I said this, her wails became louder – shrieks and pants of pain. It was wild – like a fit of grief at a funeral. She was moaning and rocking on the couch and I didn't know what to do. No one had ever ignored a request to leave before. I wondered if there was a connection between her refusal to leave the couch and her guilt at leaving her mother's deathbed. There wasn't time to discuss it.

'Susan,' I said, 'I'm sorry but I have another patient.'

Still she paid me no attention. She yelled and coughed as if she were in agony. The hour was up. I had to do something, so I got out of my chair, knelt before the couch and leaned across Susan to get a hold of her shoulders. Slowly and gently I coaxed her up from the couch. She was still crying but not as hard and she took her hands away from her face. She stared, not at me, but at something behind me. I turned to see Claudia, flashbulb-frozen in the doorway. Claudia's fidgety eyes, shining with delight or shock, shifted from me to Susan and back again. I told Claudia, in a schoolmasterly tone, to go back to the waiting room but she didn't. She stood by the door, so Susan had to squeeze past her.

I let Claudia in and realised too late that the tissue paper on the couch was wet and torn. Just before her head touched the Kleenex, she sat up.

'What was going on there?' she said.

'I'm sorry that we've started late,' I said. 'We'll continue later too. Please do try to relax.'

She lay down but her head didn't touch the pillow. She looked in better health than I'd ever seen her. She wore a black V-neck cashmere jumper, which revealed a triangle of flushed skin.

'Why were you touching her?' she said.

I didn't want to become defensive, or to talk about myself, so I tried to deflect her. 'Tell me what's on your mind,' I said. I was thinking how clever the unconscious can be. Perhaps it wasn't a coincidence that I'd allowed Susan to stay so long. Perhaps I wanted Claudia to relive that moment when she saw her father and sister in the Portakabin.

'I am pretty shocked,' she said. 'I can't believe what I've just seen.'

'Try to describe it for me,' I said. 'Does it trigger any memories?'

'Only of every man I've ever known!' she said. 'I thought you were different.' She paused. 'Why her?'

The following week Susan took off her coat and high heels without looking at me. She began by saying she was anxious about whether she could afford to carry on with therapy. I've often noticed that patients want to leave when they're on the brink of getting somewhere. I asked why she was thinking about this now and she said she couldn't afford to carry on paying me forever.

'It makes me feel guilty,' she said.

'Why should you feel guilty about therapy?' I asked.

'I don't know. It seems like an indulgence.'

'Do you think your feelings are connected to what happened at your last appointment?'

'What do you mean?' she said.

'Well, you were very open last time about something that was very difficult for you. Do you think maybe you're feeling a resistance against probing further into that?'

'I don't know,' she said. 'Maybe, but I've been worried about the expense for a long time. I just didn't say anything before now.'

'And why do you think you're mentioning it now?' I said. 'I've talked about how I saw our last meeting. I thought you made real progress. What were your feelings about it?'

'I suppose it reminded me that you don't really care. You're just listening because you're paid to. When my fifty minutes are up, that's it. You don't want to know. It made me think I should find a real friend who won't cut me off when the buzzer goes.'

We explored this. We talked about the need for boundaries and limitations on a patient's time and how that doesn't mean I don't care. I asked if she could think of any reason why she felt so angry about my not being there for her as long as she wanted but she didn't take my hint. I heard the front door open. I checked my watch and it was only half past. Claudia had never been that early before.

When I told Susan it was time, she sat up quickly and collected her clothes, as if in a race. She trod on the back of her shoe and dragged it to the door without looking at me. As the door closed behind her, I could hear the word 'what'. I collected the tissue from the couch and stood by the door. I could hear a muffled conversation. I opened the door to see the back of Claudia's leg as it disappeared into the waiting room. Susan was staring in her direction.

I told Claudia we'd have to move her session to another time of the week.

'What, so I don't walk in on you and that other woman again?' she said.

'I am trying to avoid another incident. Confidentiality is very important to therapy.'

'Why do I have to move?' she said. 'Why can't it be her?'

'Why does it matter?' I asked.

'I've got a better idea,' she said. 'Why don't I just stop coming altogether? I was in two minds about whether to come today and I can see it was a mistake.'

'Well,' I said, 'patients don't usually stop therapy suddenly like this. Normally we move slowly towards a conclusion so we're both ready. I think there are still some things you need to work on.'

'Or things you want to work on!'

'I can understand,' I said, 'why you reacted the way you did. It must have been disturbing and confusing to see me with another patient. And I can see why you interpreted that in the way you did. But have you considered another possibility? Have you considered that the patient may have been crying so hard she couldn't hear me asking her to leave? That maybe I had to touch her shoulder to remind her it was time to go?'

She paused. 'Does anyone really cry so hard they can't hear?'

'Sometimes people only hear what they want to hear, don't you think?' I said.

'Maybe,' she said.

That was the last time she came to see me. Her bill was paid by a cheque with no covering letter and for a year I heard nothing. Then I received an email:

Hey doc. I just wanted u to no I'm doing a lot better now. Check out my legs ☺☺ *LL* She attached a picture of tanned healthy legs dangling off the side of a boat.

After that, there were emails every month or two.

Sorry I walked out on u. I never told u but u really helped me. I'm dating a great guy now. No more bastards!!!

Just saw Zac again. He told me about this Japanese girl he's seeing and he was showing off about how good she was in bed. Pukesville!!!

Hiya, doc. Thought u'd like to know you're favourite legs will be walking down the catwalk at London fashion week.

I didn't reply to any of these messages. The first time I emailed Claudia was the night when Laura told me about how she'd get into Ford's bed to pose for him.

Claudia replied to my email the next morning:

Hey doc. Gr8 to hear from u! I was beginning 2 think I had the wrong address. I haven't seen Zac for a while but I'll do some digging and get back 2 U. U've got the right detective on the case! By the way, why didn't u tell me u'd written a book? That's so cool! How do I buy it? I can't get it on amazon.

9

*Hey doc. I did the digging like u asked. The word is Zac is seeing
an older woman. I've got some more details but I don't want
to put them in an email. If they can hack phones, they can hack
emails 2. Let's meet up. Are you still free at 3 p.m. on Thursdays?
Or have u replaced me with yet another?* 😟☺ *In that hotel by
Acton tube?*

Reading it now, it's so obvious I should never have met
Claudia: the schizophrenic smileys, the delusion that we
might be hacked, the suggestion we meet in a hotel. But
at the time all I could think about was who was this older
woman? [If Zac was seeing an older woman – and I am very
sceptical of everything Claudia says – it was not me.]

Although I was desperate to find out more about Laura
and Ford, I was concerned that meeting Claudia might be
unethical. I had a session with my supervisor, Ms Rosen (I
never learned her first name).

Ms Rosen liked to meet face to face in her Hampstead
flat. She used to make me sit on the overstuffed sofa in this

dark-red wallpapered room, while she sat in an armchair, like a queen receiving a guest.

She always made me speak first.

'If you needed help,' I said, 'and a former patient was the only one who could help you, it would be OK to ask them, wouldn't it?'

'What do you think?' Ms Rosen never answered questions.

'I mean,' I said, 'if I had a former patient, who knew a lot about doctors, for example, and I had to choose the best doctor, it would be OK to ask the patient for a recommendation, wouldn't it? That wouldn't be a big deal, would it?'

'Is there something you need to tell me?' she said. 'Has your cancer returned?'

'No, it's not that.'

'So why are doctors on your mind then? Can you free-associate?'

'No,' I said, 'doctors are not on my mind. It's an analogy. I got in touch with Claudia. You remember? The anorexic patient I had, with the drinking problems? She's much better now but I think she knows something about my wife and I want to find out what it is.' An ordinary person would have said something at this point, like 'What does she know?' or 'Why do you think this?' but Ms Rosen was silent so I stumbled on. 'You see my wife is spending a lot of time with a man I don't trust, a friend of Claudia's. And I just want to know what's going on.'

'Who is the doctor here?' Ms Rosen asked. 'And what is the disease?'

'Well, I suppose the disease is in my marriage and I want to know how serious it is.'

'And who is the doctor that can cure this disease?'

'It's not Claudia,' I laughed. 'She's got a disastrous history of relationships.'

'So why do you need her advice?'

'I don't,' I said. 'I just want information. I want to know if Laura's having an affair. That's all. That's the only reason I'm meeting Claudia.'

'You're meeting Claudia?' Ms Rosen's voice rose in surprise.

'Yes,' I said. 'Do you think that's a bad idea? She didn't want to talk on the phone.'

'So you're going to her for a consultation?' Ms Rosen said.

'No,' I said. 'Look, maybe the doctor analogy wasn't right.'

'Can you hear the resistance in your voice?' she said. 'I think there's some work here.' She paused.

'What do you mean?' I asked.

'Well –' she sounded annoyed that I'd asked her to explain – 'which one of you is more like a doctor?'

'Me.'

'And which one of you has been trained in curing the diseases that might infect a marriage?'

'I see,' I said, 'so you think I'm trying to reverse the roles. Make out that I'm the patient and Claudia's the therapist. But why would I do that?' I paused. Ms Rosen said nothing. The silence forced me to continue: 'Are you suggesting I'm unconsciously reversing our roles so I don't feel guilty about meeting her? So there's nothing unethical about it? Maybe. I don't know. Or maybe it was just a bad analogy. I'm not looking to Claudia for advice, just information.'

'Isn't there another way of reading this "analogy"?' she asked.

'What?' I said.

'Well,' Ms Rosen said, shuffling in her chair, 'you said there was a disease in your marriage – your wife, you suspect, is being unfaithful? Are you hoping that meeting Claudia will –' her voice lowered – 'cure that?'

'I'm not going to sleep with Claudia!' I said. 'Or is that not what you meant? Honestly, Claudia is an attractive woman but the thought has never crossed my mind ... Well, it has sort of ... but not in a real way ... just a passing thought that I would never, ever act on ...'

Neither of us spoke for several minutes.

> [I'd be lying if I said I never thought about Zac's attempt to kiss me and what would have happened on that filthy, paint-stained bed if I hadn't run away. But, like with you, these were 'passing thoughts' I would never, ever have acted on. Besides, whenever I thought about it, I always concluded that I did the right thing by leaving.
>
> I decided not to see Zac again but then I realised I'd left my phone at his studio. I called from work to ask him to send it to me and his tone was so relaxed you'd never have guessed he'd made a pass at me. He said I could pick it up from his flat any time I wanted. I thought he was going to leave it with the doorman.]

'So,' I continued, 'you think it's a bad idea. I shouldn't meet her?'

My whole life, I've always searched for someone who'd give me the answers, who'd explain who I should be, what I should do, what the point of everything was. When I was a child, it was my mother because, for me, she was the adult world. As a teenager, I turned to authors, like Tolstoy and George Eliot and Somerset Maugham, who seemed to know me. They took the tangled sensations and jumbled half-thoughts of my adolescence and smoothed them out into sentences. But I lost faith in them – they were no help when Mum got sick – so I turned to psychoanalysis. My first therapist, Mr Lightman, had this calm confidence. I couldn't imagine him worrying about death, or old age, or the purpose of life. I always hoped he'd teach me his secret but he never did. Like all the therapists and supervisors that followed, he'd just tinker with the questions, leaving me to flounder on in search of the answers.

I wanted Ms Rosen to tell me what to do. To this day, I think if she'd told me not to meet Claudia, everything would have been different. But she didn't. She just left a silence for me to fall into. The hour passed and I left without catching her eye.

Thanks for your email, Claudia. How about we meet in a café instead? Do you remember the one near Acton tube? I finish work at 5 p.m. on Thursday so we can meet around 5.15 to have a coffee and catch up. It will be great to see you. I paused. The cursor tapped its foot. I deleted '*see you*' and replaced it with '*hear your news*'.

The café was smaller than I remembered – no more than eight tables in a room the size of a squash court. A middle-aged woman, with a leather trilby so low on her head it touched her glasses, sat on a table in the far corner with a booklet of crossword puzzles. Three bags surrounded her – two handbags and one carrier bag – and there was no food or drink on her table, only a folded tabloid. In the opposite corner, with his back to the woman, a bald man with a red birthmark across his face hunched over a cheese sandwich. Neither looked up when I came in. I stood at the counter, coughing, but no one came. From an open doorway behind the counter, I could hear the sound of washing up. I took a seat, facing the door, and brushed the crumbs off the marbled plastic table. '*Now it's time for the travel news. Martha, what have you got for us?*' It was impossible not to listen to the conversation on the radio. This is a terrible place to meet, I thought.

I checked my watch and I was five minutes early. Time passed. The only sound was the radio and the slurps of cars passing through puddles. I was staring at the squeezy bottles on my table when I heard the door tinkle. A smiley man in a navy blue fleece approached the counter. A young Thai woman appeared from the kitchen and laughed.

'Coffee, sir?' she said. 'Tea?'

'Nothing like that, no,' he said and took the table behind me.

The woman in the leather hat tried to lift herself. Failed. Tried again and, taking one of her three bags, disappeared behind a yellow door. The bald man stood up, zipped up his jacket, took one last swig from his mug, then crossed the room to where the woman had been sitting. He paused for a few seconds then bent down quickly, as if he were sniffing the chair.

Around quarter past, Claudia arrived. She wasn't as skinny as when I'd last seen her – her face was rounder – but the rest of her body was still thin. Her gold bracelet slid easily up and down her bony forearm and her tight jeans could only have fitted someone with very long, slim legs. Her complexion was the yellow-brown of pale wood – the residual winter colour of someone who tans easily [or, to be more precise, someone who wears fake tan]. Dark semicircles underscored her eyes.

'You're looking good,' I said. 'I mean "well". You're looking well. Healthy.'

'Thank you,' she said in a quiet voice. She looked straight at me and her large brown eyes seemed to swell and everything else became blurry background. She stared at me in silence and I felt uncomfortable.

'Coffee?' I said.

The Thai woman had disappeared. I stood at the counter, coughing even louder than before, but nothing happened. I read the menu on the blackboard – everything involved eggs, bacon or sausages, even the 'variety dishes'. I could hear Claudia's knee jiggling. She was picking at the skin on her bottom lip and scowling. The man in the blue fleece was sat only a couple of feet from her but he never once looked her way. When I returned, she smiled and I was struck by how beautiful she was.

'When I was in rehab,' she said, 'we used to drink, like, ten coffees a day. And smoke, like, two packets of fags. All still chasing that high. I swear, the coffee makers and tobacco companies should invest in rehab.'

'The same often happens in therapy. The therapist becomes the drug. Unless you get to the cause of the problem, that's all you can do – swap one addiction for another.'

'I know,' she said. 'I had to go cold turkey to get off you.'

'Huh!' I said, grinning awkwardly. 'Well, it looks like you're well and truly past that now. You seem really healthy.'

'Oh, I am, doc. I really am.'

'And you're not in therapy anymore?'

'Don't worry,' she said in an amused and knowing voice that annoyed me. 'You were the only therapist for me!'

'Everything going well otherwise?'

'I'm single,' she said, 'if that's what you mean. But I

know now what I want. No more playboys. I want an older man who'll take care of me. Someone kind and wise. A good listener.'

'And the ...' I looked around and lowered my voice. 'The drinking?'

'Sober for a year. Coffee is my only drug.'

Well,' I said, 'if you're going to have an addiction, coffee's not too bad.'

'What's your addiction, doc?' She spoke in a girlish voice and bowed her chin so she was looking at me through her long eyelashes.

'Smoking,' I said. 'I've started smoking again.'

'Is that all?' Her lips hinted at a smile. 'Why are you so interested in Zac's love life?'

'Ahh, that. Yes. Um. Well.' I lowered my voice and leaned forward. 'The person I wrote to you about is a close friend of mine. A very close friend. And I'm worried that she's been misled by this Ford. I know all about what he did to you and I don't want him to do that to her.'

'So,' she said in a voice that could have been overheard, even in the kitchen, 'why not just tell this Laura? Laura Ferguson, right? Why not tell her Zac Ford is a shit? He'll cheat on you.'

'I thought,' I whispered, 'that might be presumptuous. I mean, I don't know for certain that she's had any kind of ... you know. She may just be friends with Ford. I want to be sure.'

'A close friend?' she said, stirring her Americano round and round. 'It's a lot of trouble to go to for a friend. How "close" are you?'

'I'm not going to go into that, Claudia.' I said.

'Chill,' she said, frowning. 'I know she's your wife. I'm not an idiot. Have you forgotten why I came to you?

111

Zac was friends with your wife – "Laura Ferguson" or whatever you like to call her. I knew there was something fishy about that. Zac said I shouldn't worry – she was too old for him. What a fucking liar.'

'Can we go outside?' I said. 'I want to smoke.'

I lit her cigarette and she took a long frowning drag. With her spare arm, she hugged herself.

'I'm not made for the cold,' she said.

'It's eighteen degrees,' I said.

'That's cold for me.'

'So,' I said, 'what exactly do you know about Laura and Ford?'

'I don't want to hurt you,' she said softly. She was looking through her eyelashes again.

'Just tell me,' I said. 'Are they in a relationship?'

She nodded, with a crumpled face as if she were about to cry. As if it were her that was being cheated on.

'How do you know?' I asked. 'Have you seen them together? Did Ford tell you something?'

'Well,' she said. 'I've not seen them together but that's not how Zac works.' She began to speak with a rising inflection, as if she were asking a series of questions rather than making statements. 'He's very clever? When we went out, he'd never kiss me or, like, hold my hand if other people were there? I used to think that was so off? He said he was just shy? It was just the way he was brought up?' It was as if she wanted my reassurance at the end of every sentence. 'But now,' she said, 'I realise he just didn't want people to know? About us?' She dipped her chin and her eyes welled. I felt a tinge of pity.

I waited for her to stop sniffling before saying, as gently as I could, 'So how do you know? I mean, if you've not

seen them together, how do you know Ford and Laura
are . . .?'

'Women know, OK?' Claudia seemed annoyed by the
question. 'I've spoken to Zac. He's got someone new in
his life. That's for sure. He's being even more evasive than
usual. He doesn't answer his phone in the evenings. He's
not going to parties. He won't say where he's been.'

'But how do you know it's Laura?'

She snorted and shook her head. 'Why would you even
be asking me if you didn't think it was her? I could tell by
the way he talks about her. Or rather the way he won't
talk about her. That's always a sign he's seeing someone.
Look, if you really want to be sure, let's follow him. I've
got an idea. On Sunday night, it's Bez's birthday party in
Soho House. Bez is Zac's best friend. I asked Zac if he was
going and he said he had something else on. I know what
that means – "something else" is a woman. We could wait
outside his flat.' I said nothing. 'You like Sherlock Holmes,
don't you? I'll be your Dr Watson. We'll go to his house,
wait in my car, then follow him.'

I laughed. 'I'm a bit too old for that kind of thing.'
Claudia's expression soured. 'Let's go inside,' I said. 'You
look like you're shivering.'

Claudia stared sulkily at her coffee cup. I asked about the
modelling and she replied with grunts. I smiled, thinking
she didn't know anything – she was just a child, playing
games. She wouldn't look at me until I said I had to go.

'Wait,' she said, holding my hand. 'I haven't told you
everything.'

'You've told me enough,' I said, squeezing her hand and
letting go. 'I have to go home.'

I stood up and she stood up too, knocking her chair into
the table behind.

She drew close to me. 'I'll be here for you,' she said, 'when you need me.'

'Thank you,' I said. We hugged and she nestled her head into my shoulder. I could feel the warmth of her breath on my neck. 'Better go!' I said.

> [The image of this nymphomaniac airhead asking for a hug so she can press her Wonderbra'd breasts up against you makes me want to retch. I don't understand how you couldn't see through her bullshit. You only have to talk to her for five minutes to realise she's a fantasist.
>
> What really hurts though, is that you told her, not me, that you'd taken up smoking again. It's not as if I'm a nagger, or someone who disapproves of smoking per se. In the old days, I used to find it sweet when you smoked: you looked so ill at ease – the smoke would get into your eyes or you'd worry about what to do with the ash. But now, after you've had cancer once, why would you take such a risk?]

It was seven minutes to the next tube. I paced up and down the platform. It would be around 6.45 by the time I was home. Laura was normally back by 6.30. She knew I finished at five on Thursdays. She might ask where I'd been. If I said I'd been for a coffee, she'd ask with whom. If I told her, that would provoke questions I didn't want to answer. I could say truthfully – or at least mostly truthfully – that I'd seen a patient.

I jogged to the end of the road, then walked to our door. I was breathing normally as I entered.

'Laura,' I called out. The flat was dark and empty.

Laura came home two hours later.

'Hi.' I said flatly. 'Where have you been?'

'At work.'

'But you're normally home two hours earlier than this.'

'I went for a drink with Julian after work.'

'Julian? I thought he'd been fired.'

'He was,' she said. 'But we've kept in touch. He was my mentor.'

'I'm not sure I liked his take on marriage.'

She pretended not to know what I was referring to. 'He's in great form. And the good news is, I might be able to work with him again. Apparently he's got this really rich backer who wants to start up a magazine on high culture – theatre, literature, opera, ballet. And he wants me to work for him. So he's asked me for dinner on Sunday evening to meet this sponsor.'

'Sunday evening?' I said.

'Yes,' she said. 'I know it's quiz night but I never know the answers. You'll still come second whether I'm there or not.'

'Actually,' I said. 'I was thinking of giving the quiz night a rest this week. How about I come with you? Meet the shareholder?'

'I don't know, Jack. It's not really your kind of thing, is it? Networking? Sucking up to rich people?'

'I don't mind,' I said. 'Or do you think I'll embarrass you?'

'No, it's not that,' she said. 'It's just ... we're going to the opera. And they've only got three tickets.'

'Opera? On a Sunday? Do they have opera on Sundays?'

'Yeah,' she said in a tone that sounded far from confident, 'sure they do. How would you know? You've never been to the opera.'

'Which opera are you going to?' She walked away into the bedroom, as if she hadn't heard so I followed her. 'Which opera?'

'Royal Opera House,' she said.

'I meant which opera is being performed?' I said.

'I don't know,' she said.

'So you're going to the opera but you don't know what you're going to see? Julian, the new editor of a magazine devoted to high culture, said "Let's go to the opera; I don't know what's on but they're all the same anyway"?'

'No, he didn't say that. He probably told me what we were seeing, but I wasn't paying attention. You know opera's not my thing. I'm not musical enough. Just going for a shower ...'

[It was like this. Julian suggested a drink. He said he might have a job offer for me. I was still committed to the magazine, despite the chippy remarks I got from Siritha every morning, but I thought 'why not?' It's not disloyal to listen. I left work early and we met in The Hansom Cab. Julian was looking younger and happier than I'd seen him in years. He was always well dressed but somehow he was even smarter than usual. He was full of his usual jolly, roguish charm. At one point, in response to his pretend flirtation, I asked him how his wife was doing and he said: 'Oh, you mean my baby mother' with this naughty, knowing smirk. He likes to tease me by making sexist remarks like this but, for some reason, I don't mind. Perhaps it's because I don't believe he really means it. Or perhaps it's because he's a different generation, where those kinds of views were considered acceptable. After a day of being demoralised and patronised at work, it was fun to see Julian again. Anyway, after a few of these Julian-style jokes, he mentioned that he knew someone who might fund a new magazine and that we should meet on Sunday evening.

I told you all this but I don't think you were paying attention until I said the word 'Sunday'.

'When on Sunday?' you said.

'Sunday evening,' I said. 'I'm not really sure but *I think* we're going to the opera as Julian said to meet at the Royal Opera House.' I could see you were worried but I thought you were just upset I'd miss the pub quiz. If you'd told me what you were thinking, I could have explained everything.]

I googled the Royal Opera House. There was nothing in their programme for Sunday evening. This time the evidence was too strong to be doubted. Even so, I couldn't believe it. She had an excuse to meet Zac twice a week. Why go to the trouble of lying about Julian and the opera? Perhaps she was bored of the sex and wanted to go on a date with him. Perhaps they thought I was so stupid and trusting they could get away with anything. Or maybe it was just paranoia on my part. Maybe she really was meeting Julian. But why had she lied that they were going to the opera? There could be no innocent explanation for that. One way or the other, I had to know.

I texted Claudia: 'Good to see you today. Can you let me know if Zac comes to the party on Sunday? Just curious.'

Claudia replied: 'OK Sherlock ☺'

10

'Have you found out which opera it is yet?' I was slumped on the couch, trying to look relaxed, but my heart was racing.

Laura appeared in tights and a bra. 'What did you say?'

'Do you know which opera you're going to tonight?' I said.

'All I know,' she said, 'is it's at the Royal Opera House.'

'What time?' I asked.

'Eight.'

'I thought opera started earlier.'

'Julian told me eight.' Laura went back into the bedroom and the hairdryer stopped the conversation. She reappeared five minutes later in a green dress – my favourite green dress. She picked out some hair clips from the bowl by the front door. 'What have you done with my keys?'

'Nothing,' I said. 'Why would I do something with your keys? Anyway, it's only seven. You've got lots of time.'

'Yeah, but I don't want to be late and . . .' She hunched into her black coat. 'Ah, found them!' she said, lifting her

keys from the pocket. 'Bye, sweetheart. Don't wait up
for me.'

What are you supposed to do when you're waiting for
your wife to return from her lover? Time hurt me. It was
unbearable to do nothing. Every thrust of the second hand
dug into me. I couldn't read – the text turned into a black
cloud, which floated between me and the book. I couldn't
watch television – even the sound of it annoyed me and
made me anxious. I had to do something, but what? I
called Laura but her phone was off. I texted Claudia: 'Has
the party started yet? Any sign of Zac?'

She replied almost immediately: 'Not yet. I'm outside the
front door of his block of flats. No sign of him in the last
hour.'

I called her. 'Claudia, what are you doing? I didn't want
you to spy on him.'

'Yes you did.'

'I never asked you to wait outside his front door. I said it
was a bad idea.'

'No, you said you were too old for it. You never said I
shouldn't. And then you asked me what Zac was doing on
Sunday and I replied "OK, Sherlock". It was obvious what
you wanted me to do. Don't you want to find out?'

'I do but . . . not this way. You shouldn't be a part of
this. I'm sorry to have dragged you in. Please go to the
party. Do you promise?' There was a silence. 'Please
promise you won't stay.'

'OK,' she said at last.

'Thanks. Before you go, what's Zac's address?'

When I stepped out of the taxi, the rain was slanting into
my face and I looked for a place to shelter. I noticed a

red Mini, parked at an angle, half of its face peering out
from behind the other cars. Claudia was sitting in the
driver's seat. I knocked on the passenger window and she
leaned across to open the door.

'What are you doing here?' I said. 'You promised
you'd go.'

'Don't be cross with me,' Claudia said. 'I couldn't leave
you standing outside in this weather.' I hesitated. 'Come
on! Get in! Are you afraid of me or something?'

Spots of rain gathered on the windscreen like sweat on a
beading back. A covered pushchair rolled past my door,
followed by a pair of legs. On the other side of the street,
umbrellas floated, like scudding clouds, above the parked
cars. Claudia was pulling skin from her lips with one hand
and smoking through a gap in the window with the other.
She turned and smiled and bit her fingers.

'Do you need the toilet?' I said.

'No.'

'It's just your legs are shaking so much. We don't need
to stay. I'm pretty sure Laura would be here by now if she
were coming. She left our flat five or ten minutes before
me.' Claudia didn't reply. She'd slid down in her chair
and was staring at Zac's front door. Her legs jiggled and
her breathing was shallow. 'Let's give it five minutes,' I
said. My heart was racing. The strange thing was I wanted
Laura to come. I wanted to be right, even if it would
crush me. Neurosis, Freud said, is an inability to tolerate
ambiguity. I wanted to be free to release the anger and
the sadness that had pent up in my heart. I wanted to be
vindicated. I'd known all along this day would come. I'd
built a concrete bunker in my soul to retreat to when the
façade of Laura's love came crashing down.

A woman, wearing tracksuit bottoms with a red stripe along the leg and a black waterproof jacket, stopped outside Ford's door. She stretched to touch her toes and looked round, flicking her long ponytailed hair over her shoulder.

'Maybe that's Zac's woman,' I said.

'Don't be ridiculous,' Claudia said. 'No one meets their lover in sweatpants.'

The woman with the ponytail jogged out of sight. Two men in hooded jackets passed. White vans squeezed up and down the street. I checked my watch. It was 7.50.

'This was a crazy idea,' I said.

'Who's that?' Claudia said, leaning forward. A blue/black woman's shape, smudged by the rain, was standing outside Ford's door.

'Turn on the windscreen wipers,' I said.

'I'm trying,' Claudia said, as she pushed and pulled on the levers around the driving wheel.

'You need the ignition on,' I said. I leaned across to turn the key and, as I did so, I brushed the inside of Claudia's thigh. She looked at me and said nothing. The wiper revealed the ponytailed jogger. 'How did she get there?' I said. 'I didn't see her go back.' The jogger caught my eye for a split second and walked towards our car. I pulled out my phone and pretended to write a text. The jogger walked past.

I heard her before I saw her. The clack of high heels. My heart was pounding with adrenalin even before I saw the black coat and the green dress. Laura stopped and tilted a brown umbrella into the wind. Claudia was holding the door handle but she wasn't looking at Laura.

'Do you know what Laura looks like?' I said.

'I think so,' Claudia said. 'I've seen photos on Facebook. Dark hair, mole on face, bit fat?' Laura stopped in front of the silver keypad. 'Wait a minute. Isn't that her?' Claudia turned to me, with a look of wild excitement.

'Let's leave,' I said quietly.

'You're just going to give in?' she said. 'Without a fight? Let them get away with it? No way.' Claudia opened the door and I reached across to stop her. She turned and looked at me with dead, angry eyes. I let her go. Claudia pushed open the door and stopped as a black cab passed. I got out. I could see Claudia crossing the street but Laura had gone.

'Wait!' I said, standing in front of the intercom. 'Please don't. I don't want her to know I've followed her. It's undignified.'

'Undignified?' Claudia said. 'I tell you what's undignified. It's letting people trample all over you. That's undignified.' She leaned in to me and reached behind my back. I could hear the doorbell whining as Claudia and I stared at each other, only a few inches apart.

'Hello,' Ford's metallised voice sounded distant. I backed up against the intercom to smother it but I still heard him say: 'Are you not inside yet?'

'Zac,' Claudia said. 'It's me.'

'Claudia?' Ford said.

'Yes,' she said.

'This is not OK, Claudia,' he said. 'I've warned you about this. You are not well. If you buzz this bell again, I'm calling the police and this time I will press charges.'

Claudia hesitated and I took her hand. 'Let's go,' I whispered. 'Come on.'

She said nothing and followed me back to the car.

['Who's this?' Zac had said suspiciously, when I rang the intercom.

'Hi Zac,' I said cheerily, 'it's me, Laura, to collect my phone. Remember? Have you left it with the doorman?'

He buzzed without replying. The doorman knew nothing about the phone. The door to Zac's flat was closed when I got out of the lift. I knocked and he didn't respond. I knocked again. I opened the letter flap and called out: 'Zac, it's Laura.'

In the same instant, I heard a click and the door opened. I pushed and the door juddered against the chain. Zac's arm came round to hand me the phone.

'Bye,' he said and shut the door.

That was it. The full extent of my meeting with Zac. I must have left his building no more than a minute after you and Claudia. If you'd looked in the mirror, as you drove away, you'd probably have seen me hailing a cab.]

I watched Claudia get into the car.

'What are you doing?' she said. 'Get in! You'll be soaked.' I hesitated. My shirt was stuck to my skin. Cold rainwater ran down my forehead. 'Come on,' she said. 'I'll drive you home.'

Claudia drove with a cigarette in her mouth and both her hands on the wheel. The rain roared and hissed. The heaters struggled to keep a circle of windscreen clear. We stopped at a T-junction. Blurry cars crossed in front of us, sloshing through puddles. Claudia's head was craned forward and she was squinting.

'Look out!' I said.

Claudia was pulling out into the main road and, through her door window, I could see something dark and large coming straight at us, impossibly fast. I put my arms round Claudia an instant before we were hit. Glass shattered and metal cracked and I held her tighter. We glided sideways across the road for what felt like ten seconds or more.

'What the hell were you doing?' I couldn't tell if it was rain or tears pouring down the young man's face as he shouted at me. He kept turning to look at the crushed face of his car.

'I'm sorry,' I said. 'We didn't see you till it was too late. Are you OK?'

'What were you doing?' He sounded heartbroken.

'I'll drive you home,' I said, 'if the car still starts.' Claudia was shrunk into her seat. She hadn't spoken since the accident.

I walked her to the front door of her block of flats. 'Here we are,' I said. 'I'll just wait here for a cab.'

Claudia didn't speak. She held a shaking ring of keys close to her face and, as she picked one out, they slid from her hand and rattled on the floor. She burst into tears.

'When you get upstairs,' I said, 'get dry and warm and make yourself a cup of tea. You're probably still in shock.'

'Don't go,' she said. 'Please don't leave me now.'

'OK,' I said. 'I'll come up to make sure you're OK and then I'll get a cab.'

In the lift we were strangers, avoiding each other's eye. I read and reread a metal plate on the wall. SCHINDLER, MAX LOAD SEVEN PERSONS, MANUFACTURED IN 1978.

As Claudia and I walked down the corridor, to Flat 16, I felt like a prisoner being led to his cell. Claudia gave me the keys as she collected her hair in a spiked clasp. I tried each of them but none seemed to work. Claudia took them back.

I hesitated as the door opened.

'I'll just get into something dry,' she said.

I felt a terrible low as I sank into Claudia's sofa. Laura was cheating on me, so all my other worst fears must be true too. My book was a failure, my career was a failure and I was a failure. I shouldn't have been surprised to find Laura preferred someone else. It was inevitable.

Claudia came back in, wearing denim shorts and a figure-hugging top. 'You look like you need a drink,' she said.

'No thanks,' I said. 'If you can just give me a local cab number . . .' She didn't seem to have heard because she disappeared into another room. She came back with two shot glasses.

'Vodka,' she said. 'Polish.'

'I thought you'd given up,' I said.

'Don't worry, she said, 'I'm OK to . . .' She stopped. 'I'm OK to not drink,' she continued. 'After all, I've been sober for a year. These are both for you.' She smiled.

'I won't,' I said. 'I'll just have a glass of water and the taxi number.'

She dimmed the lights as she left the room. It took an uncomfortably long time for her to return. She sat on the sofa, closer than she needed to be.

'You saved my life,' she said and her eyes seemed to swell as her face approached mine.

'No I didn't.'

'You did.'

'Really, I didn't. You were wearing a seat belt. The other car can't have been going more than thirty miles an hour. You'd have been fine without me.'

'You saved my life,' she said. 'And not just today.'

'I should be off,' I said.

'Please,' she said, pleading with her large brown eyes, 'before you go, will you hold me, just for a little bit? I feel so safe in your arms.'

'OK,' I said, extending my arms to keep her at as much distance as I could. She drew closer and I could feel her tight frame shuddering. Her tears welled in the hollow of my collarbone. I patted her back but she didn't let go.

My mouth was so close to her neck I could have kissed her with the smallest movement of my lips. Her heart beat fast against my chest. Her skin had a hot, sour smell that reminded me of ceiling fans and twisted white sheets and city breezes. I realised I was getting an erection and I wondered how I could stand up without showing it. Claudia placed her wrist against my crotch.

'I should go,' I said, standing in a half crouch.

'Why?' she said. 'Did I do something wrong?'

'No, you didn't do anything wrong.'

'Then what is it? Do I look fat? I thought you wanted me to be fat, like your wife. To have dumpy little legs, like her. I don't believe this.' Her voice was rising and her eyes were darkening.

'Look, you're not fat. You're a very attractive woman but I'm a married man and you were my patient . . .'

'Shh!' she said, 'there's nothing to worry about.'
She pulled at the top button of my trousers and I jumped back.

'Stop!' I said.

Claudia looked shocked, then a frown gathered on her brow.

'What are you doing?' she said.

'I'm leaving,' I said, gathering up my coat. 'This has been a mistake. I'm sorry.'

'Mistake?' She looked outraged. 'You think you can just walk out on me and leave me like this?'

'I'm sorry,' I said, fumbling with the latch.

'You can't do this to me . . .' She paused as I opened the door. 'I'm pregnant!'

I walked and walked, without bothering to think where I was going. Wet brown-grey pavements shone with puddled street lights and the rain pricked the skin round my eyes. I walked till I could no longer feel the cold in my ribs. The other people on the streets were all dressed in black and they looked down when I passed, as if they knew what I'd done. The adrenalin or the cold or the fear began to clear my mind and I checked my watch. It was only ten o'clock and I had no idea when Laura would be home. I curled up on a bench. I couldn't sleep because of the clingy feeling in my damp socks so I got up. My phone buzzed with messages from Claudia ('Come back. PLEASE!' 'Why are you not answering?' 'This is so rude!' 'Where are you?' 'Please call me immediately. It's URGENT.'). I turned my phone off and thought about what I'd say when Laura got back. Should I confront her about Ford? Or tell her about what I'd done? Or just forget about the whole sordid evening? Maybe that's why I let things get so far with Claudia. So there was a reason to forgive Laura. Or so my self-hatred would eclipse my anger.

When I reached our street, the trees that had charmed us when we first came here with the estate agent were twisted and bare, like black skeletons' hands. Without hesitating, I walked past our front door. Laura wouldn't be home and I still hadn't decided what to do. I should tell her what I'd done, especially if I was going to ask her about Ford, but how could I explain it? What form of words could mitigate the stupidity? I squelched on, not thinking where I was going, till I found myself outside the pub where we normally spent Sunday night. I felt like a Dickensian ghost looking in on the faces in the warm light. A man in the window eyed me suspiciously and I walked on till I was hidden by brickwork and I could listen to the chatter and clatter and smell the sour wafts of beer without being noticed. My mind was clouded with a sick feeling of regret, a hangover of the soul, and I continued like a madman trying to lose his shadow. I needed a plan – a speech to make to Laura – but my thoughts turned to anything else they could find: a puddle in the shape of Australia; two Chinese women huddled under a Union Jack umbrella; the smudgy red of brake lights and the glittery silver of the headlit road.

When I opened the door, the flat was quiet and dark. My jeans and trainers were soaked and I kicked them off by the door. Laura's black coat was hanging on the hatstand. I pushed the bedroom door open softly and I saw the black of Laura's hair in the midst of the twisted white duvet. I was overwhelmed by relief and I nestled up to her. She groaned as I kissed her and coiled away. I tried to turn her head round but she resisted so I rolled over the top of her and lay on the pillow opposite. Her face was striped by hair and it was too dark to tell if she was awake. I wanted to cry with happiness at the thought that she was still there.

'Sweetheart,' I whispered.

'I'm sleeping,' she mumbled.

'I just wanted to say I love you. I'm sorry for everything, everything I've done wrong. I want to spend the rest of my life with you. I always have done and I always will. I don't care what you've done in the past as long it stays in the past. Let's start afresh tomorrow. We have our whole lives ahead of us. We can still have a family. We can still do everything. Everything we've ever wanted.'

I waited for a response but there was none. I must have fallen asleep soon after because I don't remember anything else.

[Oh Jack, why did you say this when I was asleep?

I'll tell you what I remember of the evening. Julian was

waiting, with an umbrella, to meet me as I got out of the cab. With an arm round my waist, he sheltered me from the rain and guided me away from the opera house.

'What about the opera?' I said.

'We're not going to the opera tonight,' he said, 'I just wanted to meet here as it's easy to find.'

'And where's the backer?' I asked.

'Oh he'll be at dinner,' Julian said. He led me down a sleazy Soho back street to a blue door. 'My club,' he said.

We were taken to a wooden clothless table, laid for two, in a small room lit only by candles.

'What about the backer?' I said.

'I'm the backer,' he said, 'and I back you.' I nearly left but I thought I should hear him out. He said he had a lot of money and he wanted to spend it on me, fulfilling my talent. I asked why. He said he'd heard about the restructuring at the magazine and he thought I deserved better.

'What about your family?' I asked. 'Won't they be annoyed if you spend your money on me?'

'My family will be fine,' he said.

At this point, the mood of the evening changed. Julian leaned forward, took my hand and said he was tired of living a lie. He said he was in love with me and he always had been. All the urbanity and twinkle disappeared and he became urgent and humourless. Pick a country, he said. Anywhere in the world. And we'll go. You can do whatever you like. I want to spend the rest of my life making you happy. I felt awkward – Julian had been someone I'd looked up to throughout my career. I didn't want to hurt his feelings so I told him his offer was very kind but I didn't want to break up his family. He looked as if he were about to cry. He said that made him love me even more because it showed how kind I was.

He let go of my hand when the waitress came back. The atmosphere became less tense and he mentioned that he was going to New York next weekend, to meet the editor of *The New Yorker*. I said it was my favourite magazine and Julian became earnest again, saying he'd find me a job there. He said the editor owed him a favour. I explained I was happy living in London but he was insistent, saying he'd buy me a ticket.

I thought about leaving but it seemed rude – even melodramatic – especially after we'd already ordered dinner. He tried to stroke my foot and I moved it away. When I'd finished my coffee, I said I had to get home to my husband. He didn't try to get into the taxi with me. He just looked into my eyes in an adolescent sort of way and stuffed money into the driver's hand. I told him I'd be in touch but I didn't mean it. It was an awkward evening I didn't want to repeat.

I know I should have told you this before but I just wanted to forget about it. Maybe I was worried you'd misunderstand and think I'd led Julian on. The truth was the opposite. I was horrified when he made that pass. I didn't feel flattered; I felt undermined, as if all the praise he'd given me over the years was just to get me into bed.

Besides, you weren't at home when I got back and I don't remember you waking me up or saying all these things about starting afresh. Can we not start afresh now? We still have so much of our lives left.]

11

I woke up in my shirt and socks. Laura was gone. I was relieved because it meant I had more time to decide what to say. I tested the morning. The kettle still boiled just as it always had. The shower was the same temperature as the day before. The bread sprung half toasted in the usual way. All the signs were that this was going to be another normal day. Through the lens of eight hours' sleep, the night before seemed small and distant. I might even have dreamed it.

There were no new messages on my phone. The other people on the tube read their papers and hardly looked at me. It was as if they were all conspiring to pretend that nothing had happened – just another day of the Truman Show. It was only when I reached the landing outside work that I saw something unusual – unusual but not unheard of – a tongue of paper sticking out from the mouth of my letter box. My first thought was that it was just a flier so I pulled it from the door's bite, folded it and put it in my back pocket without reading it. When I'd placed a fresh Kleenex on the couch, washed and dried my hands and sat

in my chair I heard a crumple. I pulled the paper out
and read:

DON'T IGNORE ME. I HATE BEING IGNORED. I LOVE
YOU, JACK, AND I CAN CARE FOR YOU, IF ONLY YOU'LL
LET ME. BUT DON'T TREAT ME LIKE THIS. I DON'T
KNOW WHAT I'LL DO. I CAN'T TAKE THIS SILENCE. C.

I called Claudia but her phone was off. I tried again and
it rang a few times before going dead. After that, her phone
was always off. I left a voicemail saying I was sorry about
the misunderstanding. I said I'd call again when I finished
work.

It was impossible to concentrate that morning. A patient
would be in the middle of saying something and I'd realise,
with the shock of waking from a dream, that I hadn't
listened to a word. My thoughts kept turning to Claudia.
What would she do? It was unbelievably stupid to have
gone to her flat. What had I been thinking? I needed to tell
Laura everything. There was no way round it. She'd find
out in that way women always do, so it was best if it came
from me.

I turned my phone on when I'd finished work and there
were five missed calls from Claudia. The voicemails were
increasingly desperate – they started with pleas but, as they
went on, they turned into threats of what she would do, to
me and to herself, if I didn't call her. She said, in the final
one, that she couldn't wait anymore.

As I walked home, I checked my watch – there was
a long time before Laura would be back and we'd have
to have a conversation about the night before. I checked
it again and only a minute had passed. I kept checking
and that reassured me – it gave me a sense that time was

moving slowly. I felt a powerful need for a crap. There
was nowhere to go – a takeaway kebab shop; a terrace
of houses, grey estate cars crouched in driveways; a
playground of rocking horses hidden by weeds. At last
I reached an orange café overlooked by the rising sun
of the Earls Court Stadium. I ordered a cappuccino –
I didn't want them to think I was just using their toilet
– and hurried under the doorway, down the stairs, past
the chrome kitchen of deep-fat fryers, to a cramped
gents, with a sink, two urinals and a cubicle. A man
in stonewash jeans standing at the urinal let out an
unselfconscious fart. When he'd gone, I stepped into the
cubicle and coated the seat with pieces of toilet paper.
I felt a little more relaxed – inside my cell I had time to
myself; no one could expect anything. I stared at my watch
and tried to calculate how many seconds I had before
Laura would be home. If I counted in infinitesimally small
measures, it would take an infinite number before I had to
leave. I thought about this. People don't change in front of
your eyes. They only change when you go away for a long
time. If I'd watched Mum every second – if I'd never gone
away to university and left her – maybe she wouldn't have
grown old and sick.

Knuckles thudded on the cubicle door. I stood up,
collected the paper in pinches, dropped it into the toilet
and elbowed the flush. As I opened the door, a ratty man
with glasses and tight lips barged past me. With the flat of
my forearm, I pushed on the springy taps. The flow was so
short I had to press several times. I wanted to leave before
the ratty man came out but the three blasts from the hand
dryer weren't enough. He looked at me, with the flush
still roaring behind him, in a suspicious sidelong glance,
splashed his hands, pulled open the door and walked out.

I jammed my foot into the closing door and prised it open with my knee.

Underneath the froth, the cappuccino tasted of nothing. I watched Sky News for several seconds before I noticed there was no volume. The voices all around me were Spanish. An unconvincing plastic plant leaned against the wall, like a mop in a bucket. I was going to have to man up – take a deep breath, look Laura in the eye, tell her everything I saw and did and then ... And then what? Tell her to leave? Beg her to stay? Why was I so anxious? Laura had more to explain than I did, and yet I knew it wouldn't be like that – the maelstrom of her temper would upset the balance of blame. But how long could I be a cuckold? If she left me, it would be like dying, but what was the alternative? There comes a time when you have to take a stand – I loved her and I didn't want to lose her, but I was not going to be trampled on anymore. It had to be said. I needed to go home and get it over with. But first, something to eat. I ordered toast to build up my energy. When I swallowed the last crust, I felt an overwhelming urge for a smoke, so I walked to the newsagent.

I stubbed out my third cigarette. Laura must be home now and I was ready to face her. I just needed a glass of water to get over the sick feeling in my stomach. I felt ashamed asking just for tap water so I ordered another coffee. The caffeine made me light-headed so I went back to the newsagents and bought a banana and a bottle of water. I set out of the store, with my chest out, determined to walk straight home and have it out with Laura. My thoughts must have wandered because I found myself staring at the photographs in the estate agents' window. No more delays, I said to myself, and I paced home – but as I approached the turning for our street, I remembered I'd need chewing gum, so Laura wouldn't notice the cigarettes on my breath. I couldn't go back to the same newsagents a third time so I walked to another one up the road.

When I unlocked the door, the air felt wrong – too still or too heavy.

'Hi, sweetheart!' I called out.

No reply. Laura's coat was on the peg. The living room was empty but the lights were on. I turned them off and looked in the kitchen but Laura wasn't there. At last, I found her in bed, knees hugged to her chest, her face made ghostly by the glow of her phone. Oh God, I thought to myself, what's Claudia done?

'What's wrong, my love?' I asked.

'Nothing,' she said in a lifeless voice.

'Something's wrong,' I said. 'Tell me what it is.'

Laura started talking, with tears in her eyes, about something that had happened at work and I strained not to let the relief show on my face.

> ['*The something that had happened at work*' was the moment I realised I was going to lose my job – not just my job, my career. For I'd never worked anywhere else.
>
> Everyone had left the office, except Peter and me. I walked towards his desk, to see if he needed help. He looked down and moved his mouse frantically. As he swivelled round to smile at me I could see a photograph shrinking on the screen behind him.
>
> 'How are you doing?' I asked.
>
> 'Fine,' he replied anxiously.
>
> 'What are you up to?'
>
> 'Oh, just finishing an article,' he said.
>
> 'What is it? Let me look.' I reached for the mouse and he put his hand underneath mine. I took a step back and looked

at him. He was nervous. 'You're not looking at porn,
are you?'

'No. No! Of course not.' He sighed. 'You'll see it
eventually.'

An article swelled across the screen, mounted by a large
photograph of Boris Johnson – it was obviously a front-
page story.

'Who asked you to write this?' I asked.

'Don't get angry,' he said. 'Siritha said you were
overloaded.'

Overloaded?! I was outraged. She hadn't given me
anything to write for weeks.]

'Poor you,' I said. 'This Siritha sounds like a terrible
boss. Come here.' She rested her head on my collarbone
and I put my arm round her and we lay in silence for a
minute or two. I knew I'd have to confront her about Zac
at some point, but not yet. This could be the last time I
held her.

'Sweetheart,' I said, my heart pounding, still unsure
whether I could bring myself to say what I had to say.
'You know I love you. More than anything in the whole
world.' She squeezed me. 'You know I love you so much
that I think I'd forgive you just about anything.' Laura said
nothing. 'I mean, we all make mistakes, right? If you were
to own up to a mistake, almost any mistake, and promise
it would never happen again, I could . . .' Laura's back
straightened and she pulled away. I stopped.

'What are you talking about?' she said.

'Nothing,' I said. 'I'm just saying we all make
mistakes . . .'

'And?'

'And nothing . . . I see you got your phone back. Where
was it?'

'My phone? I told you, didn't I? I left it at Zac's studio.'

'Oh right. Zac's studio in east London?'

'Yes, Shoreditch, why?' she said, eyeing me warily.

'So when did you find time to pick it up? Because you didn't have it yesterday.'

'Last night,' she said.

'Oh really. Right. Hmmm. Because I thought you were at the opera last night?'

'What is this?' Laura said testily. 'If you must know, I picked up the phone on the way to the opera.'

'Did you? Hmm. Which opera was it by the way?'

She stared at me and I could tell from her expression she was calculating what to say.

'Why are you asking this?' she said.

'Because I looked it up and there was no opera.' My heart was racing. When I'd planned this conversation, this was to be the moment where Laura would burst into tears and beg my forgiveness. Instead, her face hardened, as if she were preparing for a fight.

'I didn't go to the opera last night' she said.

'I know that!' I said. 'What did you do?'

She opened her mouth and stopped. Her expression was still stern but her eyes had a cruel glint. I braced myself.

'I went dogging,' she said.

'Very amusing,' I said. 'Seriously, what were you doing?'

'I was in a car park somewhere off the A40, blowing a truck driver.'

'Seriously,' I said. 'I'm not going to stop asking till you tell me.'

'Oh for Christ's sake, I was having dinner with Julian. I thought we were going to the opera. I got it wrong. Actually, we just met at the Royal Opera House and went to a restaurant nearby.'

'So you went to Shoreditch then Covent Garden, then home?'

'I didn't say I went to Shoreditch,' she said.

'You said you left your phone in Ford's studio.'

'I did,' she said, 'but that's not where I picked it up. I picked it up from Zac's flat in Mayfair, because that's closer to Covent Garden. I'll show you.'

'Don't worry,' I said. My mind scrabbled to get a hold on what she'd just said. Could it be true?

'No,' she said. 'I do worry. You're obviously very interested in my movements so let's trace them on a map. See if that satisfies you. Here you go,' she said, pointing to her phone. 'I got out at Green Park station and walked here, then I got a cab. Anything else, Sherlock?' Sherlock, I thought to myself. Had she read Claudia's texts? I felt my pocket. The phone was still there. 'Do you want to know my timings too?' Laura continued. 'Dinner started late, around eight thirty, and I was back by eleven. Come to think of it, where were you last night? You weren't here when I got home.'

'I went for a long walk,' I said.

'To where?'

'Nowhere really,' I said. 'Just in circles. I got very wet. Don't you remember the wet clothes in the washing basket?'

'You're hiding something,' she said. 'I can always tell.'

'No,' I said in a voice that didn't sound convincing, even to me.

'Then why do you look so nervous?'

'I'm not nervous,' I said, 'only tired.'

It was only with my eyes closed in bed that I felt safe – I could free the regret and fear that cowered inside me.

Through the sleepless night I shifted from one shoulder to the other, scrambling and twisting what I'd said and done, hoping but not believing I could make it all match up.

At the usual hour on Thursday I heard the booming clangs on the metal stairs and my heart sank at the thought of seeing Susan. The doorbell didn't ring. By ten past I was worried – Susan had never missed a session before. I called her mobile but there was no answer. Once or twice, I heard footsteps outside my door and put my newspaper down in the hope that it might be Susan, but no one came in. Now I was longing for Susan to arrive. I tried to stop myself catastrophising – there could be any number of innocent reasons why Susan might be late. I turned on the hissing, coughing tap, filled the kettle and pulled out my favourite mug – the birthday present, from Laura, with MR ALWAYS RIGHT in tall gold letters. As the gargling grew louder, I thought I heard the door, but when the kettle clicked into silence, there was nothing. The box of PG Tips was empty but I had a few grains of Kenco that smelt acrid, like vomit. I scooped them into the mug and poured the murmuring water on top, tilting my head to dodge the swirling clouds of steam. I stirred till there was just one bubble left, pinballing its way round the mug.

'Did you think I'd just go away?' Claudia was standing in the doorway in a dazzling silver puffer.

'I'm glad you've come back, Claudia, because we need to talk. Where's Susan?'

'That's just typical,' Claudia said. 'You're worried about her. She'll be better off without you. Why don't you ask about me? About how I'm feeling?'

'Claudia, I understand you're upset and I'm very sorry. You have every right to be angry with me. I had no idea how bad things were with you. Otherwise, I'd never have agreed to meet with you outside work. I gave you the wrong idea and I'm sorry. Look, you need help. I can put you in touch with someone. I'll pay for it.'

'Oh yeah, pay me off like Zac did? Well, I'm not falling for that again. What about the baby?'

'Claudia, there is no baby. At least not from me. We didn't have sex. You're imagining things again. Would you please sit down for a minute?'

'Oh no, I didn't come here to be tricked. I came here to give you another chance. But I can see I've wasted my time. Well, I'm not going to let other women suffer like I've suffered. I'm going to sit outside your door and tell everyone who comes what you did to me.'

'Claudia, please be reasonable. If you do that, I'll be forced to call the police and that's not going to help either of us.'

At the mention of the police, Claudia pouted and looked at the floor. 'You won't get away with this,' she said.

For the next couple of weeks I lived on a thread. I changed the entry code and checked the landing every time I had a break. Every time a patient was late, I'd rush to the door to see if Claudia was outside. I looked into installing CCTV but it was too expensive. I was afraid Claudia would say something to Laura. If I texted Laura and she didn't reply immediately, I'd become anxious. I'd ring her up, on any pretext, so I could tell, from her tone of voice, whether Claudia had spoken to her. I should have told Laura everything, of course, but I was scared of how she'd react. One night, I found Laura crying again when I got home. I asked her, with dread in my heart, what was wrong. I nearly cried with relief, when she started talking about her performance appraisal.

[We were to have performance appraisals from now on, Siritha said, to make the magazine more professional. Of course, the real reason was to get rid of me. Siritha scored me as 'needs improvement' for 'professionalism', 'motivation' and 'target-setting'. Under line manager's comments she said I had problems with 'time management'. And then, having handed me this report and run away, she had the nerve to ask, with a smile on her face as if we were best friends, whether I was coming to the pub.

I worked for fourteen years for that magazine. People I knew from university had earned fortunes in that time, bought million-pound houses in Notting Hill with their bonuses. And I said to myself, That's OK, I don't envy them. I'm doing a job I love. I thought I was respected, in a world I respected, and that was what mattered. And then, one day, some bitch from marketing, with no fucking clue how to write a sentence, who doesn't even care whether anyone actually reads our magazine, was made editor, and now she owns me. If she fires me, I thought, my career is over. Gone. Vanished. All I'll have is fourteen years of experience in a dying industry where experience counts for nothing. That was why I agreed to go to New York with Julian. I was desperate. Of course it was a bad idea but it's like you said about Claudia – bad ideas can look like good ideas when you're desperate. I thought it was my last chance. I'm sorry if I didn't explain it at the time but we weren't really talking.]

One day a patient said she was going on holiday to try to repair her marriage. I texted Laura.

'Let's go to Mexico. You've always wanted to go. Why not now? The weather's miserable; it's a long time till Christmas. Let's just go this weekend. Get on a plane and go for three weeks. Or four. Turn it into a sabbatical.'

For the next hour, my phone was unbearably silent. I put it on vibrate when the next patient arrived, but it never moved. My hope was ebbing when, a few hours later, I felt a buzz.

'Wow! Sounds cool. Where did that come from?'

I wrote back straight away: 'I've always been spontaneous. You know that!'

The reply came instantly: 'Let's do it. But not this week. We'll need a visa.'

'No visa required. Two tickets for £400 each with Thomas Cook to Cancun, leaving on Saturday, back in three weeks. Shall I buy them?'

A long, long silence followed. I kept thinking I'd seen a flash of red light from my phone, but each time I was wrong. Then finally, I received the following:

'Just remembered. Going to New York next weekend. Work thing. Another time?'

A bitter trickle of suspicion leaked into my heart. I replied: 'Next Saturday is the 16th of October.'

The response was swift: 'I know. I have a diary ☺'

'The 16th of October is our anniversary ☹'

'We don't usually do anything on our anniversary ☺☹'

'Have you forgotten the Highlands? ☹☹'

'No, even ten years later, it stands out – as the only time we've ever done anything for our anniversary ☺☺☺'

'Who are you going to New York with?'

A pause and then another speech bubble: 'Just work.'

I wrote back immediately: 'OK. I'll come with you. Adam told me about a hostel where you can stay in central Manhattan for only $40 a night. And we get our own room.'

Another long pause. I tried calling. No answer. I left a voicemail in a cheery voice. Finally, when I was home, I got the following text:

'Already booked hotel through work. Let's go together another time. Going to be late tonight. Soz. Don't wait up.'

The injustice was exquisite. Laura was going for a dirty weekend with her lover on our anniversary. I'd been a fool to believe her story about having dinner with Julian. She was probably in bed with Ford right now, sending texts in the gaps between their lovemaking. I could have written the cruellest thing at that moment and it would have given me a sense of relief, even joy, but instead I wrote:

'If you think this "work trip" to New York is more important than our anniversary, don't let me stop you.'

She replied: 'Sorry. I'll make it up to you tonight ☺'

I wrote: 'I really don't think you understand how much this hurts me. I won't be here tonight. I'll stay at Adam's.' I sent it straight away, while my heart was still beating fast.

There was a pause. Her reply couldn't fit into one text: 'I think it's you that doesn't understand. I've waited for years for you to take me on holiday somewhere exciting, where I wanted to go, and you never did. There was always some excuse. Now, for once, it's me that says no and you throw a fit. I can't do it because I've got an important interview but you wouldn't think about that because you never think about my career, do you? Your career is the only one that matters because you're a man. Never mind the fact that I've worked longer and harder than you. That doesn't mean anything.'

I kept my cool, writing the following reply: 'That is an unfair comparison. I never went anywhere without you, or said you couldn't join me, especially not on our anniversary.'

This text was watertight, I thought to myself. Every word of it was indisputable. She'd have to concede I was right.

'You know what's unfair? It's you making me feel guilty about going on one little trip by myself. I'll be networking all weekend. I wouldn't be able to spend any time with you. I don't even want to go.'

I replied quickly: 'Why would you feel guilty, if you had nothing to feel guilty about?'

Again, I thought to myself, I have her now. Part of me really believed logic might quell her aggression and force her to admit that she was the one in the wrong, even though that had never happened in the history of our relationship.

'Don't try your fucking Jedi mind tricks on me. I'm not your patient. I'm coming home now. You've spoiled my evening. Congratulations.'

'Have you noticed how, whatever we argue about, by the end you're always, in your own mind, the victim? That's how you deal with feeling guilty.'

'Fuck off!'

> [I wanted so much to go to Mexico with you. Every year, you promised me we'd go but we never did. You said we couldn't afford it but the truth was you didn't like leaving your comfort zone. After you got Delhi belly in Turkey, we hardly ever left the UK. That was supposed to be one of the consolations of not having children – that we could drop everything, whenever we wanted, and go wherever we wanted. But we never did.]

On Saturday morning, when we could have been on a plane to Mexico City, Laura and I were sat in a dark wooden café on the Old Brompton road, with rows of tall, thin coffee-pots in the window. Our table was empty, apart from a brown bottle of Belgian beer with a pink rose forced down its throat. My phone vibrated in my pocket and it was a message from Claudia: 'I SAID YOU WOULDN'T GET AWAY WITH IT. LOOK IN THE MIRROR.'

I twisted round in my chair but I couldn't see her anywhere. This café, where I'd been so often, now seemed creepy – the banjos and violins hanging from the ceiling looked like carcasses in an abattoir; the thin black rake shackled to the wall made me think of a skeleton trying to scratch its way out of a coffin; and the brown sculpture of a priest, tilting forward off a roof beam, was on the brink of suicide.

I heard a voice say, 'This is all a lie,' and looked up to see a white-haired man dressed in jeans and a jumper. I thought Claudia might have sent him till he asked us what we'd like to order, in a different voice to the one I'd just heard. I asked for smoked salmon and scrambled eggs and told Laura I'd get the papers. I stopped outside, breathing deeply and counting from one to ten and back again.

At the entrance to Fine Food Supermarket was a near-empty carousel of postcards. A drooping tit winked at me. Underneath the brown, curling photographs of the Houses of Parliament and Big Ben was a pile of newspapers. I picked out the *Guardian* and noticed a corner of the *Mirror* underneath.

'The *Mirror*?' Laura said, when I returned to our table. 'Since when have you bought the *Mirror*?'

'I just thought I'd try it.'

I skimmed through the first few stories. When I reached page seven, my heart stopped. At first I was too stunned to read. I just sat in silence, while Laura squinted at the *Guardian*. The white-haired waiter placed a huge plate of runny eggs and cold fish in front of me.

'What's wrong?' Laura said. 'You look pale.'

'I feel sick,' I said. 'I have to go.' Laura got up. 'You stay. I'll be fine. I just need to go home. Honestly, I'd rather be alone.' I tucked the *Mirror* under my arm and ran home through the startled cars.

12

The full headline was 'SEDUCED BY MY THERAPIST: TOP MODEL SOUGHT HELP FROM MAN WHO CRUELLY ABUSED HER TRUST AND ABANDONED HER WHEN SHE GOT PREGNANT' by Steve Knaggs.

The story beneath the headline was as follows:

Claudia Alvares, top model and It girl, has opened up about how she was abused by her therapist. He sweet-talked his way into her home and had sex with her.

'I feel so cheap and used,' she said. 'I'll never trust anyone again.'

Claudia was tipped to be the next Kate Moss when cocaine and alcohol took their toll. Weighing less than eight stone she checked into the Priory but, two weeks later, she was out partying again. This cycle of self-destruction continued till Zac Ford, a friend and mentor, stepped in.

'She'd run out of money,' said Zac, one of the leading artists of his generation, 'so I paid for her to see someone. He came recommended by a friend. I had no idea what a creep he'd turn out to be.'

Aged forty-nine, 'Dr' Randall, as he styles himself, lives with his wife Laura Ferguson, a journalist, in a £500,000 flat in Earls Court. He offers 'therapy' at £125 per hour in an anonymous office block in Acton.

'He seemed so kind and thoughtful,' Claudia said, 'so much deeper than the guys I normally hang out with. I trusted him. He was old but kind of cute, with curly brown hair and piercing blue eyes, a bit like Sean Penn. I could tell he liked me but at first he seemed very professional.'

Zac Ford remained a loyal friend and confidant. In his eyes, Claudia was getting better – her weight was getting back to normal and she was staying away from drugs, so he kept paying Randall's inflated bills. Then something happened that sent Claudia crashing down again.

'I turned up as usual,' Claudia said, 'opened the door and found him all over this woman. I don't know if she was supposed to be a patient, or whether she was just his lover, but I was stunned. The worst of it was I felt jealous. I couldn't see him for what he was. I just kept thinking, "Why's he chosen her, not me?"'

Claudia told Zac all about what she'd seen and he persuaded her to stop seeing Randall. Away from Randall's clutches, Claudia's health improved. The modelling jobs returned and she stayed on the wagon.

'Then he pulled me back in,' Claudia said. 'I thought I was over him but when he emailed me out of the blue, my feelings for him came flooding back. He wanted me to spy on his wife. He said she was having an affair with Zac Ford. I was so desperate to please him I agreed to sit with him in a car outside Zac's flat.'

This was a trick. Once inside the car, Randall begged Claudia to take him home with her.

'When we were alone in my flat, all his "professional" inhibitions disappeared. He was like an animal. I felt I might

*collapse with terror and excitement. I'd waited for that moment
for so long. But then, when he'd got what he wanted, he was out
the door. I wrote to him and called him but he never replied, even
when I told him I was pregnant.'*

*Claudia says she's spoken out because it's the only way she
could stop other vulnerable women falling into his trap.*

*'I'm lucky,' she said. 'My modelling career has given me
contacts in the press who'll listen to me. What about all the other
women who don't get heard? That's who I'm doing this for.'*

*A representative for the British Psychological Society said that
it was their policy not to comment on individual cases. However,
their website revealed that it was a breach of their code of ethics
for anyone to have a relationship with a patient. Jack Randall
was unavailable for comment.*

There were several full-length photographs of Claudia,
looking as if she were modelling clothes, with captions
underneath that said things like: 'Ensnared: Claudia
Alvares – "I thought he cared about me but all he wanted
was sex"'.

My eyes have passed over that article many times in
the years since, but I still haven't absorbed every word. Its
stone lies are still so hot I have to run across them. Even
when I stare at the words, their meanings don't register.
There are only so many blows one can feel. There's still a
copy of the newspaper in my backpack – I brought it with
me to Strasbourg half deliberately, as a souvenir of my
shame.

I can think about that article now with a bitter calm –
that comes from time and resignation.

When I first read it, I was frantic. My mind was running
in circles and figures of eight, like a crazed animal in a
zoo. How could someone print such lies? What would

Laura think? Is this the end of my career? My BlackBerry moaned, and I turned to see it, writhing on the table like a landed fish. Withheld Number was calling me. I didn't answer and it called again. There were no new messages in the email inbox on my laptop. Maybe the story will go away, I thought. No one I knew read the *Mirror* anyway. Sitting on the toilet, rereading the article, I heard voices outside. I yanked the window open and put my head out.

'There he is! It's him!'

Lights flashed in my eyes, camera shutters clicked and a crowd of men and women jostled and shouted. I rammed my palms onto the curved and flaking handles of the window but it wouldn't shut. The mob separated itself into individual voices.

'Mr Randall, do you have anything to say about your relationship with Claudia Alvares?'

'How many other patients have you abused?'

I fled, leaving the toilet window open. Then the landline phone started ringing, so I picked it up:

'Mr Randall, this is the Sunday People . . .'

I put the receiver down and pulled the wire from the wall. I hugged my knees and rocked back and forth on the floor behind my sofa bed, trying to think. I turned on my mobile phone and it complained in a strident bleep of fifteen missed calls. I stared at my reflection in the curved mirror of the dead TV.

Car wheels screeched outside and doors opened. The bell rang and fists pounded against the door. I turned on the stereo as loud as I could and climbed into bed, with cushions pressed over either ear.

[Are you sure about this? After you left, I finished my breakfast, paid the bill and went to collect the dry-cleaning.

By the time I came home, no more than an hour later, there
was no 'mob' of journalists outside our door, just a bald man
with a heavy camera and a pregnant Asian woman. I thought
they were lost.]

'What are you doing?' Laura said, turning on the lights of
our bedroom.

'I'm hiding,' I said.

'From what?'

'The baying mob outside.'

'What baying mob?'

'The journalists. Outside.'

'Journalists? I saw a couple of people with cameras
but I'm not sure they're journalists. They look more like
tourists.'

'There must have been twenty or thirty of them.'

'Not now there aren't,' Laura said. She frowned at me.
'What's all this about?'

'I'm so sorry,' I said, looking at Laura's feet, 'I've made a
terrible mistake.'

'What is it?' Laura said coldly.

'I thought you were having an affair with Zac Ford,' I
said, still looking at her feet. 'And Claudia knows Zac. So
I called her and asked her to check. I had no idea it would
lead to this. It's not true what she says. She's not well. She
invents things.'

'Who does?'

I handed her the *Mirror* and Laura read agonisingly
slowly, her face darkening.

'What the fuck?'

'It's not true, I promise.'

She read on. 'I'm in it,' she said looking up with a
frown.

'I know,' I said. 'I'm sorry.'

151

Laura squinted back at the page. She snorted. 'Sean Penn!' Then her face darkened again. 'What's this about you being all over some other woman?'

'She's completely misrepresented that. A patient was very distraught, crying, couldn't get off the couch. I touched her shoulder to remind her it was time to leave. That was all.'

Laura stared at me for a few moments. I stared back and she returned to the newspaper. 'Is this true,' she said, 'that you asked her to spy on me and Zac?'

'Not exactly. I just emailed her to ask if she knew anything about who Zac was seeing. I didn't mean for her to spy on you. I just thought she might have heard some gossip.'

'So she came up with the idea of spying on me?'

I looked at Laura's feet.

'Was there more to it?'

I said nothing.

Laura drew closer. 'Look into my eyes. You've been meeting her behind my back, haven't you? When?' I'd never seen Laura so angry.

'I met her briefly in a café once,' I said, looking away. 'She didn't want to talk on the phone.'

'When?' Laura's eyes were flashing.

'I don't know. Last week. After work one day. Just for an hour.'

'An hour?' Laura's voice rose. 'What were you doing all that time?'

'Maybe it wasn't a full hour,' I said.

'What did you talk about?'

'Well, a bit about her and a bit about you. She said Ford was seeing an older woman. She thought it might be you. That's when she suggested that we wait outside Ford's flat. I told her it was a bad idea.'

'So this is a lie then? That you were sitting in a car with her?'

'No,' I sighed, 'that's not a lie. She called me to say she was there. I told her to leave but she was still there when I arrived and it was raining that day so –'

'So you were spying on me?'

'I'm sorry, sweetheart. I was desperate. I was scared I was losing you. And it wasn't just fantasy, was it? I did see you going into Zac's flat. And it was the night when you said you were going to the opera. So you can see why I was suspicious.'

'I was collecting my phone, for fuck's sake.' She looked back at the paper. 'And you went back to her flat?'

'Yes, but we didn't have sex. We didn't do anything. We were in an accident, a car crash, and she was in shock . . .' I faltered. Laura looked as if she didn't believe me. 'I'm not making this up . . .' Her sceptical expression didn't change. 'I promise, sweetheart. If she's pregnant, it's not by me. I didn't touch her.'

'I'm going to be sick,' Laura said, her face paling.

'I'm sorry. I really am. It's all my fault. I should never have emailed her. I didn't realise how ill she was. I was desperate. I thought I was losing you. If you think about it, it shows how much I love you.'

'Right,' Laura said. 'You fucking your patient shows how much you love me.'

'I didn't fuck –' Laura cut me short with a look of pure cold hatred.

'If this is all a lie, as you claim, you should sue,' Laura said.

'I can't sue an ex-patient.'

'Convenient,' Laura said.

'It wouldn't be ethical.'

'Ethical?!'

'I suppose we could sue the *Mirror*,' I said, 'but that might just draw more attention to the whole thing. If my patients read about this, my career is finished. I guess we could talk to Adam.'

'Adam!'

'He trained as a lawyer.'

'Don't make me laugh. I wouldn't go to Adam for advice on anything, except maybe where to buy weed. Dad can pay for the lawyer.'

'No,' I said. 'Your father is not going to pay. I will.'

She looked at me as if she didn't believe me. 'All right,' she continued. 'Julian will know who to speak to.'

'Why are you always talking about Julian?'

'Don't, OK? This is not the fucking time.'

The front door opened and closed. I texted Laura to ask where she was going and when she'd be back. She didn't reply. I lay in bed for several hours till I could feel pangs in my stomach. I texted Laura to say I was cooking lasagne for us. She didn't reply. I ate half on my own in front of the TV. At 1 a.m., when I was lying awake in bed, I heard the front door open. Laura slid into bed next to me and I pretended to be asleep.

> [If you'd been this apologetic, I'm sure I'd have forgiven you. I remember your being more defensive – you kept saying you hadn't had sex with Claudia as if that was all that mattered, as if sending a deranged stalker to spy on me was not big a deal.
>
> I was anxious about the story. I was anxious about the reaction at work, where the atmosphere was already poisonous. And I was anxious about Mum who'd find out about it somehow and then we'd have another conversation

about where I'd gone wrong in my life. I'll admit I was
also a bit sceptical. I didn't know then all I that know now
about Claudia and it didn't seem likely that anyone, even
a crazy person, would go to such lengths to ruin someone
else's life if they had no reason to be angry with them. You
accuse me of not telling the whole truth but are you sure
there's nothing missing from your account of that night
with Claudia? I'm not calling you a liar, I'm just suggesting
you might have rounded off the edges a bit. What is it you
used to say? 'No one's ever entirely honest, even with
themselves'?

So that's why I called Julian to ask if he knew a good
barrister. He must have realised, from the tone of my voice,
that something was wrong because he insisted on meeting
me. We went for dinner, in a French restaurant, and he was
very kind. I could hardly speak, I was crying so much, and he
just listened and held my hand.]

13

While Laura slept, I tried to reassure myself. I'd been stupid
but I hadn't done anything that bad. And maybe all my
fears were just paranoia. Laura's explanations made sense.
Maybe she wasn't having an affair. I should feel relieved.
We'd sue the *Mirror* and the truth about me and Claudia
would come out. With the damages, I'd take Laura to
Mexico and all would be forgotten or forgiven. I was still
working through this plan, when Laura's alarm went off. I
closed my eyes but I could tell from the light that she was
reading her phone. She left the room and I could hear the
shower. I waited, hoping she might come back till I heard
the front door close.

> [When I left home that morning, there were three or four
> journalists outside the door looking bored. One of them was
> eating a sandwich and slurping from a Coke can. The others
> were leaning against cars with their faces to the sun. They
> told me they were from *Kensington and Chelsea Today*. They
> didn't realise I was married to you. A scruffy short one with
> yellow teeth asked if I knew 'Jack Ramsay' (sic). I said I

didn't know any Jack Ramsay. I asked what he'd done. They said he was a doctor and he'd 'bonked' his patient.

As I walked to my desk, no one greeted me. They were unnaturally quiet – each of them absorbed by something, squinting at a screen or cupping a phone to their ear. When I sat down Sam from accounts offered me a cup of tea – something he'd never done before in seven years of working together.

'You've all read it, haven't you?' I said to the office at large, and no one caught my eye. 'It's not true. We're going to sue.'

No one replied. They were still acting like extras in an office scene. Sam brought the tea and asked what I was talking about.

'Did you not read the *Mirror* yesterday?' He said no. 'Did you?' I said, looking at Caroline and she shook her head. 'Then why are you all behaving so strangely?' They looked at their keyboards.

Later in the morning, when I was on the way to the printer, I saw Siritha opening the door of her office. She caught my eye, did a bad impression of someone who's just remembered something they left behind and closed the door again. On top of a story I'd printed off was a pile of A3 papers. I saw Siritha's name and I thought I'd take it to her. I was just trying to be helpful. I wasn't intending to read it but I could see it was an organogram. Siritha was at the top. Most people on the payroll were on the next level. And some temps were below that. I wasn't on it. I stopped and checked again. I definitely wasn't on it. In the world of this Word document I did not exist. I'd been disappeared.

Is this a mistake? I wondered. I thought of Siritha's face, when she caught my eye, and I knew it wasn't.

'When were you going to tell me about this?' I said, storming into Siritha's office and thrusting the papers at her.

Siritha pointed at the phone she was talking into. I waited. At last she hung up.

'Sorry,' she said, throwing things into a handbag. 'I have to go to a meeting. We'll discuss it when I get back.'

'No,' I said, 'we won't. We'll discuss it now. What's going on? Are you firing me?'

'No,' she said, looking past me at the door. 'You're not being fired. You just won't be employed anymore. You can still write for us, freelance. You might end up earning more. We just need more flexibility. A lower cost base. It's a tough market.'

'I know what kind of market it is. I was Acting Editor when you were making the tea at McKinsey's. I'm not just going to stand back and take this. I'm going to write to the owners.'

'It's the owners that suggested it. I tried to persuade them to keep you.'

This knocked me and I was silent for long enough for Siritha to get away. I'd never met the owners but I'd always got the impression from Julian that they loved me. I was their favourite writer, he said.]

When I walked into the living room, half an hour later, I could hear the journalists outside. Judging from the voices, there were even more than the day before. On the kitchen table was a business card from Robert Davis at Harbord and Lewis that Laura must have left for me. I called the underlined telephone number. Mr Davis's voice, cold and posh at first, warmed up when I explained why I was calling. He expressed his 'deepest sympathy' in the practised voice of an undertaker. He suggested a conference with a barrister called Richard Clarke, who'd got some 'excellent results' for him in the past. I said it was urgent. He rang back a few minutes later and confirmed an appointment for 2 p.m. that afternoon in Mr Clarke's chambers at 7 Essex Street. He said I'd need to pay £1,000, whether or not I pursued the matter any further, to cover 'counsel's fees'.

I ordered a taxi and cancelled my patients for the day. A text told me the taxi had arrived and I stepped outside. There was an eerie silence that seemed to last several seconds, as I looked at the journalists and they looked at me, before all at once they were shouting, pushing, clicking and flashing. The noise of voices and cameras and feet knocked me back.

I froze in confusion. Microphones on stalks were thrust at me. I could see my blinking, nervous face expanding in the lens of a camera. I leaned back with one hand against the door. There was a sliver of daylight in the shrinking semicircle and I ducked my head, tucked my shoulders in and charged. They parted like pigeons before a car. I ran towards the minicab, which had halted voyeuristically at the end of the road.

A bald man with stubble ran alongside me, smiling toothily. 'Where are you running to, Jack?' he panted. I didn't respond. 'Wouldn't it be better to tell your side of the story?'

I got out on the corner of Fleet Street and Essex Street, by a wine bar called Daly's – a drool of men in dark suits trailing from its jaws. As I passed, someone laughed and I turned back to catch the eye of a tall, red-faced man whose mouth hung open as if in mid-speech. His companions were looking at the pavement and smiling.

Number 7 was a Georgian town house. A pretty blonde

receptionist took my name, handed me a badge and pointed me to a leather couch next to a marble fireplace. It reminded me of Harley Street, only the magazines on the coffee table were about law, rather than fashion. Snobbery is so ingrained in English life that our best doctors and lawyers have to pretend to be aristocrats. I couldn't read so I watched the receptionist untangling headphones from her hair. After about ten minutes, my view was blocked by a man who loomed over me holding a briefcase.

'Mr Randall?' he said.

'Mr Davis?' I said, standing to greet him.

'Pleased to meet you.' He wore the smile of a shopkeeper as we shook hands. 'No trouble getting here?'

'No, I took a taxi.'

'Very sensible,' he said. 'The tubes are so unreliable these days.'

'It's not that,' I said. 'There's a pack of journalists outside my door.'

'Oh yes. Quite. Quite . . .' He looked outside the window. 'Lovely weather at the moment.'

After about fifteen minutes a tall man in an immaculate grey suit strode towards us. His cropped hair gave him a boyish look, although he must have been nearly my age, and humorous delight shone in his eyes, as if he was about to tell a joke that everyone was sure to laugh at. In his hand he held a blue exercise book and some papers with yellow highlighting all over them. Mr Davis and I stood up.

'Bob!' said the tall man in a genial manner, as if he'd met an old friend by chance.

'Good to see you, Mr Clarke,' replied my solicitor, shaking him by the hand. 'May I introduce you to Mr Randall?'

'Pleased to meet you!' said the barrister, clasping my hand in both of his. 'Do follow me.' He called across to the receptionist. 'Babs, can you let us through?'

The receptionist leaned under her desk and the doors at the back of the room spread open slowly. We went down some stairs into a room of glass and leather, in the centre of which was a long table with a tray of tea, coffee and biscuits. The barrister asked what I wanted and made some facetious remark he'd no doubt made a hundred times before, about how the coffee here tasted like tea and the tea like coffee. I drank a cup of black coffee and ate three biscuits while he fussed around with the pots and cups as if he were a child hosting a dolls' tea party. When he was satisfied that everyone had the coffee, tea, milk, sugar, water (sparkling and still) and biscuits they required, he sighed, leaned back in his chair and asked how he could help.

'You've seen the article about me, haven't you?' I asked. He nodded. 'Well, it's not true. I never slept with her. If she's pregnant, it's not by me. And that thing about my other patient is totally unfair. This story is going to ruin my career. I need to set the record straight.'

'Thank you, Mr Randall,' the barrister replied, 'for putting it so clearly.' He leaned forward and brought his fingertips together in a humpback shape. 'The first of your points was that you didn't have sexual intercourse with this young woman. Correct?'

'Correct.'

'Did you have any sort of sexual or romantic relationship with her?'

My phone started buzzing. It was Laura. I pressed silent.

[Sam and Peter stopped talking when I walked into the kitchen. Sam said there was an email he had to write and

Peter shuffled out after him, looking at his feet. I looked in the cupboards as if there was something among the crockery and teabags that might help. I found Siritha's mug. On its face was a flecked and fading photograph of Siritha, with her daughter on her shoulders. Both had open mouths and flying hair. In the fuzzy background was a brightly coloured garden and the bi-folding doors of a kitchen extension. I realised, with the shock of an alarm clock, that I was nearly forty – I had no job, no child, and my marriage was falling apart.

I called you so many times but you never picked up. I thought you were ignoring my calls because you were feeling guilty. I didn't realise you were with the lawyer. I called again and the phone rang without answer. I was crying but I was furious. What else could I do? I called Julian.

I kept the tears back in the office. It was only when the car door was closed and I was leaning on Julian's chest, that I felt able to cry. Julian said the owners would have been pushed into it by Siritha. They only knew what she told them. She was threatened by me. That was why she'd fired me. He said he knew how it felt. To give your life to something, or someone, and not be appreciated. He said I deserved better. Much better. And not just at work.

I looked up at him. 'It's not me then?' I asked. 'I'm not too rude or aggressive?'

'Not at all,' he said. 'You're not rude at all. And you're the right amount of aggressive. No,' he went on, 'sometimes in life you're just in the wrong place. You make a choice when you're young and you grow out of it. And it can be very painful leaving the ... situation you find yourself in, but you'll find life is better when you've moved on.'

'Like you,' I said.

'Exactly.'

'You're happier now you've left the magazine, aren't you?'
I asked.

He paused. 'I am,' he said. 'I feel I'm on the brink of the
life I've always wanted.' I dried my eyes. 'Have you called
Jack?'

'Yes,' I said, 'but he hasn't called back.'

'That's terrible,' Julian said. 'That guy doesn't know how
lucky he is. If I were your husband . . .' He stopped. 'Have you
been telling him all the things you've told me about what's
been going on at work?'

'Yes,' I said, 'but he doesn't seem to pay much attention.
He never used to be so distant. I suppose he's been thinking
about his own issues.'

'Terrible,' he repeated. 'Can't even be bothered to answer
your phone calls. But listen, when we go to New York, all this
is going to be behind you. You'll get a job at *The New Yorker*
and Siritha is going to look like a fool. Let's go earlier.
Tomorrow.'

'Won't it be very expensive,' I said, 'to change the
tickets?'

'No,' he said, 'I've got loads of air miles. They'll do it
for free.'

Julian drove as slowly and smoothly as he talked. He
knew the world of journalism as well as anyone and I'd be
fine. I was better off working freelance. It was insulting and
hurtful to be fired, but it would be for the best. All I had to
do was trust him and he'd make everything right. As he said
this, he turned slowly and carefully into my street, feeding
the steering wheel with both hands. 'There,' he said gently,
as we came to a stop outside our house.]

I felt guilty at cutting Laura off and wondered if I should
call her back. The lawyers were looking at me.

'Sorry,' I said, 'where were we?'

'I was asking if you had any sort of sexual or romantic relationship with Claudia?'

'No,' I said. 'I did go back to her flat once but nothing happened. It was raining, you see, and she was in a car and I didn't have an umbrella ... But I should go back a step ...' I felt weary explaining Claudia's past and what happened between us. I felt like an actor in a poor play, hurrying through my lines so I could get off stage. 'So,' I said, 'I thought I'd better make sure she was OK and then she kind of lunged at me and when I turned her down she got angry.'

There was a pause. I felt embarrassed, as if I'd told a long joke and no one had laughed.

'I see,' the barrister said. He inhaled deeply before continuing. 'When did Ms Alvares first come to see you? As a patient, I mean.'

'Last year, around summertime.'

'When Ms Alvares came to see you, was she in need of your help?'

'Yes.'

'So she could fairly have been described as a vulnerable young woman?'

'Yes.'

'How long did you treat Ms Alvares for?'

'About three months.'

'And would you say that you built up a relationship of *trust* over that time?'

'Yes,' I said, wondering why he was placing such emphasis on the word trust.

He paused and nodded, before resuming. 'How long is a normal course of treatment?'

'There's no such thing. That's like asking how long a piece of string is. There's no normal length.'

'On average though, what's the minimum time before someone of Ms Alvares's level of vulnerability is, so to speak, cured?'

'It normally takes a year or two before you see any substantial change, if that's what you mean.'

'So Ms Alvares's treatment was cut short?'

'Yes, it was.'

'And why was that?' He spoke in a soft voice, as if he were asking out of innocent curiosity.

'She just stopped coming.' I felt anxious and defensive. 'Around the time when she walked in on me with the other patient, Susan.' There was a silence as if I were expected to continue. 'Susan was crying one day ... I hadn't made her cry ... well, in a way I had, but only in the sense that I encouraged her to talk about something emotive ... that's part of my job ... Anyway, she was crying when Claudia walked in.'

'Let's take this in stages, shall we?' The barrister raised his eyebrows and gave me a fake smile. 'When Ms Alvares walked in and Susan was crying, what were you doing?'

'I was in my chair ... well, actually I was kind of kneeling on the floor trying to help Susan off the couch.'

'Do you normally help your patients off the couch?'

'No ... no.'

'Was this lady injured in some way that required special assistance?' I wondered if he was being ironic but I couldn't see it in his face.

'No, she was just crying a lot and it was the end of the session and she didn't respond when I told her she had to leave. I thought a gentle touch might do the job better.'

'So you did touch your patient at your place of work?'

'Well, yes –' Mr Clarke started writing in his exercise book – 'but not in the way Claudia describes. I touched

Susan once on the shoulder or arm. There was nothing sexual about it.'

'And this is what you were doing when Ms Alvares came in – you were kneeling in front of the couch touching another patient . . . on the shoulder or arm?'

'Yes.'

'I see,' he said, as if that had cleared up some doubt he'd had. 'Let's go back to the timings. Your working relationship with Ms Alvares ceased after three months, you said?'

'Yes.'

'So that would be around autumn last year?' The barrister seemed to be enjoying himself – his cheeks were flushed and his eyes were sparkling.

'I suppose so.'

'And that must mean that you went to Ms Alvares's home around a year after the end of your therapeutic relationship, correct?'

'Yes.'

'And that's less time than it normally takes to be cured. So, when you contacted her, you knew, or should have known, that she was likely still to be suffering from the same vulnerabilities that she had when she was your patient?'

'I should have known, true.' He took up his pen and wrote something. I leaned forward but I couldn't make it out. 'But I wasn't thinking sensibly. It wasn't just her that was in shock. I'd just seen my wife coming out of another man's front door.'

To my irritation, he didn't write any of this down.

'Is there likely to be CCTV footage of you and Ms Alvares at the entrance of her block of flats?'

'I don't know. Why does it matter? I'm not going to lie and say I didn't go to her flat,' I said.

166

'I'm not suggesting you lie, Mr Randall.' Mr Clarke smiled like a forbearing teacher. 'I'm just wondering if there might be footage of you and Ms Alvares at the front door. She might have rested her arm on yours when you arrived. Little gestures like that – even perfectly innocent ones – can be misread by a jury.'

'Jury?' I said. 'What are you talking about? I'm not on trial here. I haven't committed a crime.'

'I'm so sorry, Mr Randall. I was getting ahead of myself. I should have explained. You're not on trial. Of course not. But, if you were to sue the *Mirror* for defamation, and they did not settle, there would be a trial and that trial would be heard by a jury. Defamation is one of the few areas of civil law that is still heard by a jury.'

'Right, OK.' I pictured myself in the witness box, a jury of *Mirror* readers staring at me. 'What were you saying?'

'I was saying that juries don't always get things right. It's not the criminal standard, you see. The newspaper doesn't have to prove beyond reasonable doubt that you slept with her. They just have to show it's more likely than not. They see a young, pretty woman inviting an older man into her flat late at night. The woman is leaning on the man's arm.'

[I leaned on Julian's arm as he walked me to my door. He said he didn't like leaving me in the state I was in. I said I'd be fine. I just want to see you settled, he said, sidling past as I stood at the door. I'll help you pack, he said, and before I could stop him he was in our bedroom. I was worried I might have left my underwear on the floor so I rushed after him but there was nothing. For once I was grateful for your tidiness. It's fine, I said. He sat springily on the edge of the bed, as if he were testing it.

'It's hot in here,' he said. 'I'm going to take off my cardigan.'

'I'll pack later,' I said. 'Come into the kitchen and let's have a cup of tea.' He stood up slowly and followed me. 'I would offer you a drink,' I said, 'but I don't think we have anything. I don't really like alcohol. Well, I like champagne, but . . .'

'I love champagne,' Julian said.

The front door of the building opened and he stood up.

'Don't worry,' I said. 'That's just the neighbours.'

He didn't sit down. He checked his watch. I told him it was fine if he wanted to go.

'OK,' he said, 'unless you want me to stay . . .' He paused. 'For any reason.'

'No thanks,' I said. 'You go.']

'Are you saying no one will believe me?' I asked.

'Not at all. I believe you, of course,' the barrister said, with a fake smile that made me dislike him even more. 'But juries are not infallible. It's one person's word against another. They have to choose between a pretty young woman in tears and a married man who followed his vulnerable patient back to her home at night. Besides, the case won't necessarily turn on whether you had sex with her.'

'What do you mean?' I said.

He shuffled through the papers on the table, as if he hadn't heard me.

'Mr Randall, are you aware of the Code of Conduct of the British Psychological Society?'

'Yes.'

'Do you consider yourself bound by it?'

'Well, not exactly. I'm not a member of the BPS but –'

He cut in. 'Let me read one paragraph of it to you: "Psychologists should . . . refrain from engaging in any form of sexual or romantic relationship with persons to whom they are providing professional services, or to whom they owe a continuing duty of care, *or* –' another damned rhetorical pause – 'with whom they have a *relationship of trust*.' He looked up at me, before continuing. 'This might include a *former patient*, a student or trainee, or a junior staff member.'"

'I wouldn't disagree with any of that. But it wasn't a romantic relationship, at least not for me. I'm not saying I'm blameless, but surely newspapers can't just print whatever lies a mentally ill person tells them and get away with it?'

While I was speaking, he seemed to be looking for a document from among his papers. At last he found it.

'Can I read something else to you, Mr Randall?' He continued without waiting for a reply. 'It's from the General Medical Council's code of conduct. They say this on maintaining boundaries: "If you are not sure whether you are – or could be seen to be – abusing your professional position, it may help to discuss your situation with an impartial colleague, a defence body, medical association or (confidentially) with a member of the GMC Standards and Ethics team." Mr Randall, did you discuss your situation with an impartial colleague, supervisor or anyone else who could have given you guidance?'

[When Julian had gone, I called Mum.

'What's happened?' she said in a tone of alarm that annoyed me.

'Why do you assume something bad has happened?'

'Because you never call unless there's been a disaster.'

'That's not true,' I said. 'I call you all the time.'

'When,' she said, 'did you last call?'

'I don't remember the exact date but look, Mum, I don't

want to get into an argument. I've got something to tell you. I got fired this morning.'

She sucked in her breath. 'I knew it,' she said. 'When did it happen?'

'I just told you. This morning. That's why I said "I got fired this morning".'

'Why didn't you call?' she said.

'I am calling!'

'This is awful,' she said. 'But don't worry. Your father will lend you some money.'

'Mum,' I said. 'I don't need money.'

'This is terrible,' she said.

Although it did feel terrible, I was annoyed to hear her say it.

'Mum,' I said. 'It's OK! My career's not over. There'll be other, better jobs. As a matter of fact, I have a job offer from *The New Yorker*. I'm going to New York with Julian to meet the editor.'

'Julian?' she said in a nosy tone of voice that irritated me.

'Yes, Julian,' I said. 'My old boss.'

'Isn't he a bit old for you, dear?' she said.

'He's not my lover, Mum! He's just a friend.'

'You always liked older men, didn't you?' she said. 'Even when you were a girl. You had a crush on that English teacher. What was he called?'

'Mother, I was sixteen!'

'Exactly. He must have been twenty years older than you. And how old is this Julian? Sixty? Sixty-five?'

'I don't know,' I said.

'He might not be able to have any more children,' she said. 'Have you thought about that? Men of that age can't always, you know. They can't get it up and even if they can –'

'Mother! Please stop!'

'I'm only thinking of you,' she continued. 'A few years down the line and he may go back to his wife. And then where will you be?'

'For the last time,' I said, 'I'm not having an affair with Julian.'

'I don't judge,' Mum said.

'Yes you do!']

'Sort of, I did kind of mention it to my supervisor.'

'And did she condone the notion of going to Ms Alvares's flat?'

'No,' I replied, 'she did not. But I'm not a predator, for God's sake. This article makes out I'm one of those therapists that abuse their patients.' The barrister clicked and unclicked his pen. I looked to Mr Davis for support but he wouldn't catch my eye. I took a slug of coffee. 'I'm not saying what I did – asking her about Laura, meeting her, going to her flat – I'm not saying any of that was appropriate or sensible. It wasn't. It was stupid. But it wasn't predatory or sexual, like they've made out. I've always been crap with boundaries, I know that. And maybe that means I'm not a very good therapist. But I'm not one of those therapists that has sex with their patients. I'd never do that. It's a line I'd never cross. But no one is ever going to believe me unless I sue.'

'Mr Randall –' he put down his pen and leaned back – 'I do understand. Lies have been told about you in a major newspaper and so, naturally, you think of suing. The action you have, in law, is one of defamation.' His eyes rolled upwards and he continued, as if reading from the ceiling.

'A defamatory statement is one that lowers the reputation of the subject in the eyes of reasonable men. It's not enough, for an action to succeed, to prove that a defamatory statement was false. The law of defamation does not require newspapers to ensure that their stories are true. The law gives newspapers several defences to claims for defamation, two of which are important for present purposes: justification and qualified privilege.' I looked at my phone to check the time and there were four missed calls from Laura.

'The defence of justification arises when the defendant is able to establish that the sting of the defamatory allegations is true. The defendant does not need to show that everything they have said is true, merely that the sting is true. If I falsely accuse you of having murdered X, whereas in fact you murdered Y, not X, I will have a defence of justification because the sting of the allegation, that you are a murderer, is true. The defence of qualified privilege, on the other hand, lies when the defendant is writing on matters of public interest after having taken reasonable steps to verify the accuracy of their information.

'As I see it, the sting of the allegation against you is that you had a sexual relationship with Ms Alvares. On that we have an admission that you went to her flat and one person's word against another as to what happened next.

'Now let's take the best-case scenario –' he flicked his eyes from the ceiling to the floor – 'the jury believe you. There can be no doubt, can there, that the sexual abuse, by therapists, of their patients is a matter of public interest?' He left no pause for an answer. 'So, qualified privilege comes into play. The defendant news organisation had a first-hand source for the allegation. Was there any reason they shouldn't have believed that source? She had undergone therapy, true, but so have many people. That doesn't make her story unbelievable. And they were under no obligation to consult you.

'And there's another matter, Mr Randall, which you should bear in mind – newspapers fight dirty. If you bring this case, they'll rake up whatever they can find against you – every ex-girlfriend, every drunken mistake you made when you were a student, every embarrassing photograph, every disenchanted former patient. If you have any skeletons in your cupboard, rest assured they will be aired. Newspapers do this to scare off litigants and in the hope that if they throw enough mud some of it will stick.

'So, in conclusion, I'm afraid that your prospects of success are not good. I don't say they are hopeless, but they are not good. There's one last factor to bear in mind – bringing a case will be very expensive. You've chosen a good firm. There's none better.' The two lawyers exchanged congratulatory eye contact. 'But good firms in London have to charge high rates. Bob will have a better idea than me but you should budget on tens of thousands of pounds at least. And if you lose, you'll be ordered to pay the newspaper's costs as well and they will be even higher.'

I tried to make a show of considering his advice, whereas in truth I just wanted to get out of the room as quickly as possible.

'I'm sorry to be the bearer of bad news, Mr Randall,' said the barrister, without a trace of sorrow in his voice or expression, 'but I'd be failing in my duties to you if I didn't give you my frank opinion. Take some time to think about it. If you do decide to take the case on, I'd be happy to fight it as best as I can but you must be aware of the risks ... I'm sorry. I've probably been talking too much. Is there anything you'd like to say or to ask me ...? No ... Well, in that case –' he stood up – 'Do help yourself to one of the pens. They're complimentary.' He nodded at a glass of pens, emblazoned with 7 ESSEX STREET, in the middle of the table.

I stood up slowly and bowed to him and Mr Davis, miming words of thanks, and turned to leave. The barrister bounded ahead of me, opening each of the sets of doors, until we reached the entrance where he stopped and, with a broad grin, stuck out his hand. I offered mine meekly and he shook it vigorously and said with cheery warmth: 'Good day! Tubes on the left, taxis on the right. Best of luck!'

I could hardly feel my legs as I walked down the narrow steps to the tube station; my throat was dry and my head was spinning. I'd just spent £1,000 to be humiliated.

The reporters had gone by the time I got home. I found Laura in our bedroom, packing the brown leather suitcase I bought for her thirtieth birthday.

'What are you doing?' I said.

She turned to me and her eyes were red with tears. 'Have you not even listened to my messages?' she said.

'No,' I said. 'Sorry, sweetheart. I was in the conference with the defamation lawyer. What's happened?' I moved to put my arm round her and she flinched.

'That bitch ... That bitch has ...' She sobbed and my heart froze. What had Claudia done now? 'That bitch has fired me.'

'I'm so sorry,' I said, although in my heart I was relieved it wasn't something I'd done. 'They don't deserve you. That magazine is going downhill fast and they've lost their best writer. You're going to show them. Come here.' I put my arms round her but it was like hugging a statue.

'You don't get it, Jack,' Laura said. 'I called you so many times and you never called back.'

'I'm sorry. I was at the conference with the lawyer. I

had to have my phone off. I had no idea you were calling about ...' I stroked her hair but she wouldn't turn to me. 'Sweetheart, this has been a terrible day for both of us but at least we have each other. We can go away, like you always wanted. I can be a teacher and you can be a freelance writer. Think of it that way.' She said nothing. 'I mean, my career's finished. You're leaving your job. We can go anywhere. There's nothing to stop us. We'll find work. What does work matter, when we have each other? This could turn out to be the best thing that ever happened to us. I loved my career but it's nothing compared to how much I love you. You choose where you want to go. Make it somewhere sunny. There's no point leaving England and going somewhere even colder! We can see the world together. Fuck London. Fuck England. Fuck horrible bosses and lying newspapers and smug lawyers and rain and friends we never see. We'll give notice on this flat and leave in a month. We can find jobs when we're out there. Just say where you want to go and I'll start looking for flights.'

Laura didn't react.

'It looks like you've started already,' I said, nodding to her suitcase, with a half-hearted smile. Then I felt myself shrinking. The room was blurry and unreal, as if I were somewhere else, watching it on television. 'Wait. Why are you packing?' I asked.

'It's a bit late, Jack.' Laura closed the suitcase. It had leather buckles and a metal clasp, like an old-fashioned portmanteau, but there were wheels on the bottom and a metal handle that Laura was extending. It was one of the best presents I ever gave her. I'll always remember her face when she opened it, and the way she flaunted it up and down the front room, like a game-show hostess with the star prize.

'Late for what?' I said.

'For all this talk of going away. If you'd wanted to travel the world with me the first hundred times I asked, maybe. To do it now, as a way of getting away from the trouble you've caused by screwing your patient, well, it's not quite so romantic.'

'I didn't screw ... Wait. Where are you going?'

'New York.'

'But that's not till the weekend, you said.'

'I moved the flights forward.'

'Isn't it supposed to be a work trip?'

'You've no right, Jack, to ask these kind of questions. Not after all you've been hiding from me. If you must know, Julian is going to introduce me to the editor of *The New Yorker*.'

'Julian?'

'Yes, Julian. He's been very kind to me recently. I needed someone to talk to and you've been too busy fucking your patients.'

'I did not ... Hang on. It was Julian you had dinner with on the "opera" night, wasn't it? Have I got the wrong –'

'I'm not interested in this.'

'How long are you and "Julian" going to be in New York?'

'I'm not sure. If it works out, I may not come back at all.'

'What do you mean?' I felt like I was shrinking into a tiny dot within myself.

'Jack,' she said, 'I think we need to have some time apart.'

'Time apart?' Every word she said was painful but I wanted more of them. 'What does that mean? If you're leaving me, just get it over with. Tell me now.' She hesitated and I made the mistake of continuing. 'Because if you walk out that door now, you're walking out on our marriage. I'm not going to wait around here, to see if your little romantic adventure with "Julian" works out.'

'Fine,' she said coldly.

'Fuck off, then!' I yelled. 'Fuck off to America and don't come back, if our marriage means nothing to you!'

I lay back on the bed, formerly our bed, the bed we'd chosen together from that converted church on the North End Road, when we'd jumped, hand in hand, on all the mattresses. It was good that I'd told her what I really thought, good that I'd released all that anger. What I was watching her do wasn't real. It was just a bluff. Laura couldn't be leaving me. This was someone else's life I was watching.

Laura didn't turn back as she left but the wheel of her suitcase got stuck in the door. This stopped her, like a dog pulling back on its lead and, for one absurd instant, I thought it might be a sign that Laura wasn't leaving after all, that she realised I didn't want her to go, that we'd see this nightmare through together, that we were still a couple, that we were still going to spend the rest of our lives together as we'd always promised. But, with a twist, the suitcase was free and Laura was gone.

[This isn't how I remember it. I tried to explain that I was going to New York to save my career, and that I had no desire to sleep with Julian, but you were so angry you wouldn't listen. That made me angry and I said something about you and Claudia and that upset you and it escalated until it was out of control. I remember your face at the end – your jaw set, your mouth tight, your eyes as hard as a wall. I remember trying to be as cold as you, when all the while I was more scared and unhappy than I'd ever been.

I did hesitate at the door. There was a moment, a flicker, when I thought of going back and throwing my arms round you and saying sorry, even though I didn't feel like I'd done anything wrong. And now, my God, there hasn't been a day, or an hour, or a minute where I haven't relived that awful evening. But what else could I have done?

Oh, Jack, I don't even know if you're even going to read this. Can you imagine how hard that is for me? If you knew how much I miss you. Do you think it's easy for me, to live without the person I know best in the world? To hear nothing from you? To know nothing about you? About where you are? About whether you're OK? It's not fucking easy. It's not fair to pretend it was all my fault and that I left you, when really it was you that left me. It fucking hurt and it still fucking hurts but we can't take that evening back now. Too many things have changed. But we can still be friends. It doesn't have to be all or nothing. I really fucking miss you.]

From: Laura Ferguson
Sent: 5 March 2011 23.16
To: Jack Randall
Subject: Re: Call me!
⌀ The [Edited] Strasbourg Diaries [Part 2]

Dear Jack,

I've calmed down now, you'll be pleased to hear, and read a bit more of your diary. See my comments in the attached. I stopped when I got to an interesting passage about you and your new 'friend' Nathalie. Why didn't you mention her before? Is this diary you're making me read just a long-winded way of telling me you've found someone else? If you have, that's fine, but you could have just told me straight out without all this sepia-tinged detail. Congratulations by the way. I looked her up on Facebook. You've done well.

Laura

The [Edited] Strasbourg Diaries [Part 2]

14

When the door closed behind Laura, my heart was beating fast but I didn't feel like crying or shouting. I didn't feel anything. I had a sense that something important had happened that I couldn't make sense of, like screams from a neighbour's house. Laura and I had been together for so long I couldn't remember life without her. I was a different person before I met her. For nearly twenty years she'd been the only family I had. It was impossible to accept she'd play no further part in my life. The change was too stark, too abrupt to be real. I knew, even then, it was the end of our marriage, but only in the way that I know I'll die – my brain accepted it but my heart could not believe it. I tried to imagine life without Laura. Seeing her again once or twice, at a wedding or a funeral or somewhere insignificant on the way to somewhere else. Her with someone else, not letting go of his hand, to show him and to show me. A minute of awkwardness, shifting eye contact, searching for an excuse to leave. Or, worse, stopping to chat. Catching up. Reducing the enormity

of what we'd lost to banality – '*A dentist! That's great.
No, I didn't remarry* . . .' If she'd died it would have been
unbearable but at least our life together would have
been preserved. Instead, I'm going to be a footnote –
the first husband, the bit of Mummy's life we don't
talk about.

> [Darling, don't be so melodramatic. It's not that bad.
> I'd never marry a dentist. In fact, if you'd only reply to my
> bloody emails, we can meet up tomorrow, in the flesh, and
> not wait for anyone's wedding or funeral.]

These were just some of my thoughts as I sat at the
kitchen table (the most expensive item on our John Lewis
wedding list) and drank the neat Pimm's I'd found in the
cupboard. There were many other thoughts too, I'm sure,
but they're buried now. I looked through the contacts on
my phone and the mass of names bewildered me. I didn't
recognise half of them. The only person I could bear to call
was Adam. He sounded stoned but his voice sharpened
when I told him what had happened.

'I'm sorry, Jack,' he said. 'Come and stay with me as
long as you need. I'm at home now, just watching TV.'

I filled a backpack with enough clothes to last a week
and turned off the lights. Before I left, I looked around the
room to see if there was anything I'd forgotten. Almost
everything was Laura's – the standard lamp with the
domed hood I'd carried back from Kensal Green as it
wouldn't fit in the car; the red glass bottles she wouldn't
tell me how much she paid for; the rusted iron she bought
in a flea market, when I begged her not to, which became a
bookend. My eye was caught by a framed photograph on
the bookshelf. We were at a concert in Hyde Park. I was
wearing a purple cowboy hat and kissing Laura on the side
of her cheek. Laura's eyes were closed and she was smiling.

She looked happy and proud. I stuffed the photograph in my bag and left.

Adam looked concerned as he opened the door.

'Come in,' he said. I knocked over a pizza box as I squeezed my backpack into his flat. 'I'm sorry. I don't have a proper bed. I hope the sofa'll be OK. It folds out.'

A low grey sofa crouched in front of a massive TV. On the far wall was a tiled fireplace. Six or seven beer cans stood like candles on the mantelpiece. A small brown table was covered in exhibits of Adam's life: uncased DVDs; an overflowing ashtray; a cereal bowl of grey sludge; a mug with a dried teabag inside; and a green upside-down Frisbee containing a plastic bag of weed, a mutilated pack of Rizlas and a small box of Marlboro Lights.

'We'll tidy this up, obviously,' Adam said. 'I'll move the table. Sorry. I should have done this before. I just didn't know when you'd be getting here.'

Adam picked up the cereal bowl and the mug, while I put down my backpack.

'Don't worry, Adam,' I said. 'I'll do it.'

'No, no,' he said. 'You put your feet up.' He picked up the Frisbee, looked around the room, frowned and put it back on the table. 'Are you hungry? Because look what I've got for us. He left the room and came back with a Pizza Express frozen pizza. 'Ta-da! Shall I put it on? And also ... wait ...' He put the pizza on the sofa and rummaged in a cupboard in the corner. 'Look at this. A boxset of every movie Tom Cruise has ever made!' He smiled. 'Guaranteed to cheer anyone up! What's wrong?' he said, catching my expression and frowning. 'Don't you like Tom Cruise? I thought you loved *Top Gun*.'

'I do, Adam. I do. Don't worry. I'm just a bit fragile at the moment. I'm . . . I don't know what to say.'

'You don't need to say anything,' he said, looking embarrassed. 'I'll put the pizza on.'

Two of my patients didn't turn up the following day. One of them left a message saying she'd decided to stop coming. Others came but behaved oddly, looking at me suspiciously and holding things back. Most worrying of all, I didn't care. All this talking about oneself, I thought, what does it really achieve? Susan, for example, had seen me for two years and was just as depressed as when she started. Maybe she had more insight but so what? How did that help? In the afternoon, Graham, a management consultant with depression and drinking problems, said he wanted an 'audit' of what he was getting for his money. I asked what he thought he was getting.

'Nothing,' he said.

'Maybe you're right,' I said.

This seemed to take him by surprise and he paused. 'Well,' he said with a snort, 'at least you're honest, I'll say that for you! But, if you didn't think it was working, why didn't you say something? Why do you keep taking my money every week?'

'Why didn't *you* say something?'

'I didn't know how this works,' he said. 'I thought I had to give it time.'

'And what were you hoping would change over time?'

'I don't know,' he said. 'That you'd figure out what was wrong with me. That you'd tell me what I needed to do to get myself out of this rut. All I seem to do here is talk about myself, while you just sit there and ask questions. I mean, you haven't given me one positive suggestion.'

'You want a positive suggestion? OK. How about this?
Accept the possibility of failure. Your career has trained
you to think that problems are "challenges" and that, with
the right advice, you can find "solutions". Well, maybe
life isn't like that. Maybe you'll never overcome your
depression. Maybe you'll drink until it kills you. Maybe
all this sitting around and talking about yourself is a waste
of your time and money. If you can accept all of that, who
knows, you might actually get somewhere. You might not
be any happier, but at least you'd be plugged into the real
world.'

'Are you all right?' he said.

'Why do you ask?' I said.

'You just seem to be in a strange mood today.'

'It's time,' I said.

Graham got up from the couch and looked at me
inquisitively. I looked down at the ground, waiting for him
to leave.

'I need to pay you for the past month,' he said. He took
a cheque book and a fountain pen from his jacket pocket.
He shook the pen and slowly unscrewed the top. I can't
do this anymore, I thought to myself. He scratched at the
cheque book. 'This pen isn't working,' he said. 'Do you
have one?'

'No,' I said. 'You can pay me later.'

'What about that?' He pointed at the 7 Essex Street pen,
which I'd forgotten I was holding.

'It's run out,' I said. 'Pay me whenever. I'm going to be
off work for a bit. I'll let you know.'

When I got back to Adam's flat, he was out. I filled a
bin bag with all the debris I could find – the beer cans,
the pizza box, the old cigarette packets. When I finished,

the bag was as full as a balloon. I couldn't force the
rubbish down far enough to tie a knot so I put the bag
down and it coughed up a carton of fruit juice. There
were no other bin bags so I left it there and collected all
the crockery – the bowls in front of the TV, the plates in
the kitchen, and the half dozen mugs and glasses hidden,
like Easter eggs, around the living room. I opened the
dishwasher and it was full of clean plates and glasses. I
couldn't face taking them out. I thought I should at least
turn my bed back into a sofa, so Adam could watch TV,
but I couldn't figure out how it worked. I found a lever
that I turned but even when I pressed with all my strength
the bed wouldn't bend. I gave up and lay back, looking at
the ceiling.

I emailed all my patients to say I was taking a break
from work for health reasons. I gave them the names and
numbers of other therapists. Most didn't reply.

I settled into Adam's routine. We'd wake up around
ten or eleven and wash up two of the dirty bowls and
spoons that lived in the sink to use for our cereal. A copy
of the *Telegraph* was pushed through the letter box and
Adam would read it and do the crossword. I'd mostly
stare at the cereal packet as I'd given up reading the news.
He'd have the first shower. He'd be in the bathroom for
twenty minutes before the water would come on. I'd go
after him. By the time we were both changed, it was nearly
midday and there was only an hour to kill before we had
to start thinking about lunch. We'd perch on the end of my
sofa bed (which we never folded) and look at what was
on TV. If there was golf, tennis, cricket or football, we'd
watch it. If not, we'd have what Adam called 'the agony
of choice'. He always held the remote control. He'd flick
through the channels on Sky, never spending longer than

a few minutes on any programme, like a security guard checking CCTV cameras. In the days when I was leaving the flat we might go out to Greggs or McDonald's for lunch. Otherwise, it was usually a Scotch egg and some chocolate in front of the TV. Adam would have his first spliff of the day after lunch – 'the postprandial', he called it. It was a point of principle, he told me, never to have spliff before lunch.

'How long have you lived like this?' I asked one afternoon.

'Like what?' he said, looking at the remote control.

'Like this. You know. With no job and nothing to do all day but watch TV.' He looked at me suspiciously. 'I mean, you were a scholar at school, right?'

'Music scholar,' he said.

'But, still, you got a 2:1 in Law from Warwick, which was something of a miracle given how much time you spent in the pub. You're such a bright guy. You could do anything.'

Adam sighed. 'Have you forgotten what happened when I did pupillage?'

'But that's a stressful job. You don't have to be a barrister. When I came to see you in Strasbourg, you were happy.'

'That's because I wasn't doing any work.'

'But you were doing an internship at the European Court of Human Rights. That's very prestigious. They must have made you do some work.'

'Nope,' he said.

'But there are so many other things you could do,' I said. 'It doesn't have to be law.'

'Uh-huh,' he said, changing the channel.

'You could be a teacher,' I said, 'or, I don't know, a

script reader. You could read film scripts for a production company and tell them what's good. You know so much about movies. You'd be brilliant at it.'

Adam turned to me. 'Thanks, yeah, good idea,' he said in a deflated voice. The wounded sadness in his eyes told me to stop, so I did. Here was an opportunity to discuss something that really mattered with someone who really mattered and, as so often, it slipped away. With everyone I've ever cared about, there's a conversation I've never had.

We developed an unspoken agreement. I never mentioned Adam's unemployment and he never mentioned my impending divorce. Except once.

'I'm sorry,' Adam said, as he knelt down to retrieve *Cocktail* from the DVD player. 'About you and Laura. I don't think I've said that yet. It must be awful. I don't know what to say. I've never come anywhere near what you must be feeling. I imagine you must be angry.'

'Sometimes,' I said. 'And sometimes I think it's all my fault and I made a terrible mistake. You see I still don't know for certain that she was having an affair. I thought I knew her as well as I knew myself but this whole thing made me realise you never really know anyone else.'

'Right,' he said, looking at me briefly, as he packed the DVD into its box.

'I mean, you and I have known each other for more than twenty years, but there are lots of things you don't know about me.'

'You think so?' he said in a nervous tone of voice that made me think he was regretting the conversation.

'Sure. My sexual fantasies for example. It's OK,' I added quickly, as he was looking anxious. 'I'm not going to tell you about them. I'm just trying to point out there are lots of things that are really important to our identity that we never share with anyone. Not even with our spouse. Especially not with our spouse.'

'I guess,' he said, standing up quickly. 'I'll put on the pizzas.'

The only message I got from Laura was a text to say I still had to collect my clothes from the flat. She told me to come on Saturday as she was away for the weekend.

> [I'm sorry if the text was curt. I was hoping you'd write to me. Also, you have to understand the mood I was in when I wrote to you. While you'd been getting stoned in front of eighties movies with Adam, I was being dragged round New York by the drunken and increasingly lecherous Julian. Of course the *New Yorker* job offer was a lie. What else could I do, dead-hearted and hopeless as I was, but drink with him? We had five days of restaurants and bars, phony appointments with executives who always cancelled at the last minute. It was a sick blur of blue cocktails and starched white tablecloths.
>
> So, when I got home, after a night of small-screen movies and small-bottled champagne on the red-eye flight, I was exhausted. I opened the door and called out your name, still hoping you might be there. That little flat echoed with sadness when it was empty. I just about kept it together until, looking in the drawers for my pyjamas, I found your sky-blue Pavement T-shirt – the one you used to wear in bed. I was upset. I thought that, if you were going to leave me, the least you could do was take your stuff and not leave mementos of our marriage to torture me.]

I scrolled up through the history of our text messages. Only a few bubbles above, she'd written 'I love you, my only. Come back soon.' She must still love me, I thought.

The human heart can't have a shorter memory than a phone. I wrote a letter.

My dearest Laura,

Something has gone terribly wrong. I love you as much as I always have and, I may be wrong, but I think you still love me too. So why are we splitting up? It can only be some failure of communication – the wrong words at the wrong time. If you could look inside my heart and see how much I miss you every day, every second, you wouldn't want to leave me. We've been through so much together. Too much.

Do you remember when we lay on that beach in Turkey, holding hands and looking at the stars, too happy to go back to the hotel? Or your cousin's wedding, where you got the giggles so badly they stopped the service and we had to leave? What about Heathrow, when you were leaving for a month, and you turned back and pushed your way through the queue for one last hug?

And do you remember in the hospital, when you lay next to me in the ward, and ignored the curfew, and found nurses when no one answered the bell. It was you that cleared up my vomit, and lifted me from the bed, and scratched my back when I couldn't sleep. It was you that persuaded me to continue with the radiotherapy when I couldn't bear it anymore, and reassured me that the voices weren't real and that everything would be OK. It was your vision of our future together that kept me going. It was you that I lived for.

The past is everything, Laura. It's everything that's ever happened. It's what makes us. You can't ignore it because it's you. I can't bear for the happiest memories of my life to become the most painful. What was the point of all those years together, if you leave me now? Have we just wasted our lives? I don't believe that. I can't believe that.

We just have to find a way to forgive each other. I know I've

*been jealous but that's just because I love you and I was scared
you didn't love me as much. Maybe I was wrong about Ford and
maybe I'm wrong about Julian. Maybe I'm the only one who
needs to apologise. And if so, I'm terribly, terribly sorry. But
please don't do this. Don't leave my life. I can't live without you.
At least, I can live but it's no kind of life. Let's start again. Let's
go somewhere and make new friends and find new jobs and leave
this miserable country behind. Maybe, if we're living somewhere
sunny, with none of the stress of our careers, we'll have what
we always wanted. The doctor said that lots of couples go
through IVF with no luck and then get pregnant when they stop
worrying. And what a child we would have – with my sense of
direction, and your dark skin, and my sense of humour and your
organisational skills (for which read bossiness). And we'd love
that child so much. No child would ever be more loved. It would
grow up so happy.*

*Please, Laura, for both of our sakes, forgive me and take me
back. No one could ever love you as much as I do.*

Jack

[Oh, Jack, what a letter! Why are you showing it to me
now? Are you trying to make me feel guilty? Because, if you
are, it's working. I feel wretched. What's the good of all this
now? And if you really can't live without me, why aren't you
answering my phone calls?]

When I came back to the flat, with Adam, to collect
the rest of my things, I left this letter in an envelope on
the kitchen table, leaning against a mug. The flat still
smelt of Laura. It was surreal to think she'd trodden on
the same floors only a few hours before. I stared at the
shelves, wondering which books were mine. Adam asked
what he should do and I told him to collect my suits and
ties from the bedroom. When he'd finished, he asked if I

wanted him to continue with the rest of the clothes. No, I said, I'll do it.

I bent down and opened the drawer where I kept my socks and underwear and began shovelling them into a cardboard box. The socks weren't in pairs. Laura must have done a wash. I was matching the pairs on the floor when I saw something that made my heart stop – under the bed was a large grey men's cardigan I didn't recognise. I pulled it out. It was ribbed cashmere, from Paul Smith, extra large. In the rush to get into bed with Laura, Zac must have tossed it under the bed and forgotten it. [No, no! It was Julian's and completely innocent – see above.] I laid it out on our bed or, I should say, Laura's bed. I picked the envelope off the kitchen table and replaced it with a note: 'I've taken what I could carry and left what doesn't belong to me. If there are other things you want me to collect, kindly let me know what they are.' [If you meant all the things in that letter, why would a stupid fucking cardigan make you change your mind?]

I still couldn't believe we were separating forever, even as the abstract concept of divorce turned into concrete reality – into Excel spreadsheets of possessions, letters from lawyers and appointments at the county court. I refused to accept I'd been guilty of 'adultery' or 'unreasonable behaviour' so, after charging me more than £2,000, my lawyer (Mr Felton) agreed with her lawyer (Ms Raines) on 'the cheap option' – two years separation, a no-fault divorce. Mr Felton was appropriately gloomy, even before I started speaking. He wore a dark suit and white shirt. No tie. Was that to make me feel relaxed? I wondered. Or was he losing it too? His skin was grey, he had at least a day's stubble, and his eyes were red and lined with bags.

He looked like a man who'd recently lost his life savings in a casino. Was it just the job or had he been through it himself? Laughed a bitter laugh at his own 'no fault' divorce? Compressed his pain and bewilderment into ironic inverted commas.

[It wasn't my idea to say you'd been guilty of unreasonable behaviour or adultery. I didn't even want a divorce. I just wanted you to say sorry for leaving me, to tell me you loved me and to beg me to come back. But you didn't write. You never wrote. It didn't have to be a grand, romantic letter. Just a fucking email. What was I supposed to do? I couldn't live in limbo, waiting to see if you'd change your mind. Ms Raines, or Suki as she insisted on being called, said I could get the divorce over with more quickly if there was 'unreasonable behaviour' or adultery. That's why I, or rather she, made those allegations.

Do you remember, when you were sick, you used to ask me if I'd marry again, after you died? And I didn't want to talk about it, but you insisted? When I told you I might, you looked shocked and said something like 'I'm definitely not dying then.' I didn't want to break up but what good would it have done, if I'd frozen my life, after *you* walked out? How could you expect that of me?]

15

I sunk into the world of Adam's basement flat. From the barred window of the front room, other people were just a traffic of clacking shoes. We pulled each other through the day, from game show to microwave meal to sitcom, like two old drunks on a pub crawl. Adam would go out sometimes. He'd never explain where he was going or what he was doing. He'd just say he was 'ticking things off the list.'

I took to smoking dope with Adam, as there was nothing else to do. It sorted out my sleeping problems – I could sleep till the afternoon – and it made TV funny and pot noodles tasty. I worried less about whether I should apologise to Laura or she should apologise to me. It was difficult and I couldn't cope with anything more complicated than Uno.

[It wasn't metaphysics. You left so you were the one who had to come back. You do overcomplicate things.]

I can remember laughing a lot but I can't remember what about. I sometimes sent myself emails but they were

incomprehensible the next morning ('Adam killd snail
with Morden sea salt – farmer's markey stylee!' 'gratude =
reverse guilt').

'How do you deal with the guilt?' I asked one day when
we were both drinking coffee in front of the TV.

'What guilt?' said Adam, looking guilty.

'The guilt that we're just wasting our time, getting
stoned to avoid the real world?'

'Oh,' said Adam, visibly relaxing, 'you mean the 'noia.'

''Noia?'

'The paranoia will destroy ya.'

'But is it paranoia? Or is it just a reasonable anxiety?'

'What's the difference?' said Adam, leaning forward and
frowning.

'One's reasonable and one's not,' I said, feeling anxious
that I was taking Adam into a subject he'd rather not
confront.

'But who defines whether an anxiety's reasonable?'
Adam said.

'I see your point,' I said, nodding. Adam still looked
tense. 'But I don't know, maybe it's just me but I still
think I should be doing something. You know, working.
Or helping someone in some way. Or learning something.
Some kind of action.'

'Uh-huh. Uh-huh. Yup,' said Adam in a tone that
suggested he couldn't wait for me to stop talking.

'Have you seen *Touching the Void*?' I said.

'Of course,' said Adam.

'When that climber's stuck on the mountain with a
broken leg, not knowing which direction he should go,
he says something I've been thinking about a lot. He says,
"You gotta keep making decisions, even if they're wrong
decisions, you know. If you don't make decisions, you're

stuffed." That's kind of how I feel. I need to keep moving, you know?'

'Sure.' I couldn't tell whether Adam was relieved or hurt or indifferent, or still too stoned to take in what I meant.

'I mean, I love being here but it can't go on forever and I thought, if I go abroad, put a bit of distance between Laura and me, maybe that will help.'

'Do a geographical,' Adam said.

'Yeah,' I said. Then I stopped. 'What's that?'

'When you get away from your problems by moving to another part of the world. People in NA do it all the time.'

'Does it work?'

'I dunno,' he said. 'I never see them again. Maybe that means it works.'

'Well, you'll see me again, won't you? You'll come to visit?'

'Sure, sure. I've just got to get a new passport. It's on the list. Where are you going?'

'I was thinking of France, maybe Strasbourg.'

'Strasbourg? Why Strasbourg?'

'I liked it when I stayed with you there. It was small and pretty and very un-English. And it doesn't remind me of Laura.'

It was a relief, at first, to be alone in a foreign country where no one knew me. I never had to pretend. And I had places to explore, a flat to find and a new hobby – calculating how long my savings would last. I had just under £6,000 in my savings account when I arrived and about £10,000 more if I used up all my overdraft and maxed out my credit cards. With my rent and about fifteen Euros a day for food and drink, I could survive for about two years. It gave me a perverse pleasure when I spent more than fifteen Euros in a day as it took me one step closer to some sort of an ending.

Christmas Day was the hardest. Strasbourg was ablaze in the evening. Every street wore a necklace of lights. Gigantic Christmas trees loomed over every square. Market stalls sold candies and toys and drinks and trinkets. The sweet smells of waffles and hot chocolate and roasted nuts filled the ice-sharp air. Families and lovers walked hand in woollen-mitted hand. I seemed to be the only person on their own. I felt awkward under the gaze of the strangers, so I walked back to my flat through the drifts of starlit snow.

[Christmas in London with Mum was far worse, trust me. She talked constantly about the divorce (and Julian, whom she insisted on calling John, no matter how many times I corrected her). Sometimes, she'd overdramatise it, as if I had no chance of ever being married again, which annoyed me. Other times, she made too little of it ('It's for the best'), which was even more irritating. Even when she wasn't talking about the divorce, she'd look at me with this expression of pity and excitement that infuriated me. Do you remember what you used to say about her – how she only ever came alive when something terrible happened? Well, she was having a high old time with our divorce. I was constantly angry with her, never more so than when I could see that she was actually trying to help.

I gave her such a good Christmas present – the Nespresso machine she'd been so amazed by at Andrea's. When she'd unwrapped it, she paused, temporarily at a loss for something negative to say about it.

'How much did it cost, dear?' she said at last. 'Shall I pay you back?'

I don't think I'd realised how irritating Mum becomes when you're not there. There's no one I can laugh with. If I say anything even remotely critical of Mum, Andrea makes me feel guilty by saying something like, 'Poor Mum, she means well', as if I don't. And so Mum-scenes that would have been funny with you there, become enraging. If you'd given me the choice, I'd have jumped at a few days on my own in Alsace. I like your description of the Christmas markets. Let's go together some time. I'll bring mittens.]

When the New Year came, I made a friend by accident. I was eating out every night in the cheapest restaurants and bars in town. I'd never go to any of them more than once in a week as I didn't want anyone to notice me, or ask why I was always alone. Then, one night, a big man walked into La Lanterne, wearing a Man City football shirt. He stood next to me at the bar and before I could leave, he said in a loud, English accent:

'Are you waiting, mate?'

His eyes were smiling and he had an easy warmth that drew me to him.

'No, mate,' I said. 'Are you a City fan, then?'

'Yes. Who do you support?'

'City.' (This was half true – my cousins were City fans.)

For the next two weeks I spent almost every evening with Wilf (as he was called), full of a false camaraderie born of loneliness and alcohol. To my intense embarrassment, he kept trying to high-five me. Whenever I made a joke, or criticised the Tories, or said something about Man City, and sometimes for no obvious reason at all, he'd lift up his palm in excited readiness, and I didn't have the heart to let him down.

One day Wilf sent me a text: 'Jackyboy. Footy at 7 in
the pub. You. Me. Lager. You know the rest.' This pseudo-
poem made me recognise something I'd been avoiding
– Wilf and I had nothing in common. I don't even like
football. I made an excuse (unspecified 'plans') and he's not
been in touch again. I worried that I'd hurt his feelings,
but I couldn't bear to spend another evening pretending to
have fun.

[I like the idea of your trying to pass yourself off as a
Mancunian football fan. Aye, that be our Jack. He's just
your average salt-of-the-earth working-class northern
psychotherapist, off to play tennis with his old-Etonian
pal, Adam. Then he'll get home and polish off t'problem of
Freud's hermeneutics before tea. That's a full working day,
lad, and don't you forget it.]

I didn't want to bump into Wilf again so for a month
or two after his text, I didn't leave my flat, except to go to
the supermarket in the shopping mall next door. I bought
a French dictionary and tried to learn a page a day. After
a couple of weeks, when I went back to the first page,
I'd forgotten everything. I tried watching French TV but
most of the time I couldn't understand it and, when I
did, it annoyed me. Most programmes seemed to involve
smug men in suits talking to pretty women who'd laugh
for reasons I didn't understand. I signed up for French
Conversation Level 1 at an adult-education centre. The
classes were in a dusty room with cracked windows
near the university. I'm not sure it was free but no one
ever asked me to pay. There were two other students
– a large woman from Poland and an elderly Japanese
man. The teacher, Monsieur Laurent, was an earnest
man with a saggy moustache, who discoursed (as far as
I could understand) on grand subjects: reform, justice,

communism, etc. He had a withered hand, which he'd hide, except when he was excited. He probably had ambitions to lecture at university. He'd ask us each, in turn, for our views on the subject of the day and pause, with an earnest expression, while he waited for our replies. The Polish woman would say it was all '*Très, très compliqué.*' The Japanese man would grin and fidget until we all looked away. If M. Laurent was disappointed by the answers we gave, he didn't show it. I felt a lot of sympathy for M. Laurent and, one afternoon, after class, I asked if he wanted to go for a drink. He looked scared, as if I were making a pass at him, and said he was busy as he had a wife and children. I never went back after that.

Many times I thought of writing to Laura. I drafted and redrafted a letter but I could never get the tone right. My aim was to write something that would hurt her without appearing vindictive – something emotive, but not maudlin, which would remind her of what she'd thrown away and, without criticising her directly, make her feel like she'd made a terrible mistake. But the words would either fall short of what I wanted or they'd go too far and drag me with them. The long descriptions of happy moments from our past, which were supposed to make her feel sad, would bring tears to my eyes and I'd find myself making the promises I wanted her to make. When I reread these letters, with the objectivity of time, they seemed too manipulative and self-pitying so I'd tear them up.

In the internet café, I used to toy with the idea of sending Laura a jokey email about what I was doing, but it seemed too trivial so I just followed her life through Facebook instead. Facebook became like porn, only without the gratification. Just one more photograph, I'd say to myself, knowing it wouldn't be just one, each click dragging me deeper into the envy and the self-loathing. Nearly every day a new photograph would be posted of Laura in a party or a nightclub. She was often surrounded by two girls I didn't recognise who'd pose for the camera – pouting or tilting an eyebrow – while Laura sat between them with a relaxed 'I'm-going-to-look-much-prettier-than-either-of-you' smile. I've never seen a bad photograph of Laura. Her eyebrows are too dark and her skin too olive for the camera to miss.

I was not the only 'friend' taking a close interest in Laura's Facebook life. There were others who didn't have the decency to stalk her silently, like me. Instead, they were constantly hitting on her – liking her posts, poking her, writing comments like 'Megababe!' I couldn't tell whether she liked any of them but there was no doubt that she was having fun, far more fun than me, probably more fun than when she'd lived with me. Of course, I didn't want her to be miserable – not forever anyway – but I was hoping for a grieving period. I wouldn't want – to be more accurate, I wouldn't expect – her to be celibate indefinitely. I'd be happy (sort of) to see a photograph of her, on a walking holiday, say, with a mature man, maybe a divorcé in his late fifties, who'd lost his hair. Then I'd know she was happy and cared for, without there being too much sex. Instead, she was always photographed next to dreadful shiny Made-in-Chelsea types, with V-neck T-shirts and lecherous smiles and names like 'Jeremy À. Michel' – men with profile pictures that said 'I'm too rich to bother with irony' (standing, in swimming trunks and Ray-Bans, at the wheel of a speedboat), men with photograph albums titled 'Verbier' or 'Klosters', or 'Mustique 2009'.

[I don't know any 'shiny Made-in-Chelsea types'. From
what I recall of the TV programme, I'm old enough to be
their mother. Jeremy Michel, as I know him, is a perfectly
nice man from Andrea's year at school whom I've met twice
in my life. I wasn't out partying all the time. Most nights I
was alone in front of the TV. I moved out of our flat to a dank
studio in Shepherd's Bush above a girl who was always
having screaming rows with her boyfriend or noisy sex or
both. Emily and Aoibheann, the two very beautiful women
you describe somewhat uncharitably, were people I met in
a spinning class. They insisted on taking me out once or
twice, but my heart wasn't in it.]

One black afternoon, Laura posted a photograph
that made my heart stop – her and Zac Ford, scored by
sunlight, on the edge of an Alpine terrace. We'd been
separated for nearly a year and it shouldn't have mattered
so much but it did. Nothing mattered more. I spent hours
on the internet, looking for more photographs of them
together. I read every article and review about Ford I could
find. I learned a lot about him, including some things I
might use one day, but I never found anything to suggest
that Laura had written an article about him – I guess that
was just a pretext to meet him.

[It was not a pretext. I did start an article about him, but
I put it on hold when he started my portrait. Then, when
he tried to kiss me, I stopped seeing him and shelved the
article.

It was nearly a year later, after I'd given up hope of
hearing from you, that I got in touch with Zac again to finish
the interview we'd started. I was desperate. No one was
hiring. No one was going to pay to read my reviews when
there were countless free ones online. Celebrity interviews
were the only kind of work a freelance journalist could still

get paid for. It wasn't my fault if Zac misinterpreted my phone call and invited me to Nobu. What was I supposed to do – refuse so I could have another TV dinner alone?

I did write the article about Zac in the end. It started off as an in-depth interview and analysis of his work but Siritha said it had to be 'glossier'. It was edited and edited until it became the following puff piece that got spiked to make way for an article on sex shops:

Zac Ford On Being Alone
The celebrated artist talks love and art
By Laura Ferguson

'There's a tension,' says leading British artist Zac Ford, 'between explanation and creation. Sometimes I try to explain the ideas that were behind my work and it feels like air bleeding from a tyre. The reason I'm an artist is because I prefer to express my emotions through non-verbal means. The temptation is always there, to explain, because people so often misunderstand, but I try to resist. When an artist explains his own work, it's like shooting one of those toy guns, where a flag comes out and says "Bang".'

The irony of this is that Ford is a beautiful talker. When he speaks, everyone listens. He began his career ten years ago, selling his own work from the kitchen of his parents' house. It sold so well he decided to give up his place at Goldsmiths. 'I don't really see the point of being taught if you're an artist,' Ford says. 'I've spent most of my life trying to "unlearn" everything I've learned because that's the only way you can hope to be original. And that's the point of being an artist.'

His success since that first exhibition has been meteoric – he has sold to Gwyneth Paltrow, Bono and Bob Geldof among others. But, despite the critical acclaim, and the huge sums of money he's been offered, Ford will only sell his work to people that, in his words 'get it'. He estimates that he turns down ninety-five per cent of offers.

'Money is a distraction,' he says. 'I hate thinking about it or talking about it. I could be paid in paints and bread. I'd still do what I'm doing.'

I first met Ford when I was researching an article on Great Ormond Street. He was working with some of the children there on a project he called Self-Destruction where children destroyed and recreated Ford's portraits of them.

'The children,' Ford said, 'were amazing. In spite of everything, they had so much energy and creativity. It was humbling.'

Ford is coy when asked if he'd like to have children of his own. 'I feel like I have hundreds of children already from Self-Destruction. We developed such a bond. I'd do anything for them.' Ford keeps his cards close to his chest when it comes to his love life. He's been seen on the arm of the supermodel Iris Willan, but he says they're just good friends. 'I'm really an introvert,' he says. 'My best work has been created when I've been alone. I can take myself away from external influences and find something within me.']

When I left the internet café and walked home, I felt irritated by the pseudo-medieval pennants that hung above the narrow streets. The dark shop windows were revoltingly bourgeois – all these expensive products crammed into little boxes for the affluent consumer: tiny tins of caviar; shining triangles of foie gras; ribboned chocolate gifts; jam jars with faux handwritten labels; perfume in bottles shaped like women's bodies. Everything and everyone was vulgar. I wanted to be alone, even though I hated being alone. I loathed this cold, lonely city, but I had no thought of leaving it. I preferred to loathe myself for not leaving it.

Clients with depression often told me that exercise helped – Graham used to say an hour with a personal trainer was better for his mental health, and a lot cheaper,

than an hour with me. I tried jogging but each step
jarred my knees. So I signed up to the local tennis club.
And it was there I met someone who's helped me turn my
life round.

> [Oh God. Am I about to read about some tennis-playing
> cougar?]

16

Édouard was a silver-haired man in his fifties with small
round spectacles that made him look nerdy and shy. He
wore a yellowing frayed Lacoste shirt with tight elastic
round his skinny biceps. In the knock-up, he moved
gingerly, like an old man, but in the real game, he was
fitter and faster than me. I had to stop, at times, because I
was panting and coughing so hard. He struck his forehand
so clean and flat you could almost read the words on the
ball. His sliced backhand would kiss the ground and scoot
through at ankle height. He thrashed me with polite smiles
and nods at the changeovers.

After the match, we drank Oranginas in cold glass
bottles and I congratulated him in pre-prepared French on
how he'd played. With vocabulary I'd learned when I was
fifteen, and never used since, I told him what it was like to
be an Englishman in France. I said something like '*Tout le
monde boit beaucoup plus à Londres qu'ici*' and he smiled.
I had a sense he was encouraging me to talk – it was as if
he knew I'd not spoken more than a few words in months.

I asked him as many questions as I could formulate, each
one beginning '*est-ce que*', and he answered slowly and
clearly.

I asked him how I could find work as an English teacher.
He suggested I put an advert on the noticeboard at the
Conseil de l'Europe. After a silence, he asked whether
I'd like to come to dinner on Friday night. I'd meet some
English friends who might be able to help.

'*Es-tu célibataire?*' he said.

What does that mean? I thought. Am I celibate? [No,
it means 'Are you a bachelor?'] I thought I'd make a joke,
something like 'not on purpose'.

'*Pas volontiers!*' I said. [That means 'not gladly'.]
Édouard looked confused. I was embarrassed and I wanted
another drink so I turned to look for the waiter.

'*Tu cherches un garçon?*'

'*Pas du tout!*' I said, offended that he'd assumed I was
gay. Then I remembered that '*garçon*' means waiter as well
as boy. 'Ah!' I said. '*Garçon! Pardon. Je veux dire "oui". Je
cherche un garçon pour une autre boisson. Pas pour autre
chose parce que ...*' I must sound like a gay man in denial.
I was drowning in French. 'I'm in the middle of a divorce,'
I gasped.

'Ah, I see,' Édouard said in near perfect English. 'You
will not mind if I invite a colleague of mine, who's single?'

'No,' I said.

Édouard lives in a grand, high-ceilinged apartment in Place
du Marché Neuf. The cobbled courtyard is tarnished by a
jumble of cars under the broken canopy of an old oak tree.
The doorway's in a corner with Roman numerals carved
into the stone.

I was late, because I'd been writing, and I raced up the

stairs. The other guests were sat on couches on either side of a long rectangular drawing room. There was a British couple, Matt and Clare, and a woman, called Nathalie, who was introduced as Édouard's colleague. My heart sank. Nathalie had a handsome face and warm sparkly eyes but her hair was grey and frizzy and her skin looked old – her neck, in particular, had the texture of a burst balloon. This was my level now, I thought. I'd never have gone out with a woman as beautiful as Laura if I hadn't been her tutor. And Claudia was only attracted to me because she'd been my patient. Take away the position of power and I'm no catch – a divorcé in his fifties of slightly less than average height, with no money, no career and no prospects.

[Is this the 'Nathalie Piccard' that's now your friend on Facebook? If so, you're being as uncharitable to her as you are to yourself. I can see from her photographs that she has quite a sense of style. Very original clothes. It looks like she made them herself. And I like the fact that she doesn't pretend to be younger than she is. I respect women who don't wear make-up. She does have a prominent nose, I suppose, if one were being hyper-critical, but all in all, she's much more attractive than Claudia, for example.]

'So,' I said to Nathalie, when we'd all sat down, 'you work with Édouard?'

'Yes,' Nathalie replied.

'He's a fantastic tennis player, did you know that?'

'No,' Nathalie said, 'I did not.'

'Really, he is,' I went on, as if she'd disagreed with me. 'He could have been a professional . . . very graceful on the court.'

'Well, he is a man that is graceful in everything.'
She smiled.

I smiled too. 'What subject do you teach?'

'French literature.'

'Oh, great,' I said.

'And you,' she said, 'what do you do when you are not playing tennis?'

'*J'essaie d'apprendre français*,' I said.

'What?' She frowned and leaned towards me.

'I'm trying to learn French.'

'*Eh bien, parlons en français.*'

'*Non. Je parle trop mal. Ça serait énervant pour toi.*'

'*Mais, tu parles bien.* Very "graceful",' she smiled.

I made a few trite observations in French till I felt tired. My head was blank. I was ashamed to switch back to English. I used a cough as an excuse to go to the toilet. I locked myself in and read the back of the shampoo bottles, in English and in French, till I thought I'd have to go back.

When I took back my seat, Matt leaned across the table to me. 'Do you like cricket?' Matt asked. Clare rolled her eyes and groaned and Matt smiled knowingly. 'I'm thinking of starting a team.'

'That was the main reason,' Clare said, 'why I agreed to leave England. No more bloody cricket teas with the other bloody wives.'

I laughed and said how much I missed English tea.

'I know!' Clare said, leaning in conspiratorially. 'Whenever we have a visitor from Britain, I make them bring Earl Grey and Cheddar cheese. The stuff you get from those Lipton bags is just –'

'A cooked breakfast on Sunday,' Matt cut in. 'That's what I really miss. That and cricket of course. I've looked everywhere. There's a cafeteria above the Museum of Modern Art that does something it calls an English Breakfast but the sausages –'

'They're wet,' said Clare, 'like frankfurters. It's all wrong.'

I felt a surge of love for them. Ideas, observations and stories – about Strasbourg, about the French, about home – scurried and slipped over one another in a race for expression. I told them about my beginners' French class and did impressions of the other students. I was elated by their laughter – it was as if I'd rediscovered something I thought I'd lost forever. I told them about my twinkly-eyed French GP, who only wanted to talk about Russian prostitutes.

Matt and Clare promised to put me in touch with an English family who were looking for a tutor. I was so excited to be talking to them I forgot about Nathalie. Out of the corner of my eye I could see her smiling but she never joined in. It was only when Matt and Clare had gone home that I turned to Nathalie, who was next to me on the sofa. Was it just the alcohol, or was she more attractive than I'd first thought? Her long thin legs were folded over one another at the knee and she played with her shoe, cupping and uncupping her heel. Her hair looked softer and smoother and, in the lamplight, she looked younger. It was unrealistic, I thought, to compare everyone to Laura. I was still in my twenties when I met Laura. And I'd never been in love before. If I were to wait till I had feelings like that again, I'd be waiting forever. I stretched my arm so my little finger touched Nathalie's thumb and we caught each other's eye. Her expression was hard to read – neither pleased, nor disappointed, nor surprised, just steady and knowing. I was too nervous to speak. Édouard walked in and smiled as he saw us. He said he had to go to bed and asked if I would walk Nathalie home.

Nathalie and I walked in humid silence down the empty, curving streets. The only noise was the occasional rattle of a bicycle. A naked pair of women's legs posed, trunkless, in a shop window.

'*J'habite ici*,' I said, '*depuis six mois et je deviens perdu toujours. Est-ce que ca se passe avec toi?*'

'*Non, mais je suis Strasbourgeoise. Je peux être ton guide.*'

Nathalie was walking down the centre of the road in the storm drain. I was a couple of feet to her right and the slope was pushing me towards her, but I resisted. A sleek and snaky tram crept up on me and hooted. I jumped sideways and touched Nathalie's shoulder with my hand. She shot me a look of surprise and smiled – it was a warm smile that made me feel like I'd known her for years. We carried on through Petite France and crossed a bridge by a watermill, which split the water in two – upstream it was still as ice, downstream it was white and frothy. Underneath us was a bottle-smooth waterfall. A hundred yards away a wooden restaurant loomed on stilts over the flecks and stars of the bubbling canal.

A few minutes later, we reached her door. There was a silver plaque by the entrance announcing that M. Blanc, ophthalmologist, lived there. Nathalie tapped some numbers into a keypad, pushed open the door, turned and paused in the entrance. I hesitated, embarrassed and unsure what to do. My heart beat fast at the thought she might invite me upstairs. It felt like it wasn't me there, standing in silence at the doorway of this woman I barely knew. It was another person, whom I couldn't control, and I didn't know what he was going to do. I was just a spectator.

Nathalie looked at my lips. I leaned in to kiss her and she closed her eyes. At the last moment, as if they were matching poles of a magnet, my mouth turned from hers and gave her a glancing kiss, half on the lip and half on the cheek. Maybe it was the dry, frizzy hair that put me off. I imagined pressing it to her head and watching it bounce back. Or maybe it was the memory of that disastrous night in Claudia's flat. [Or maybe it was the nose that could have taken your eye out.] I said goodnight.

'That was not so graceful,' she said with a laugh. 'Do you not want to come in my house? For a coffee?'

'Yes. No. I do.'

17

Nathalie's flat was tiny, even smaller than mine.
Amateurish pencil sketches and watercolours of Strasbourg
lined the red walls of the hallway. In the humming light
of the kitchen, as we waited for the coffee to boil, she
looked as plain as when I'd first seen her. 'You made the
paintings outside?' I said.

'Yes.'

'They're good,' I said.

'Thanks.'

[That's about all I could get out of Zac. I spent a lot of
time with him, writing the article, but he seemed more and
more reluctant to talk about his work the better I got to
know him. I thought, at first, that it was like a magician not
wanting to explain his tricks and that when he trusted me
enough, he'd let me into his secrets. But over time I grew
to suspect there weren't any secrets. He'd always answer
my literal questions with metaphors, as if that were the
only language he could speak. And I heard him using the
same metaphors again and again. He'd repeat sentences,

even whole stories, word for word with the freshness and enthusiasm of someone telling them for the first time. And I realised that was why he kept travelling to new places and making new friends. He didn't have to say anything new if the audience was always new. Like that line about the toy gun. I thought it was clever, even poetic, the first time I heard it. After several repetitions to admiring women, I realised it was little more than a chat-up line.

We went to an exhibition once. I wish you'd been there. The main piece was a tower of Lego about three feet high, one block on top of another. I said something about how my four-year-old niece makes towers like that and Zac gave me one of his pat speeches about how artists need to be more like children.

'Do you actually know any children?' I asked. He said of course he did and he began listing all the children's hospitals he'd been to. 'No,' I said, 'that doesn't count. You don't really know any of the children in those hospitals. I mean, do you actually know any children? Because my experience of my nieces is they're not very original. In fact, they spend most of their time copying. That's how they learn. My niece doesn't put the Lego blocks one by one on top of each other because she has an "interest in formal structure" or whatever it says in this bullshit programme. She does it because she hasn't got the imagination or the fine motor skills to do anything else.'

'But that's the point,' Zac said loudly. 'Western children are given building blocks and Monopoly and plastic cash tills to turn them into good little capitalists. Lego is to children's creativity what Le Corbusier was to architecture.' I was going to come back at him but, as he was speaking we passed a box that made a fart noise. I laughed and Zac stopped in his tracks. 'What are you laughing at?'

The veins rose from his neck and he looked like he wanted to hit me.

'I'm not laughing at you,' I said. 'I'm just laughing at the noise. Look.' I walked past and the box farted again.

'What's funny about that?' he said, a little calmer. 'That's a serious work of art.'

'Give over,' I said.

'Of course it is,' he said. 'The artist is ridiculing the critic, blowing a raspberry at the narrow-minded people who think art has to be something you can see and touch.'

God, I missed you then. I nearly called you that afternoon. The only thing that stopped me was that Zac had bought a ticket for us (not just for the two of us but for several other friends too) to go to Istanbul that weekend for an opening of his work. I really wanted to go as I'd never been to Istanbul and I knew if I talked to you, I wouldn't feel like it. So I made up my mind to call you when I got back.]

I leaned in to kiss Natalie. Our teeth clashed and I pulled back. There was a silence and I couldn't bear to look at her. We kissed again and she pressed her crotch against mine. I didn't have an erection. I felt empty – why was I pretending to want this woman? I was deliberately mistranslating my desire for her friendship as sexual. I could see it. I could stand above myself and see the disconnect – the parallel lines of my thoughts and my actions. The coffee machine clicked and I pulled away.

'Perhaps I should go,' I said.

'As you want,' she said.

We kissed again in the doorway. I held her buttock and it was firmer than I'd expected. As she pressed against me, I felt a stirring of desire.

*

I don't remember either of us undressing, or getting into
Nathalie's bed, or whether she touched me or I touched
her. I remember she had condoms in the drawer and I
remember the silence that seemed to watch over us. It
was as if we were in a speechless battle, like strangers on
a tube fighting for an armrest. I couldn't tell what she
wanted. She smiled, but her brow was furrowed, which
made me wonder whether she was just concentrating, or
whether she disapproved of something I was doing.
I wanted her to turn round, as Laura would have done,
but I was too embarrassed to ask. We were on the edge
of the bed and my knee kept slipping off. I listened
carefully to her breathing and, when it got shorter, I let
myself go in the hope that she might come too. She didn't
and when I'd finished, she got up almost immediately, to
go to the toilet.

I threw the wrinkled, shrunken bag into a wastepaper
basket and lay back on the bed. For a few moments, I
floated contentedly amid the flotsam and jetsam of dream
fragments, while guilt and anxiety sank beneath their
own weight. I dreamed that I was in bed, next to Laura
and I felt a deep peace until I was disturbed by a shaft
of consciousness. Laura left me, I said to myself, this
must be a dream. Hold on, came the reply, it can't be a
dream because everything's right. This is our bedroom.
Everything's where it's meant to be. And, for a moment,
I was satisfied, but then the doubts returned. Why are we
in our old flat? I don't live there anymore. I live in France.
Yes, I said to myself, that's right, it was a dream but look
– now you're waking up from that dream and see where
you are – you're in bed with Laura. What a relief! I relaxed
again until a drip of suspicion entered my heart. And so
I stumbled on, hitting the walls of this house of mirrors,

till Nathalie's voice cut in, asking me to get up. She was wearing a satin dress and she held a corner of the duvet that I was lying on. I stood up, wondering if it would be rude to leave, while she got in.

'That was nice,' she said.

'Yes,' I said, getting back into bed.

'Let us do it again,' she said.

'You might have to wait a bit,' I said.

'No,' she said smiling. 'Another day.'

[This is a bit gross. Could you not have deleted these icky details before forwarding me your diaries? I'm not condemning you. I do understand how it can happen (even with a woman whose nose is as big as a leg). I myself did, very, very occasionally, out of loneliness or drunkenness or simple biological need, find myself, briefly, in bed with Zac Ford. It was always perfectly clear to him that I didn't love him, and he certainly didn't love me. It meant nothing.]

When at last Nathalie had fallen asleep, I slipped out of bed and trod on something crinkly. I looked down. The condom packet, splayed down the centre like a Valentine heart, was stuck to the base of my foot. I kicked it off and put on my shoes, without lacing them. I let myself out of the room with my shirt and jacket still in my hand.

[You sound like Zac! On the very, very few occasions we ended up in bed together, I'd always catch him sneaking out when he thought I was asleep. I think, with his great vanity, he thought I'd fall in love with him if I woke up next to him. He went to elaborate lengths to remind me we weren't in a relationship – he'd even leave his phone behind in bed so I could read all the texts from his other women. It was absurd as the one thing I liked about sleeping with him was the fact that it wasn't going to lead anywhere.]

*

The family that Clare and Matt put me in touch with were called Beefton and they lived in Robertsau, an expensive suburb in the north of Strasbourg. Virginia Beefton was a middle-aged woman with downy cheeks and a short crop of greying hair. We sat on high stools at a Formica island in her tidy kitchen, while a silver fridge hummed behind us. A French window revealed an uncut suburban lawn, a cherry tree and a deflated football.

'So Clare tells me you're looking for a tutoring job. What's your experience?'

'When I was doing my PhD, I taught a couple of courses to English undergraduates.'

She looked surprised. 'So no experience with children?'

'Well, no.'

'And where did you go to university?' she asked.

'My first degree was at Warwick.'

'Warwick?' she said in a tone of disgust. 'Clare said you went to Oxford.'

'I did. My first degree was at Warwick and then I did a master's and PhD in Oxford.'

'I see,' she said, frowning. 'What subject?'

'I started with English and then I switched to Psychology.'

'Psychology!?' She looked at me as if I'd said something obscene. 'So, why are you living in Strasbourg looking for teaching jobs at your age?'

I paused. Was that a trick question? Had she read the *Mirror*? No, I decided. She was just one of those rude people who pride themselves on being 'direct'. If she'd known, she'd have said something.

'I'm writing something,' I said.

'Oh really,' she said warily. 'What's it about?'

'Strasbourg.'

'Thank God for that,' she said. 'I thought you were
going to say it was your life story. There's nothing worse
than when someone says they've given up their career
to write about themselves. Why do they think anyone
cares? So ...' she continued, 'we want you to teach Harry
English. They don't teach it properly here. Piers, Harry's
older brother, is so gifted it didn't matter. He got the fourth
highest scholarship to Harrow,' she said. 'But Harry ...'
We both turned to see a worried blond boy in the doorway.
He walked softly towards us and came to an obedient stop
just a few inches short of his mother's waist. With her eyes
on me, Virginia spanned her fingers round the boy's head.
He stared at me with sad, honest eyes. 'Harry's not as
bright as Piers. He's going to need a lot of help this year for
the Harrow entrance exams.'

Harry was sent on his way so Virginia and I could talk
money. As Harry left, I caught his eye and smiled. He
paused, in suspicious contemplation, and then ran into the
garden. While Virginia explained what the 'position' would
involve (as if I were a governess), I watched Harry at the
far end of the lawn toe-punting the football into a wooden
fence. He reminded me of someone.

Harry and I have our lessons in a dining room with dark
green wallpaper and unsmiling portraits in heavy gold
frames. We sit at the corner of a long mahogany table.
Books and papers slide across its polished surface but
if you look closely, you can see a history of black scars
underneath the veneer. The walls must be thick because we
can't hear anything from outside.

We've been reading *The Catcher in the Rye*. I told him
to read at least four chapters a week. Each week he reads
exactly four chapters. Never more. Never less. Like it's a job.

'What do you think of Holden?' I said.

'Dunno.'

'Do you like him?' I asked.

'He's rude,' Harry said. 'About other people.'

'Yes, but that can be likeable, don't you think?' Harry said nothing. 'I mean, some people need to be laughed at, don't they? When everyone makes too much of a fuss of them.' Harry looked up at me suspiciously from between strands of hair, as if I were trying to trap him. For the rest of the hour, he said almost nothing and his gaze wandered.

The following week, I tried a different tack.

'What do you think of Stradlater?' I said.

'Dunno,' Harry said.

'Do you think he's a moron?'

'Kind of.'

'Do you think someone can get good grades at school and still be a moron in other ways?'

'Definitely,' Harry said through a half-buried smile.

We trudged on like this, all my leading questions and therapeutic tricks getting nowhere until a few months in – our last class on Salinger. We'd run through all the essay questions and how we might answer them and there were fifteen minutes left.

'Have you enjoyed reading this book, Harry?'

'Yeah,' he said with a qualifying hesitation.

'It sounds like there's something you didn't like.'

'There's just one thing. I don't get why it's called *The Catcher in the Rye*.'

'Do you remember what Holden says he wants to be?' I asked.

'Not really.'

'He says he wants to be a "catcher in the rye" like in the Burns poem. Only that's not what the poem says – it says "Gin a body meet a body *coming* thro' the rye". Holden thinks the poem's about children on the edge of a cliff, with someone trying to catch them before they fall.'

'Oh OK,' he said, sounding unsatisfied.

'So what does the scene tell you about Holden?'

'Dunno.' He frowned. 'That he's crazy?'

'What do you mean by that?'

'You know ...' Harry sounded frustrated, as if I were deliberately misunderstanding him. 'A bit mad.'

'You have to be precise with words in a subject like English, as it's all about words. Do you mean "mad"? How else could you describe him?'

'Different. He sees things differently.'

'Yes,' I said. 'Absolutely. Can you think of an example?'

'That thing about the ducks. In the van. What happens to them in the winter.'

'Exactly. Brilliant example. So the catcher in the rye is just like that. Holden sees the poem differently. He's original. And what else does that scene tell you about Holden?'

'That he's a nice guy ...' Harry looked downhearted again, like a tired walker who's just been told that there's another hill they hadn't seen before. 'That he wants to help people?'

'Yes,' I said, 'but what kind of people?'

'Children.'

'And how does that connect to the rest of the book?'

'Well –' the confidence was returning to his voice – 'his sister is a child and she's the person he seems to care most about.'

'And Holden? Is he a child or an adult?'

'I don't know. He's sort of in the middle.'

'And where does the catcher in the rye stand?'

'On the edge of the cliff.'

'Which is in the middle, isn't it, between the field and the cliff?'

'Right,' he said. 'Are you saying that's on purpose? So, what, like the field is childhood and falling off the cliff is growing up?' He hesitated. 'That's kind of cool. But is it right? Did Salinger mean that?'

'Does it matter?'

'Yeah.' Harry frowned again suspiciously.

'Why?'

'Because otherwise it's just made up.'

'Let me tell you a secret. No one knows what the author meant. We all just guess, even the teachers. And your guess, Harry, is as good as anyone's.' I paused. 'What I'm saying to you, Harry, is next time you have an idea about something you've read, don't hold on to it for fear it's wrong. Let it go. If no one else has thought of it, so much the better. It's like the catcher in the rye – that's much more memorable than a poem about "coming" through the rye.'

'I wish I'd known Salinger,' Harry said. 'It's like Holden says – when you like an author you want to be friends with him.'

'But you do know him,' I said. 'You may not know what he looks like, or where he lives, or who his friends are, but you know his ideas and that's the richest thing you can know about a person.' I held his gaze to make sure I had his attention. 'That's all you have to do, Harry. Share your ideas. You have loads of great ideas, I know. You're as bright as anyone. Don't let anyone tell you different. You just need a bit more confidence.'

Harry looked at the floor and blushed. I was suffused with warmth. For the first time in months, if not years, I felt I was doing something worthwhile.

I heard a knock and the door opened before either of us could say anything. Mr Beefton bustled in, all red face and red corduroys, and Harry stood up. I got up too (after a deliberate delay) and took the puffy signet-ringed hand that was offered to me. Mr Beefton asked how it was going. I answered enthusiastically, but I tailed off when I realised he wasn't listening.

He nodded gravely, his slick hair shining like fresh paint. 'His brother Piers came top in English at Harrow,' he said.

Harry was just outside my field of vision as his father said this. I stopped myself from looking at him. I said nothing and Mr Beefton nodded again, mumbling something about leaving us in peace, and left the way he'd come. After that, I told Harry we'd done enough studying; it was time for football.

'Look what I've got!' I said, pulling a new ball from my backpack. Harry said nothing. I led the way to the garden and Harry slipped off his chair and followed me with a hunched show of reluctance. When I placed the ball on the ground, with my foot on top, and challenged Harry to tackle me, he pretended not to be interested, but then ran at me. When he was just about to kick the ball, I dragged it backwards, leaving him charging at the air and squealing in delighted frustration. He ran at me again and again, stretching and missing, reacting rather than anticipating, like a cat chasing a torch. Eventually, I let him take the ball off me, and he celebrated by running to the other end of the garden, kicking it against a tree and sliding onto his knees with his fists clenched.

When we returned to the kitchen, for something to

drink, Mrs Beefton walked in and frowned at Harry's
trousers. 'Take those off!' she said. 'Maria can wash them.'
Harry ran out of the room and she looked at me. 'You
don't have to play football.'

'I wanted to,' I said. 'He enjoyed it. We both enjoyed it.
The ball's a present by the way.'

She screwed up her face in an imitation of a smile and
peeled out, with great deliberation, three twenty-Euro
notes from her wallet. I held out my hand but she placed
them on the table.

> [It's funny but I cried when I read about you and Harry.
> Do you remember when we talked about adopting a child?
> You said we should keep trying as you thought you wouldn't
> love the child as much if they weren't 'yours'. I knew you
> were wrong. You were always so good with Andrea's kids.
> If we'd adopted a child, they'd have loved you so quickly
> and then you'd have loved them for loving you. Think about
> the jobs you've enjoyed most – teaching children and
> counselling children. It's your calling – to love children, to
> catch them before they fall off the cliff.
>
> By the way, FYI, 'Coming thro' the Rye' is actually a
> poem about how sex is not that big a deal. *Gin a body kiss a*
> *body – need a body cry ... Gin a body kiss a body – need the*
> *warld ken!*]

'*Ça va*' ('It goes') is more accurate than 'OK'. For a basic
level of well-being, you don't need things to be 'orl korrect',
you just need a feeling of movement. With that comes the
possibility of change for the better. Teaching Harry, getting
better at tennis, learning French. I have a sense of progress.
Perhaps it was the process of writing down the past that
freed me to look to the future. I feel not exactly happy, but
not unhappy. I wouldn't say I was over Laura, but I can think

of her now without pain. For example, there's this car – a little white bubble-shaped Nissan hatchback like Laura used to drive – which parks near my flat. For a long time, the sight of it would send adrenalin coursing through my body, as if I were on the edge of a tall building, even though I could see it wasn't her car. Just this morning, however, I walked past it on the way to the Beeftons' and I barely noticed it. And I have something new to look forward to – Adam has finally got a passport and booked a ticket. For a man who doesn't like going anywhere that requires changing tube line, that's a touching gesture.

There's just one thing that troubles my conscience – Nathalie. She's a single woman in her early forties. She doesn't want to be going out with a man like me, who hasn't got over his ex-wife and probably can't have children. I thought I might leave it, after our night together, but then I got a postcard in my letter box. On the front was a black-and-white photo of a man with a thin moustache in cricket whites holding a wooden tennis racket. On the other side was a page of twirly French handwriting:

Cher Jacques,
You left without giving me your number. I was a little timid but I find your address from Édouard. I hope this is OK. My number is 0033748659124. Please do call me. I hope we will see each other soon. I amused myself very well with you the other night. It is rare, in Strasbourg, to meet someone with such a large spirit.
Yours gracefully,
Nathalie

I will have to have a frank conversation with her, but how do you say, in French, 'I like you but I don't love you' when 'like' and 'love' are the same word?

[Well, you don't have to say it in French for a start. You could just say 'Thanks very much, Nathalie, it's been fun, but I want to go back to my wife now.' If you want the translation, '*Au revoir, je retourne à ma femme maintenant*' should do the trick. But I'm not sure you really want to leave her, do you?]

18

Mrs Beefton called out 'Harry' and I stood in the kitchen, rereading the spines of the books on the shelves, trying to figure out what kind of person has the complete works of Proust and Joanna Trollope. A shoe scuff made me look up. Harry's tousled hair and anxious frown made me want to pick him up and hug him. Instead, I just smiled and nodded.

'How are you enjoying *The Great Gatsby*?' I asked, when we were alone.

'I like the parties. But I don't see the point of Nick Carraway and Jordan Baker. They don't even love each other. I just want to get to the bits about Gatsby and Daisy.'

'Well,' I said, 'how would the novel change if you took out Nick and Jordan?'

'It would be shorter.'

I laughed. 'Yes and ... what else?'

'More exciting.'

'But would it? You listen to music, don't you? Do you know Nirvana?'

'Who?'

'Doesn't matter. Whatever you listen to, you must have noticed how a lot of songs have quiet bits and loud bits. Why do you think they do that?'

'To make it more exciting when you get to the loud bit?'

'That's one way of looking at it.'

'So, you have to have the boring bits with Nick and Jordan to make it more exciting when you get to Daisy and Gatsby?'

I laughed. 'I suppose some people might see it that way.'

'How do you see it?'

'For me, it's almost the other way round. When I first read the book, I was around your age. I loved Gatsby. But now, reading it again, I've got a lot more time for Nick. In his heart, he'd like to be the romantic hero, but he can't because he's too cautious and too realistic. Nick is what people are actually like, and Gatsby is what they wish they were like. When a man finds out his childhood sweetheart has married someone else, he might be hurt, he might even be heartbroken, but he doesn't spend the rest of his life trying to win her back. If he did, people would think he was a loser. You see real relationships aren't like Daisy and Gatsby. They're more like Nick and Jordan. There's this beautiful bit near the end –'

'Hey! I haven't got there yet.'

'Sorry. But you don't care about them anyway. Nick describes leaving Jordan. He says, "Angry, and half in love with her and tremendously sorry, I turned away." Just before that he said "I'm five years too old to lie to myself and call it honour." You see, Nick's sorry not so much because he's lost Jordan, but because he's lost the romantic capacity for hope that young people have. He's grown up.

And, as we know from *The Catcher in the Rye*, growing up can be like falling off a cliff.'

> [Oh right, so you're Nick Carraway, are you? Does that make me Jordan, the dishonest golfer? Were you 'angry and half in love with me' when you left? Well, I do hope Mlle Piccard enjoys the other half of your love.]

The restaurant overlooking the pond in the orangerie had a musty smell of houseplants. Nathalie and I sat under an orange canopy. The wicker chair creaked under my weight.

'*C'est joli, ici*,' I said.

'*Oui*.'

I couldn't think of anything else to say. The fountain in the middle of the pond hissed like a deflating tyre. Jets of water rose twenty feet in the air. The shadow of their spray bent in the wind like a dandelion.

> [I'm sorry. I don't think I can read anymore tonight. When I started, I thought I was going to read some sort of apology or explanation for why you left me. I didn't realise I'd be wading through sub-Mills-and-Boon chick lit starring you and Madame Big Nose. I'll come back to this tomorrow, when I'm less tired and I've got my sick bucket at the ready.]

From: Laura Ferguson
Sent: 6 March 2011 23.53
To: Jack Randall
Subject: Re: Call me!
📎 The [Edited] Strasbourg Diaries [Part 3]

Dear Jack,

I've finished your diary now and I'm scared. It isn't what I think
it is, is it? Please reply. It's cruel to torture me in this way. See
the attached.

Laura

The [Edited] Strasbourg Diaries [Part 3]

'*T'es bien silencieux aujourd'hui,*' Nathalie said. I looked back anxiously – when Laura said something like that, it usually meant trouble – but Nathalie was smiling. Her teeth were short and her gums were long. I thought 'horse' and then got angry with myself. I was distancing myself from her for the most superficial of reasons. It's a defence mechanism. The shape of her mouth is not important. Besides, she doesn't show her teeth that often.

'*Pardon. Je pensais d'un roman que je lis avec Harry.*' Empty rowing boats clacked against one another in a corner of the pond. A couple – the man pulling one oar, the woman reclining – turned a slow circle.

'*Quel roman?*'

'*The Great Gatsby.*'

'Oh,' she said and she looked sad, as if she'd guessed that I was thinking of Laura. The air was so still that, even in the shade, I was sweating. I tried to change the subject.

'*Quand j'habitais en Angleterre, je ne remarquais pas comment le printemps, il est beau en Angleterre – je voulais*

233

un printemps plus chaud, comme ici. Mais maintenant, ici,
je veux un printemps plus froid, comme en Angleterre.'

'*Pourquoi tu ne rentres pas?'*

[And? What's the answer?]

I was worried I'd offended her by saying I didn't like
the French spring, and I thought how I might rephrase
it. Then I realised what it was that I was missing. It
wasn't the English spring in general, but a particular day
in a particular English spring, which stood out for no
other reason than it may just have been the happiest day
of my life. It was the first warm day of the year and it
transformed Oxford – strangers were smiling at each other
and the streets were full of beautiful people I hadn't seen all
winter. My PhD was nearly finished and Laura had come
from London to visit. Her hair was long then and twisted
in a plait, and she wore a yellow sleeveless dress that was
tugged by the breeze. We lay on a bank in the botanical
garden, her head on my shoulder, among the daffodils
and the sweet polleny smell of first love. She was reading
a book in that intense way of hers, as if her mind were
pointing at each word in turn, and I was just watching
her, thinking how lucky I was, feeling almost as sad as I
was happy because I knew such happiness couldn't last. It
was as if my heart couldn't hold that much love and it was
being wasted, spilling onto the floor while I tried in vain to
catch it with my memory.

'Sorry,' I said to Nathalie, 'I don't think I can explain in
French. What I'm trying to say, I suppose, is that, there's
a fragility to the English spring, which is more ... I don't
know ... poignant than here. I mean, to be really beautiful,
something has to be a little bit vulnerable, don't you
think?' Nathalie was smiling. 'I mean, there's no beauty
without some sadness, or damage, or at least the potential

for damage. If something's unbreakable, you can't love
it because it doesn't need your love. It's the things that
don't last that really move us. The English sun can be
heartbreakingly wonderful because you know it won't last.'
Nathalie's smile remained fixed. 'You haven't understood a
word I've said, have you?'

'You like England when it is sunny?' Nathalie said with
an apologetic expression.

'Yes, I suppose that's it. It's not exactly what I meant,
but maybe I didn't express it well. I like the way you
French say '*Je veux dire*' for 'I mean'. In English we blame
others for not understanding us when really it's our fault
for not saying what we wanted to say.'

'I know what you want to say,' she said.

'Hmm.' I smiled. 'I'm glad you sent that postcard.'

'Me too.' Nathalie smiled.

'I didn't mean to run away,' I said. 'It's just I'm still ...'

'I know, I know. You still love your wife.'

'Soon to be ex-wife.' The waiter came with the menu. I
waited till he'd gone. 'And you don't care?'

'I do care about you, Jacques.'

'No, I mean, you don't care about my ... wife.'

'No. I do not know her.'

'I mean, it doesn't bother you. How I feel about her?'

'*Je m'en fou*. Everyone has a history.'

'So we can just be friends?' I said.

Nathalie placed her hand on mine. I looked back at the
pond. 'Yes,' she said, 'we will be friends.'

The reflected trees were spliced by the wind, like
interference on a television picture.

'What's "*cerf*"?' I said.

'Deer.'

'So the choice is rabbit, deer or duck's liver?'

'You don't like Alsace cuisine?'

'No, I mean, yes, I do. It's good for me to try new things,' I said.

> [Incidentally, that's all Zac was to me – a new thing. I was bored and lonely and, with him, it was always new places and new people – hotels in Marrakesh and squats in Berlin, parties and raves, artists, socialites, neighbours, friends, enemies, people he'd met in a club and people who'd met people who'd met him in a club.]

Nathalie smiled and again something felt wrong. Maybe it wasn't her teeth. Maybe her jaw was too wide. [Keep guessing.] Anyway, it was something superficial I'd get used to, especially if I looked at her from more of an angle. I pushed my chair alongside hers. A stork nosed up the hill, watching us from the black bead of its truculent eye. Children shrieked in the distance and the stork took off. Nathalie stroked my hand with her thumb. The stork circled above us, trailing its fingered wings, too lazy to flap.

'*Ça va?*'

'*Ça va*,' I said. '*Je suis allé au médecin il y a une semaine, mais il était plus interessé par les prostitués que ...*' Her eyes dulled. 'I told you this before, didn't I?'

'Yes,' she said, 'but in English. I prefer when you talk in French. You talk with the hands and face more.' She looked at me. 'I know a good doctor. I'll go with you.'

> [This reads a little strangely. Did you cut something out here? Why did you start telling her about your trip to the doctor? And why were you going to a doctor? You did look gaunt when I saw you. I'm worried now. You don't have to tell me whether you've gone back to Nathalie. You don't have to meet me. Just tell me why you were seeing a doctor and what he said.]

*

I met Adam at the station.

'Sorry I'm late,' I said. 'I've just been with a friend.'

'Is this friend a girl?' he asked.

'Yes.'

'So she's what might be called a girlfriend?' Adam said, smiling.

'Not really,' I said, smiling back in spite of myself.

The view as we stepped out of my block of flats was a rippled white sea of bus tops in the car park beneath us. We passed through the shopping centre, out of the sliding doors, down the steps and onto the bridge. The streets were full of people. We walked under the giant metal halo of Homme de Fer and into Place Kléber. The sun was beating down and the tables at the café at the end of the square were all full. A young man on a bicycle stopped at the fountains and dipped his front tyre into the water, like a rider giving his horse a drink. At the last turning the narrow streets revealed the cathedral in all its dizzying height.

The inside of Maison Kammerzell was too gloomy – its ancient bottle-glass windows shut out the light – so we sat down at a table outside, Adam facing the cathedral. I ordered beers. Circles of tourists formed and broke. Schoolchildren took turns to put their heads into the face hole of a flat wooden statue in Alsatian dress. A man with night-dark skin wandered around with a tower of hats on his head, selling souvenirs.

Adam seemed pleased to be back in Strasbourg and I felt proud of my adopted city. When we were drinking our third beer I became conscious of something unusual about my mood – an emotion I hadn't experienced in a long time – something like contentment. I was getting slowly drunk with my best friend on a sunny afternoon in a beautiful city. What could be better?

When the sun went down, we walked to Épicerie, a small café tucked into the elbow of a back street, where they serve only tartines (i.e. food on toast) – it's the only restaurant I can afford, serving the only kind of food I can make myself. We sat outside at a table covered in a red-and-white checked cloth, next to a blackboard with the menu in curling French chalk script. Inside, a spotlight picked out the woman behind the antique cash till, as if she were about to perform a solo. She had a mannish build and a square jaw and was dressed like a 1930s starlet, with glittering red lipstick and a flower in her tightly coiled hair.

'So,' Adam said, 'tell me about this friend who's "not really" your girlfriend.'

'She's great,' I said. 'I don't know her that well but she seems like a really kind person. And I think she's funny too, although it's a bit difficult to tell because we don't really speak the same language. I mean, her English is OK but it's not ... you know, perfect, and my French is poor.'

'But that will get easier,' Adam said.

'Right. Sure. Yeah. There's another thing though. And I'm not sure if it should be a problem but it's just ... I feel bad saying this, but I don't actually fancy her that much. It's not that I don't find her attractive at all. I do. I totally do ... except for when I don't.'

'Wood is king.'

'What?' I said.

'Don't you remember?' Adam said. 'We used to say that, back when we were at university. You can't be going out with a girl that doesn't give you wood.'

'We used to say that?'

'Sure we did,' Adam said. 'Well, I'd say it and you'd agree with me.'

'But where's that got us? I fell in love with someone out of my league and she cheated on me. And, no offence, but you've never had a relationship for more than three months. I don't think Nathalie would cheat on me. So what if I don't always want to have sex with her? The older I get the less important that seems. Besides, Laura and I hardly ever had sex in the end anyway.'

'Everything ends badly,' Adam said. 'Otherwise it wouldn't end.'

'*Top Gun*?'

'No,' Adam said, '*Cocktail*.'

We moved on to La Lanterne and ordered *tartes flambées* and pints of home-made beer. By now we were drunk and, a couple of times, we laughed so loud other people turned to stare. Wilf walked in and my swollen spirits were burst by a stab of anxiety – I felt guilty because I hadn't called him. I caught his eye and he waved cheerily.

'All right, Jackyboy!' Wilf said, with his great hairy arm round me, making my head bow awkwardly. 'Great to see you. Sorry I've not been in touch. What are you having?'

As Adam was buying our second, Wilf's friend Ned arrived – a middle-aged divorcé from Sheffield. He stood hesitantly in the doorway in a jacket two sizes too big. He'd been a bystander in a few evenings I'd spent with Wilf and I'd formed an impression that he was nerdy and (sorry, Ned) kind of dull. No doubt people have said the same about me.

'Ned! Over here!' Wilf bellowed. 'This man,' Wilf said to Adam, nodding at Ned and chuckling to himself, as if he were recalling some fond memory, 'is a legend!'

Adam looked at me and stifled a smile. Ned took the stool by my side and nodded.

'Wilfmeister,' Ned said. Then, turning to us and nodding, he added, 'Gentlemen.'

Adam offered Ned a drink and Wilf cut in: 'That'll be a Kronenbourg.' Wilf chuckled again. 'Ned's a numbers man.'

'Numbers?' Adam asked.

'Sixteen sixty-four,' Wilf explained with a smile. 'Pint of numbers for the Nedster,' shouted Wilf to the barman, who seemed to understand.

Talking to Ned meant pushing the conversation up a hill. Half of my attention was on the conversation between Wilf and Adam who were shouting at each other about how great Strasbourg was. Wilf said he was never going home.

La Lanterne closed and we moved to Les Aviateurs, a thin, ersatz American bar. The evening was slipping away from me. I wanted to talk to Adam about Laura, but the music was too loud and Wilf and Ned were always nearby.

I woke up, fully clothed and cigarette-sick, with a sense I was late for something. Adam was asleep on the sofa. In the shopping centre the compressed air made me want to retch, so I rushed home with espressos and pains au chocolat. When I got back, Adam was in his boxer shorts, smoking on the balcony and staring at the rooftops.

'What do you want to do before you go?' I asked.

'Dunno,' he said. 'Shall we go up the cathedral?'

The nave was as cool as a vault.

'I think the stairs are over there,' Adam said.

'You know that conversation we were having,' I said, 'about Nathalie.'

'Uh-huh,' Adam said. I could only see his feet, as we curled round the spiral stairs.

'I've been thinking about it,' I said. 'The problem is not really that I don't fancy her. I usually do. Enough.' Adam was out of sight now, so I had to speed up. 'It's more that I don't feel excited about seeing her. With Laura, I was always excited.'

'Right,' Adam said.

'But then again, I can't expect to feel like that again. I was so much younger when I met Laura. And besides, if you take away Laura's good looks, and the twenty years of memories, what's she got that Nathalie hasn't?'

'Right,' Adam said with a chuckle. 'Apart from the medicine and the roads, what have the Romans ever done for us?'

'No, but I mean Nathalie is kinder and more reasonable. And that's ultimately what matters. When I think of relationships I know that have lasted, it's more about whether they trust each other than whether they have a spark.' I could see, through the slits in the wall, that we were getting higher and higher above the city. 'I'm not saying Laura was a bad person. Melanie Klein says ...' I stopped because I couldn't see Adam. 'Are you listening to this?'

'Sure.' Adam stopped and I caught up with him.

'Klein says when we're children we think of adults in schizophrenic terms – either all good or all bad. Growing up is the depressing process of realising that people are somewhere in the middle. I don't think Laura's evil, just because she cheated on me, but nor is she ...'

I paused to catch my breath but Adam kept on walking.

[Do you get breathless often? Have you told the doctor about this? What did they say? Oh please, Jack, talk to me!]

Even at the top, there was no breeze. A bank of clouds rested like a stripe of paint above the blue sky. Strasbourg lay before us in all its apricot glory. A fat boy in a black T-shirt saying GO F**K YOURSELF came out from the steps behind me and looked around, unimpressed.

'There's something I wanted to ask you about,' I said, leaning on the green copper railings.

'What?' Adam said.

'Laura. How is she? What's she doing? You must have heard something.' Adam stiffened and I felt scared. I cut in. 'If she's seeing someone else, don't tell me. I just want to know if she's OK. I was thinking of calling her. It's been over a year and we're due to be divorced in a few months. I just thought I'd check in with her ... Or do you think that would be a very bad idea?'

'I haven't seen her,' he said.

'But have you heard about her?'

'Coughlin's Law,' Adam said. 'Bury the dead. They stink up the place.'

'Does it ever occur to you,' I said, smiling, 'that the dialogue of a mediocre eighties movie may not be the best guide to life?'

'Never,' he said.

I felt a heavy end-of-summer-holiday sadness, as we approached the train station. Neither of us spoke. I wanted to tell Adam how grateful I was that he'd come, how much I loved him and how much I'd miss him.

'What time's your train again?' I said.

'Six,' he replied.

'Right,' I said. 'You should have plenty of time.'

We stopped at the foot of the steps to the platform. I didn't want to leave, but sitting on the platform next to him was only going to make me feel lower. He must have sensed what I was thinking because he told me to go home. I hugged him and he tapped me on the shoulder blade.

'Why do you have such a sad air?' Nathalie said, as she opened the door.

'I just said goodbye to Adam. He's only been here a couple of days so it's silly to be upset I know ... Sometimes I feel like the pain of ending things is so bad it's not worth starting them.' Nathalie's face clouded. 'Can I stay here tonight?' I said.

'Of course,' Nathalie said, smiling toothily.

'I'll just lie down next door. I'm a bit hungover.'

'OK. I'm just making the kitchen.'

My mind was roaming the free ground between sleeping and waking when my phone went off. I ignored it for a couple of rings, hoping it would go away, but then I thought Adam might have forgotten something. The phone was lodged tight inside the pocket of my jeans so I had to inch my fingers in to grip it. Still half asleep, I held it above my head: 'Laura' it pulsed, like a warning. I hesitated, my thumb above the phone. Would it be better not to answer? I could listen to the voicemail and decide whether to call back. But what if she didn't leave a voicemail? I pressed the green button and lifted the phone to my ear.

[I'm so sorry. If I'd known I was interrupting your night with Nathalie, I wouldn't have called. I'd moved back in with Mum and she was giving me a hard time. She'd say things like:

'I don't understand you. Why have no boyfriend when you could have a boyfriend with a chalet in Verbier?'

243

'I don't love Zac,' I'd reply. 'And I don't think he even wants to be my boyfriend.'

'Of course he does, dear. Why else would he take you on those fancy holidays?'

'He just does that with everyone. He's very rich. He buys friends.'

'Nonsense,' she'd say. 'I've been around the block, you know. I know your generation tries to pretend money's not important and it's all about being "in love". Well, life's not like that. Without your father –'

'Dad walked out on you. You're always saying he ruined your life.'

'Rubbish! I never do! The things you say to upset me . . . Your father may not have been the best of husbands, but he paid for our house and your school fees, not to mention clothes and food. I don't know how we'd have survived without his money.'

I wanted so much to talk to you then. You were always my antidote to Mum-rage and there were so many other things to tell you. I looked at my phone. I'd been longing to talk to you for so long I'd forgotten it was even possible. 'Why not?' I thought to myself. Why shouldn't I call him? The worst that could happen is he doesn't answer.]

19

'Hello,' I said tentatively.

'Hey, Jack,' Laura said. I'd forgotten how much I loved her voice – how low and soft and confident it was. It was her face and body I'd obsessed over, clicking on photo after photo down the tunnel of Facebook despair, but it was the voice that undid me. All of the emotions of the last two years – the pain, the pride, the humiliation, the determination, the self-hating indecision, the circular night arguments – all of it melted in the warmth of those two syllables. It was obvious. I had to be with Laura.

'Laura!' I said.

'Jack! Is that really ...?' Her voice caught and she paused. 'Hang on ...' There was a noise and her voice continued from further away. 'I'm just going to another room.' I could hear footsteps, breathing and a door click. 'Jack, are you still there?' She was panting.

'Yes.'

'Is it really you?' she said.

'Of course,' I said. Laura said nothing and I could hear a

sound that could have been a sob or a cough. 'Are
you OK?'

'I'm fine,' she said, sniffing. 'I'm just a bit emotional.
I've missed you so, so much.'

'Me too,' I said and for a moment I felt a wild
happiness. With her voice next to me, it was like holding
her again.

'I'm sorry, Jack,' Laura said.

'Me too,' I said. 'I'm so sorry for everything.'

'I think about you every day.'

'I think about you every minute.' I thought about Laura
so much she'd changed from a person to a concept. She'd
lost the constancy of a physical thing and become a symbol
for a world view. When I thought people were dishonest
and selfish and cynical, Laura was a cold hypocrite who'd
cheated on me without remorse. Other times, when I was
nostalgic, Laura was the beautiful girl of twenty stood
outside my door on St Clement's roundabout, too shy to
ask if she could come in. When I was pessimistic, Laura
was a restless flirt, who'd been on the lookout for a lover
for years. At my most detached and philosophical, she was
neither good nor bad, just someone who'd once loved me
quite a lot (though not as much as I'd thought), but had
grown tired of our uneventful marriage and found herself
attracted to someone else. But now it seemed that she was
the best of all the Lauras: the Laura I'd never let myself
believe in – the Laura that had loved me all along, that had
never loved or even desired anyone else, the Laura who'd
pined for me as I'd pined for her and who wanted me back
as badly as I wanted her. And so, it seemed, everything in
the world must be for the best.

'When can I see you?' she said.

'Whenever you want.'

'It sounded, from the ringtone, like you were abroad.'

'I am.' I heard Nathalie's footsteps approaching. 'But I'll come back.'

'What?' she said. 'I can't hear you.'

'I'm sorry,' I said. 'It's the phone. Can I call you back?' There was a silence. 'I promise I'll call you back. I've been looking forward to this conversation for so long. There's so much to say and . . .' Laura didn't say anything and I heard Nathalie knock. 'I love you,' I whispered, and hung up.

> [I didn't know what I was doing calling you. I thought it would just feel like talking to an old friend. I thought that time would insulate me. But when I heard you say my name those years apart vanished. All I could think about was the fact you were still there, somewhere. If I could talk to you, I could see you. And that was a wild and dizzying thought that blocked out everything else.]

'I'm sorry, Nathalie,' I said. 'I think I need to go.' I saw her face harden and I realised why she repelled me. It wasn't her teeth or her jaw or her English. It was the fact she wasn't Laura.

Twenty minutes later, in my sitting room, my brain buzzing with nicotine, I called Laura back.

'I can't wait to see you,' I said.

'Me too,' she said.

'I'm in Strasbourg now. I've just bought a ticket for the Eurostar on Monday. It gets into St Pancras at 5 p.m.'

'You've booked a ticket for Monday?'

'What's wrong?' I said. 'Have you changed your mind?'

'No, no,' she said. 'It's not that.'

'Is that too far away? Or too soon? They're the cheapest tickets so I don't know if I can change them. It's just I have to pack and say some goodbyes.'

'I've waited over a year, Jack,' she said. 'I can wait another week.'

'So,' I said, 'why did you sound sad?'

'I'm not sad,' she said.

'What is it?'

'Nothing.'

'I know it's something really bad when you say it's nothing.'

'I can't wait to see you.'

'Are you in love with someone else?'

'No.'

'Sure?'

'Sure.'

[I know I should have said more on the phone. But you'd bought a ticket and you seemed so excited, and I was excited too.]

I phoned Adam to ask if I could stay at his again.

'It shouldn't be for too long,' I said.

'Stay as long as you want,' he said.

'I'm hoping to give it another go with Laura.'

The line went silent for a few seconds.

'Have you spoken to her?' he said.

'Yes,' I said.

'And ... what did she say?'

'Not much. We kind of got cut off.'

'What about the French girlfriend?' Adam said.

'She's not my girlfriend.'

'But I thought you liked her. I thought she was nicer than Laura. Wouldn't cheat on you.'

I laughed. 'What about "wood is king"?'

'You told me you don't believe in that anymore.'

'I don't,' I said. 'Look, it's not about what Nathalie's

like or what Laura's like. It's not a contest. Who ticks more
boxes. You know I never was much good as a therapist
and one of the reasons was I was never sure of anything – I
could never tell whether their problems were because of
their childhood, or their relationships or just bad luck. But
now there's something I am sure of. I love Laura and she
still loves me.'

'Did she say that?'

'Not in so many words, but I could hear it in her voice.
Besides, it's what my heart is telling me to do. I love her
and I'll always love her. It doesn't matter whether there are
other women who'd be better for me or make me happier.
I'm tied to her and I always will be and there's no point
pretending otherwise. It's like ... you know in *Titanic*?
Kate Winslet has this affair with DiCaprio for a few days,
he drowns and then she spends the rest of her life married
to someone else, right? But, right at the end, she's an old
woman and she dies and you see her going to heaven. And
heaven is that big staircase on the *Titanic* and who is there,
right in the middle, waiting for her?'

'DiCaprio.'

'Exactly,' I said. 'And there's no sign of the husband.
The guy she spent the last thirty years of her life with is
nowhere. Unless he's one of the extras in tailcoats.
Anyway, I don't want to do that. I don't want to live out
whatever time I have left with someone I don't really
know or love.'

'Whatever time you have left?' Adam said quizzically.
'You're not that old.'

'All the more reason to be with the woman I love now.'

'Was Winslet definitely dead at the end?' he said. 'I
thought she was just sleeping. I thought the staircase thing
was a dream.'

'Maybe she was just sleeping, but even so that means, after thirty years of marriage, she's dreaming about someone else. I don't want to be doing that.'

I had one last lesson with Harry. He looked upset when I found him in the dining room. My copy of *The Great Gatsby* had been forced face down onto the table, cracking the spine.

'Everything OK, Harry?' I asked.

'I feel tricked,' he said.

'But why?' I said. 'Your exams are in a few weeks. We've done all the preparation. You'll do brilliantly. You don't need any more lessons from me. You just keep writing down what you think and you'll blow them away.'

'It's not that,' he said, picking up the book. 'It's this book you made me read. It says, right in the beginning, "Gatsby turned out all right at the end." So I read the whole thing, thinking Gatsby was going to be OK; he was going to win back Daisy and they'd live happily ever after. But instead, Daisy breaks his heart, he dies and no one comes to his funeral. So, how exactly is that "turning out all right"?'

I smiled. 'What do you think?'

'I don't know,' Harry said, annoyed. 'That's what I'm asking you.'

'Is there a way in which Gatsby did turn out all right?'

'Not really,' Harry said.

'Well, what does Carraway think of him at the end?'

'He likes him.'

'Yes,' I said, 'he tells Gatsby he's better than the whole rotten lot of them. And that's the first compliment he's paid Gatsby. And why is he better than the whole lot of them?'

'I dunno. Because he's romantic?'

'Absolutely. And what does it mean if you're romantic?'

'You love someone a lot.'

'That's one way of describing it. I like the way Nick describes Gatsby as having an "extraordinary gift for hope".'

'So,' Harry said, frowning, 'you mean Gatsby turned out all right because he didn't give up hope? But that doesn't make sense. It's like, literally, the opposite of what you said last time. You said that, in the real world, if you can't get over someone who's dumped you, that makes you a loser.' I smiled and his frown deepened. 'That's what you said.'

'Some of my biggest heroes are losers. Besides, you can only be a loser if you think you are. Before I became a teacher I used to be a therapist and one of the things I'd often try to do was to help my patients be a bit more rational – to show them that the world was not really as they saw it. But you can have too much reality. Hope is transformative. It's like us now, saying goodbye. You'll move on to your new school and make friends and have great teachers. And we may not meet again. But if I thought like that, I'd be sad. Instead, I'm full of hope that we'll stay in touch and I'll get to watch you grow up into the fine person I know you'll be.'

'We'll still write to each other, won't we?' Harry said, with pleading eyes.

'Of course we will,' I said, smiling and trying to swallow the lump in my throat. 'And you can Skype me any time. And if you want, I'll come and visit you at Harrow. Because I know you're going to get in.'

There was just one last thing to do, the saddest and hardest thing of all. Nathalie walked by my side, holding my hand. The narrow streets were cut with shadows. An old man was wrapping the carousel at Place Gutenberg in faded cloth. The chandelier lamps next to the French flag were beginning to light up. The ting-ting of a bell let me know I was in the bicycle lane. As we passed Épicerie, where I'd spent so many nights alone, I remembered something Adam once told me – that nostalgia means 'the pain of the homecoming' in ancient Greek. It seemed odd, when Adam said it, because it's so different to what I thought nostalgia meant but, looking at the empty tables outside Épicerie and thinking of what awaited me at home, I felt the connection – the pain of the homecoming is the pain of longing for the past. It was a feeling more than an understanding. Even now I struggle to articulate it. I suppose it's because, when we return home after a long absence, we're forced to reflect on what time has taken from us. The staircase may be the same, but we'll never again be the child that would race up its steps.

As we walked, I could hear the whistle and buzz of bicycles all around. The sun was blinding when it appeared above the houses. We turned right at the canal and walked along the towpath. A sun-tipped willow wept onto the bank. Two ducks slid past, cutting chevrons into the mirror of the water. An empty tourist boat hummed along behind them, flat and white like an ice tray. The only person on it was walking up and down the aisles scrubbing the seats.

'So,' Nathalie said, 'why did you leave last night?'

'Let's sit down,' I said.

We found a table by the canal in Petite France. I was in the shadows, but Nathalie was gilded by the late-afternoon sun. A hazy silhouette of light framed her, like the filter they use in films for flashbacks and dreams. Flies thronged between the trees – golden dots that seemed to be falling, at one moment, like motes of dust, but would then dance with life.

'*Je vais rentrer en Angleterre*,' I said at last. Nathalie gave me a quick, pained look. '*Désolé*.' Nathalie put a hand up to her face, as if the sun were in her eyes, and her lips pursed. '*Ça va?*' I said, stretching my hand across the table.

She snapped hers away. '*C'est rien. C'est qu'une déception*,' she said.

'Deception?' I said. 'But we agreed at the start we'd just be friends.' ['*Déception*' in French means 'disappointment' in English.]

'*Oui*,' she said, laughing half-heartedly. 'Friends.'

'You've been wonderful to me,' I said. 'Really. I'll never forget it. I feel so lucky to have met you. And I wish I could stay here and love you in the way you deserve to be loved, but I know I can't. I need to go home.'

'London is at three hours. Plus, you said you were more happy here than in London.'

'I was, but now I'm not. I don't know how to explain. It's like these shutters,' I said, nodding at the houses behind her. 'I think they're beautiful. In fact, they're so pretty it makes my heart hurt, but it also makes me want to go home. It's a kind of beauty that doesn't belong to me. I could never feel at home in a country with such pretty shutters – I'd feel like I was pretending. I don't want to pretend anymore.'

'What are shatters?' Nathalie said.

'You see,' I said. 'That's part of the problem. We don't speak the same language. And I know I could learn French eventually, but it'd be like learning to write with my left hand. I'm sorry. I really don't want to hurt you, as you're a good person and you've been kind to me.'

'*Comme si la plénitude de l'âme ne débordait pas quelquefois par les métaphores les plus vides.*'

'I don't even understand what that means,' I said. 'Something about the fullness of your arms starting with empty metaphors.'

['As if the fullness of the soul did not sometimes overflow in the emptiest of metaphors.' It's from *Madame Bovary*. You might remember the bit that comes afterwards: 'since none of us can ever express the exact measure of our needs, or our ideas, or our sorrows, and human speech is like a cracked kettle on which we beat out tunes for bears to dance to, when all the while we long to move the stars to pity.']

'There are not two people who speak exactly the same language, Jacques. But I understand you, even without the language. You don't love me and you think you can make it better for me if you say this stupid thing about shatters. Some things,' Nathalie said, with a crack in her voice, 'cannot be made better. I will go now –' she paused, and it seemed like she might cry but she recovered herself – 'as I have shame. *Au revoir.*'

Watching her walk away, for what would surely be the last time, I wished I could make her feel better – run after her and say I'd made a mistake.

[I guess it wasn't too late.]

Once over the bridge, it was a short walk to the station. Red lights flashed on the bollards, as if to warn me against my journey. I recognised shops I'd not seen since I arrived. A boy in a pushchair stretched out both hands towards his father. The station appeared straight ahead – a mushroom of glass haloed by the sun. A reflection of the city swelled above me as I approached the entrance. Inside, I joined a long queue at Paul but, when I reached the front, I realised I didn't want anything. I thought it would seem foolish to have waited so long for nothing, so I ordered a croissant. The woman in the chef's hat ignored my cupped hand and dropped the change into the wooden bowl on the counter.

There was a girl in a panama hat sitting on the only spare bench. The train to Paris was announced and the girl stood up. I didn't want her to think I was following her, so I waited a couple of minutes before walking up to the platform. Night had closed in and only one or two of the dark clouds still had an underscore of pink. As the train pulled away I had one last glimpse of Strasbourg – a row of trees, standing like needles against the pale cream of the sky.

20

I've been trying to write down some things to say to Laura, but I can't concentrate. I'm pinned into a corner of my seat by the long legs of the man opposite and the overspilling flab of the snoring man to my side. I know I shouldn't expect to find Laura at the station – I've texted my arrival time, but she's not replied – yet I feel sick with nerves as if I were about to see her. Someone else's iPod is playing rock music and it makes me feel pumped up, like I'm about to walk into a boxing ring. We've pulled in. No one's moving.

The station is Ebbsfleet, not St Pancras – we're told this in three languages: English, French and one I don't recognise (Flemish?). The platform is streaked with puddles, but the sun is breaking through the duvets of cloud, creating ripples of silver and grey. The approach to London is bleak: factories, high-rise estates, power cables, wire fences. In a moment we're thrust into a tunnel of darkness and my ears pop. The blackness whistles and the carriage rocks.

Three pings. People stand up. I wait. We pass through a building site: mud, piles of concrete, yellow vests, scaffolds and the skeletons of tower blocks. The train glides at walking pace.

I'm the last one out of the carriage and down the sloping escalator. Beyond the brick wall is a room of hospital blue. Two men with IDs round their necks are talking to each other. For a moment, I think they are talking about me. At last, the sliding doors part to reveal a small gaggle of people at the base of some stairs: an old woman with a walking stick; a young woman reading a newspaper with her foot on the railings; a girl sitting on a pink roller suitcase; and an Asian man with an earpiece holding out a piece of paper saying FARLEY. That's it. As I stare ahead, the traffic of pedestrians flows across me, breaking the view and brushing me with the edges of their bags and coats. No Laura.

Laura's phone went straight to voicemail. [My battery was dead.] I looked at the other names in my phone. Apart from Adam, I hadn't called any of them for years. Aidan, Alasdair, Albert. They were just names now. Alina used to be friends with Laura. I called her. The number wasn't recognised. I tried Beverley but there was no answer. I went on like this, no one answering, until I got to Toby, my old friend from Warwick whose wife, Marika, used to be friends with Laura.

'Jack!' Toby said in a loud, friendly voice. Voices and glasses fuzzed in the background. 'How are you doing?'

'Good, good,' I said. 'I hope all's well. Listen, I'm calling because –'

'How've you been buddy?' Toby shouted over me.

'Fine,' I said a bit louder. 'Is Marika with you? It's just I wanted to ask her about Laura.'

'Can't hear you, mate. I'm in the pub!' he shouted. 'With Mark. The Walmer Castle. Come and join us.'

'I'd love to, but will Marika be there?' I said. 'Can I talk to her?'

'Come soon!' he shouted and hung up.

I walked from Notting Hill tube station. I was still carrying the backpack, with everything I owned in the world, and the lower part of my neck ached and a bead of sweat was dripping from my armpit, tickling me as it fell. The pub was overflowing with people. They burst out onto the street, drinking and smoking and laughing.

I saw Toby and Mark standing at a corner of the brass-rimmed bar. Mark saluted me with a pint glass and elbowed Toby. I was shocked by how much they'd aged. In my mind they were young and athletic. Now Mark had soft padding about his jaw. A wrinkle in his untucked shirt hinted at a beer belly. Toby's once dark hair was strewn with grey and folds of pallid skin sagged under his eyes.

Their smiles were warm as they hugged me. I was touched. Even with all the terrible things they must have heard and read about me, they still welcomed me as their friend.

'Jeez, buddy,' Mark said. 'You look like you've been on a three-week bender.'

'It's just a bit heavy, this backpack,' I said, leaning it against the bar.

'We're watching Murray-Nadal,' Mark said, pointing at a television fixed high up in a corner of the room. In the background, behind the clatter of conversation, I could hear squeaking clay and shrieking line judges. Toby wasn't watching the television: his eyes slanted down at the pretty girl of no more than twenty who was balanced on the heavy arm of a swarming sofa.

'He's going to bottle it again,' Mark said, and Toby mumbled agreement. I drank my pint without speaking, following the match through Mark's winces of disappointment and the far off echo of a television crowd. I sought the eye of the harassed barman, who was frowning and hurrying from till to pump and back again, and pausing, after each sale, to decide between the customers who clamoured for his attention.

'So, Toby,' I said. 'You're still with Marika, right?'

His gaze snapped back to me guiltily. 'Yeah. Why wouldn't I be?'

'No reason,' I said. 'And how are ... the kids?' I was sure he had children but I couldn't remember anything about them.

'All good,' Toby said. 'Oscar's just started at the big school. Just had number four. Angie. Marika's over the moon. And you? I can't remember. Have you got two or three?'

Mark turned back from the TV and frowned at Toby.

'None actually. Laura and I never managed to have any ...' I filled the silence. 'And now Laura and I are separated. But we're not divorced. Which is why I want to get hold of Marika. Is she still friends with Laura?'

'Yeah,' Toby said. 'But we don't see her very much. With kids, your social life kind of dies off. Mark here's pretty much the only person I see. Committee night, we call it. Once a month. You should join us.'

'Yeah, mate,' said Mark. 'I heard about you and Laura. That's rough, man. Still, plenty more fish in the sea, eh?'

'Well, not for me,' I said. 'I still love my old fish. That's why I've come back.' They looked confused. 'You do realise,' I said, 'that I've not been in London for nearly two years.'

'Really?' said Toby. 'Did you have a sabbatical? I've always wanted to do that if I made partner. Too late now.'

'You've got to do it, mate,' said Mark, whose attention had been drifting but who was now part of the circle again. 'Nina and I took a month to go round Thailand on a yacht. Best thing we ever did. Left the kids with the grandparents. Where did you go, Jack?'

'Strasbourg,' I said, suspicious that I might be the victim of a joke. 'It wasn't a sabbatical though. I don't have a career anymore.'

'Sorry to hear it,' Mark said. 'I got made redundant too. Credit crunch they said. What bullshit. I know a good employment solicitor but you're probably a bit late ...'

'No,' I said. 'I wasn't made redundant. I was a therapist. Surely I've seen you guys since I became a therapist? Anyway, I had to stop after that story about me in the papers.' They looked blank. 'The story about me and Claudia Alvares. It was all over the news for days.'

'Oh yeah!' Toby said. 'I remember something. Didn't you bone some model?'

'What was it like?' said Mark, leaning in.

'No,' I said, 'I didn't bone her. She made it up.'

'Come on,' said Toby with a hint of a leer, 'you can tell us. We're in the circle of trust here.'

'I swear I didn't have sex with her. She was my patient. She was mentally ill. I would never have slept with her. The whole thing was fantasy. I was going to sue the newspaper that wrote the story. I even went to see a barrister but he said the jury wouldn't believe me. No one believed me.'

There was a silence. Mark's gaze slid back to the TV.

With one last look at the girl on the sofa, Toby downed his pint and slammed it onto the bar. 'Got to go,' he said.

'Me too,' said Mark. 'I've got to get back to look after the kids. Nina's doing the marathon next month. You guys should come.'

I followed Toby home, to a basement kitchen with an atmosphere of barely suppressed panic: toys, towels, food, chairs all lying on the floor and in the middle Marika cradling a baby and staring at Toby with pure hatred.

'My fault we're back late,' I said. 'I was just so happy to see Toby again.'

Marika looked at me coldly, then turned back to Toby. 'You said you'd be back to help with homework,' she said.

'He really wanted to get back earlier,' I said, 'but I kept him. You see I've been in France for two years. I've come back to find Laura. Do you know where she is by the way? I really need to get hold of her and her phone is off.'

An adolescent girl shouted from upstairs, the baby bawled and I was forgotten. Marika shrieked to 'get the dummy' and Toby sprang into action, tearing through the pillows of the sofa and throwing himself to the floor to sift through the shagpile carpet.

'Not there,' Marika said irritably.

'Well, where then?' Toby replied defensively.

'I don't bloody know,' Marika said. 'Is it my responsibility to look after the dummies?'

'You must have had it last,' Toby said.

'What, because you go off to the pub with your mates, I'm in charge of everything?'

'Sorry,' I said. 'I'm intruding. I'll leave you two in peace. If you could just tell me where Laura might be.'

Marika sighed and looked at me. 'Last I heard she was living with an artist called Zac … Zac … something.'

'Ford. Thank you.'

> [I haven't seen Marika in years. I don't know where she got this idea from. I never lived with Zac, honestly. I just stayed over once or twice.]

Walking to Montclare Street, it felt like I was carrying a man on my shoulders. I took off the backpack and sat on it. What was I doing? What could I achieve, turning up after two years at Ford's apartment? All I could do was make a fool of myself. I should wait till Laura replied to my messages. But she called me first. And there was love in her voice. If I'm wrong about that, I'm wrong about everything. Either way, I had to find out. I lifted the bag and trudged on.

I stood in front of the intercom, where I'd stood with Claudia two years before. What would I say? Just press the button and it would come to me.

'Hello,' said Ford.

'Hello. It's Jack Randall. I want to see Laura.'

'Who are you?'

'Look, Ford, you know who I am. I'm Laura's husband. Let me speak to her please.'

'Laura's not here.'

'When will she be back?'

There was no reply. A window opened and Ford leaned out. 'James!' he shouted down. 'It really is you. And what a stylish suitcase you've brought! Were you hoping to move in?'

'I want to talk to my wife and I'm not going to leave until you tell me where she is.'

'Have you been interrailing?' he yelled. 'You look like one of those "Bad Dad" backpackers.'

'Tell me where she is!' I screamed.

He closed the window. I waited by the intercom. Nothing happened. I pressed the bell again. No response. I leaned on the buzzer for a minute. Still no reply.

'I've called the police,' he said. 'And told them I'm being harassed by a hobo.'

'You're a fucking coward, Zac Ford,' I said in the intercom. 'A fraud and a coward.'

I waited at the corner of Davies Street. Laura couldn't be in Zac's flat, or she'd have said something. She wasn't one to miss a fight. Perhaps she'd left him. Or maybe she was just out for the evening. It was impossible to know and pointless to guess. I lay down on the pavement with my head on the backpack. I closed my eyes and was woken by a drop on my forehead. The clouds were pavement grey. I should go to Adam's. He'd be home by now. I looked again in my wallet. I had a twenty-pound note. The rain was hardening, but I could ill afford a taxi. If Laura had left Zac, where would she go? I heard the chug and screech of a black cab behind me and I held out my arm.

The navy blue door of Mrs Ferguson's house was at the top of four stone steps. The room to my right was hidden by net curtains – I could see nothing inside, even when I pressed my forehead against the icy pane. There was a brass knocker in the shape of a lion's head and a bell to the right. I rapped the knocker. No one came. I pressed the bell.

Twenty minutes later, as the rain was thinning, and I was thinking of giving up, a black SUV with ATLAS CARS on the door pulled up. I recognised the flurry of white hair and witch-black clothing coming out of the back. Mrs Ferguson hooked her handbag round one arm and rummaged urgently. She pulled out a packet of cigarettes and a purse in the same hand.

'Want a light?' I said.

Mrs Ferguson shrieked. The handbag dropped to the floor, sending coins and mirrors and cigarette packets spilling out. I knelt down to pick them up. Mrs Ferguson's face was still ashen when I handed the bag back.

'I've come to find Laura,' I said. 'Where is she?'

'You're too late,' she said.

'What do you mean?' I said. 'I spoke to Laura on the phone only a few days ago. We agreed to meet.'

'Well, I've just seen her and she definitely doesn't want to see you. She made that clear.'

'Where is she?' Mrs Ferguson turned her head and walked towards the door. 'Please, Mrs Ferguson. I do love her, you know. And that story in the papers was not true. I never cheated on her. Please just let me know where she is.' The door opened and I thought, for an instant, of putting my foot in it. While I hesitated the door closed. I rang the bell but she didn't answer.

'Please,' I shouted through the keyhole. 'Laura's phone's dead. Just tell me where she is and I'll go.'

Mrs Ferguson didn't answer. I was so tired I thought I'd fall asleep if I sat down. I had no money left for another taxi so I shouldered the bag and set off on foot.

Staring at my Shreddies the next morning, my head was still turning over ideas to find Laura. Could I follow Mrs Ferguson? Not without a car. On the kitchen table was a train ticket with a quarter torn off. Adam must have used it for a joint. I don't have a car but neither did Mrs Ferguson. Hadn't I seen her in a taxi? Then I had an idea. I called Atlas Cars.

'Hello,' I said, 'my name's Jeremy Ferguson. My mother, Diana Ferguson, booked one of your taxis yesterday. She was dropped off at our home, 22 Colville Terrace, around eight p.m. She's lost all her jewellery. She has Alzheimer's, you see. We're trying to find it. Did any of your drivers find any rings or bracelets in the back of their taxi?'

'I'll just have a look, sir.' I held my breath. 'No, sorry, sir. No one found any jewellery.'

'She must have left it somewhere else. The only problem is she can't remember where she was yesterday. Do you have a record of where you picked her up from?'

'Should do. Just wait.' My heart soared. 'Guy's and St Thomas' Hospital.'

'A hospital! Can you take me there now?'

'We can get a taxi to 22 Colville Terrace around ten a.m., sir.'

'I'm not at 22 Colville Terrace. I'm ... visiting a friend at Flat 2, 14 Sterndale Road. Please pick me up there as soon as you can.'

2I

Please God, I said to myself, let it not be serious. I promise I'll look after her my whole life. I don't care if she has a hundred lovers. I'll never leave her.

'Sorry about your mother,' said a voice.

Was that the taxi driver? I thought of Mum in hospital, the first time I saw her after the stroke, the way the light reflected off her irises. The same face, the same hair, the same body, but inside? No way of knowing. No way of reaching her. A scared old lady in a hospital gown clutching at sheets. No sign she recognised her only child. Why did I leave her? She never left me. 'Where's your mother?' she'd said once, when she was back at home, supposedly getting better. 'Don't worry, they're only words,' she added, when she saw my face.

'I cared for my mother when she had Alzheimer's,' the voice continued, 'so I know what it's like. But I must say –' we stopped at the lights and the driver turned to face me – 'I didn't notice anything wrong with your mum yesterday when I drove her. She must be in the early stages. They can be so good at hiding it.'

I nodded. I was working on what to say to Laura. I'd kneel by her bed and, before she could say anything, I'd say 'Laura, I love you. I always have and I always will. I know I wasn't always the best husband for you. I was too jealous. Too controlling. I've realised what it feels like to lose you and I never, ever want to do it again. I'll change in whatever way you want me to change. I don't care if you slept with Ford or not. It's not important. Just please don't divorce me. Give me another chance. I've spent so much of the last two years, so much of my life, unsure of what I wanted but there's one thing I know for sure. I can't live without you.' This speech looped round my head again and again.

'I'm here to see Laura Ferguson,' I said, when I'd at last been directed to the private ward. Mum was over sixty when she had her stroke. Laura was only thirty-nine. It had to be less serious.

'Are you a relative?' the nurse said.

'Yes,' I said. 'I'm her husband.'

'That can't be,' she said. 'Ms Ferguson's husband is here already.'

I swallowed. 'There must be some mistake,' I said. 'She'll recognise me if you take me to her.' The nurse looked doubtful. 'Please. If she doesn't want me to stay, I'll go, I promise.'

The nurse led me to a white heavy door and stopped. I tried not to show the fear that filled my heart. She turned the handle and pushed. I heard laughter before I could see them. Mrs Ferguson was stood by the window, her smile freezing. Zac Ford was leaning back on his chair, eyes closed and snorting. And Laura was lying on a bed, propped up by pillows, gazing lovingly at Ford, red-cheeked, sparkly-eyed and pregnant. Unmistakably happy, and unmistakably pregnant.

The room was full of silence. The silence of laughter cut short.

'Fuck,' said Laura.

'This man said he was your husband,' the nurse said.

'He was,' Laura said.

The nurse left. The door followed her slowly, hushing, till a soft click told me I was alone with them. I'd imagined so many kinds of reunion with Laura. Tearful embraces. Romantic kisses. Angry shouts. Cold rejection. I'd never imagined this. Being a ghost at a family feast.

'Look at his face,' Zac chuckled. 'Did you not know? Did Laura not tell you? Oh, Laura, you are priceless.'

'Is this your doing, Mum?' Laura said.

'No,' Mrs Ferguson said, still staring at me. 'No, I promise.'

'Because it's a pretty shitty trick to pull,' Laura said.

'It's not her,' I said. 'She told me you didn't want to see me. I thought that was just because she doesn't like me. I didn't realise ...' I turned to leave.

'Jack, wait,' Laura said. I stopped, the door half open, still half hoping. 'Don't be a stranger.'

And that, dear Laura, is a fitting end to this diary. I know, I know – Zac was just picking up a mobile phone that he'd left at the hospital, you weren't pregnant, you just had a strange stomach infection, and you weren't really happy, you were just posing for a photo. Don't bother – I've heard it all before. I won't be answering your emails or phone calls. I'm going away for good this time.

[I can't believe you mean that. I am going to explain everything, but I have to go back a few steps. I am pregnant and Zac is the father. We didn't use protection because I thought I couldn't have a baby – that's what the doctors said, as you know. In Istanbul I had a dizzy spell, but I thought it was just the heat. The next morning I was sick so, when Zac was having a siesta I left the hotel and wandered the streets till I found a pharmacy.

Do you remember the last time we did one of those tests? You lifting me up in the air? Me shrieking at you to be careful? That's what I was thinking of alone on the bathroom floor with Zac snoring next door. That and the horrible drive we had back from the hospital with the empty baby seat in the back.

What am I supposed to do? I didn't choose to have a baby with Zac. I wish I'd had a baby with you, but this could be my last chance. I'm sorry I didn't tell you earlier. I was going to, but I wanted to see you so much and I thought you might not come if I told you. Besides, there have been so many false alarms before, I thought I wouldn't jinx it. I still can't believe it's going to happen.

Guess what Zac said when I told him? He said he loved kids, but wasn't sure he could commit as 'the pram in the hall is the enemy of the artist'. Even when he's being a shit, he does it a phony way.

So I moved in with Mum. She nagged me all the time to be careful, which made me do the opposite. I was up a ladder, trying to paint over the stars on my bedroom ceiling, when I felt a tight cramp in my stomach and something cold and wet in my knickers. I put my hand in and there was blood on my finger.

In the taxi on the way to the hospital, my phone blacked out. I never got a chance to charge it. That's why I didn't get your phone calls when you came back to London. And I wanted to talk to you so badly. It was just like last time. The contractions. The bleeding. I kept thinking of the little grey sack that splashed into the loo. It was you that had to pick it out and put it in a Tupperware box. I couldn't touch it. I kept wondering – if it happens again, will I have to look at it?

'We won't know for a few hours,' the doctor said. 'We'll keep you in overnight, to be safe.'

'Will you be here?' I asked.

'I'll be around,' the doctor said.

'Promise me,' I said. 'Promise me you won't leave the hospital.'

'I promise.'

He left and it was just Mum and me for five minutes that felt like five hours.

'This is terrible,' Mum said. 'I can't bear this. How long are they going to keep us waiting? I'm going to find that doctor. He should be here in this room right now.'

When the doctor reappeared, he looked serious. I couldn't believe it was happening again. And this time it was my fault.

'No,' I said. 'Please.'

'The baby's alive,' he said. Mum swooned and I yelled. 'But you need to be very careful from now on. You've had a lucky escape.'

Mum was still smiling when the doctor left. I'd not seen her look so happy for years. 'He's wonderful,' she said. 'I think I'm in love with him.'

'Me too,' I said. 'Come here, Mum,' I said, 'and give me a hug.'

She leaned over the bed and for a few seconds I felt nothing but love for her. She has her faults, but she does care. Of course I had no idea what she was plotting.

The next day she appeared with armfuls of flowers.

'Why did you bring the flowers, Mum?' I said. 'I'm being released today. You could have just left them at home.'

'I just thought they'd brighten up the room,' she said with a sparkle in her eyes. She took the chair by the window.

'Why don't you sit in the chair next to the bed?' I said. 'Rather than all the way over there.'

'Oh, I thought I'd look at the view,' she said, standing up to look out of the window.

'It's only a car park.'

The door opened and Mum stood up. It was the nurse, coming to check my blood pressure. Mum sat down with a disappointed expression and looked at her watch.

'Have you got somewhere to go?' I said.

'No, no, dear.' She smiled archly. 'Just checking I had the right time. The doctor told me visiting hours are ten to twelve.'

'Well,' I said, 'it's just after ten now so there's plenty of time.'

I tried to talk to her, to reassure her that the worry was over and the baby was healthy, but she seemed distracted. She kept standing up to look out of the window. At 10.30 the door opened and Zac walked in.

'Hello,' Mum said, smiling. 'I'm just going out for a cigarette. I'll leave you two alone.'

'You don't look very pleased to see me,' Zac said.

'I'm just surprised,' I said.

'Really?' he said. 'Your mother told me you've been asking for me all night.'

'Did she? Well, you're here now so you might as well sit down.'

'OK,' he said, picking a strand of grapes from my bowl.

271

'So, you're OK then?' he said, crossing his legs and looking at the ceiling.

'Yes,' I said. 'It was a scary moment, but the baby's still healthy and I'm fine. They're just keeping me here for observation . . .' I stopped because Zac was leaning forward and twisting his shoe round to look at the sole. 'Am I boring you?'

'No, no,' he said, giving me a quick guilty look.

'Why are you here?'

'Well, your mum told me you were sick and you might lose the baby. She said you needed me by your side.'

'It's OK,' I said, 'I'm fine now. Don't feel like you have to stay.'

'No, it's cool,' he said.

I said nothing. Zac hummed. After a few minutes he got up and said he was going for a 'wander'.

'Where's he gone?' Mum said, when she came back in.

'For a wander,' I said.

'Still,' she said. 'It was nice of him to come, wasn't it?'

Zac came back in, out of breath. He looked anxious. I thought there might be bad news from the doctor.

'There's paparazzi here,' he said in a low voice.

'What?' I said.

'I went out to the car park and this guy tried to photograph me. Luckily I got him to delete it.'

'You got him to delete it?'

'I know. I had to grab the camera.'

I burst out laughing. 'Tell me, Zac. Who in the world is going to be remotely interested in the fact that you've visited a hospital?'

'The press.'

'The press? Rubbish. It was just some random guy, minding his own business, trying to photograph the hospital where his child was born and you got in the way of his picture.' I could see from Zac's expression that he hadn't thought of this and I laughed. 'The poor man! He must have thought he was being mugged!'

That's what I was laughing about when you walked in. If I was happy, it was because I was still on a high that I hadn't lost the baby. I'd forgotten that you were back in London and I was shocked to see you in the hospital. I said 'fuck' because I was annoyed with myself for not calling you. I could see, from your expression, that you were anxious and I guessed you'd probably called me lots of times. I wasn't saying 'fuck' because I was unhappy to see you.

I don't know why I said you 'were' my husband. It must have been the shock. Or maybe it was the fact you looked so different. The more I think about how thin and pale you looked, the more worried I am.

When I said to Mum that she'd pulled a shitty trick, I meant that she'd pulled a shitty trick on you, not on me. I thought she'd planned it so that you'd walk in on me and Zac together and jump to the wrong conclusions. I see now it wasn't her fault.

I feel bad about the stupid joke at the end. 'Don't be a stranger' is what the wife says in *Don't Look Back in Anger* when the husband leaves. Don't you remember? We had an argument about what it meant.

When you left the room I shouted for you. I looked for my phone, but the battery was still dead and I didn't have a charger. I tried to run after you but when I stood up, I had a head rush and had to sit down. By the time I got past Mum and out of the door, you were gone. I came back to the bed to rest and when I closed my eyes for a moment Mum had slipped out and left me with Zac.

'I suppose,' Zac said, 'we could give it a go.'

'What do you mean?'

'You and me,' he said, 'living together. I mean, not forever,' he added quickly, 'because I don't think either of us believe in the whole till-death-do-us-part thing.'

'You know what, Zac? You're even stupider than you look. Why don't you understand that I don't want to live with you? I didn't leave because you were cheating on me. I left because I don't respect you. I don't respect your work or your intellect or your character. Don't get me wrong. You're not the worst man I've ever met. You're generous and you're kind of fun to be with and you're not a completely bad person, but you're also vain and self-obsessed and, frankly, a bit stupid. That man who left here earlier, that fine man whom you so gracelessly laughed at, is a hundred times a better person than you will ever be. I'd rather be a single mother than be with you. I don't want you involved, in any way, with my child who, by the way, since you haven't asked, is going to be a boy. Seeing as you obviously have no interest in being a father, I'd say it was a pretty ideal arrangement. So piss off and take your flowers, and don't answer my mother's calls.'

So, as you can see, it wasn't how it looked. I don't love Zac and I have no intention of seeing him any more than I have to. I'm not asking you to be a father to my child. I just want to see you. I thought you weren't replying to my messages because you were angry with me, but is that not the real reason? Are you sick again, Jack? Is that it? I know you think your mother was heroic, hiding her illness so you'd still go to university, but I don't want you to be a hero, Jack. Besides, you're not saving me from worrying. Being cut off from you, unable to help, knowing you may be ill, I worry more than ever. Even if you don't want to see me, please let me know you're OK.]

Dear Laura,

I'm sorry it's taken me so long to reply. I've enjoyed
reading your comments. They remind me of you – funny
and clever and not entirely honest. I'm impressed, and
even quite touched, that you figured out about my scare.
I did delete some passages from the diary so as not to
worry you. It was just a cough but, with my history, I
thought I should check it out. I was going to tell you
about it when we met, but it seemed like you had enough
going on.

Anyway, it turns out there was nothing to worry about.
There was a shadow on the X-ray, but Dr Kumar says it's
benign. In fact, it's so small and so unthreatening they're
wondering whether they should even treat it, or just leave it
and monitor it.

But I can't pretend that was the only reason I didn't reply
to your messages. I was hurt and angry at what I saw in
the hospital. I've read your explanation and it's all very
neat and plausible. There's just a few things you've missed.
Like why did you say, in your article about Ford, that the
first time you met him was at Great Ormond Street? You
always told me it was at my book launch. And have you
forgotten telling me, on our sofa, how Ford was painting
a second portrait of you? That doesn't really fit with your
story about what happened after Zac's tantrum, does it?

You were so outraged by his making a pass you went back for a second portrait! And would Julian, the Establishment man always in Savile Row suits, really wear a Paul Smith cardigan? And why would you risk your marriage to go to New York because that someone you knew was a liar promised you a job there? And why did you tell Zac you 'left' him because you didn't respect him? Can you leave someone you're not living with or even going out with? And why did Marika think you were living at Zac's flat?

I'd really like to believe every square-bracketed word but do you know how often I've had patients tell me stories like these about their unfaithful spouses, desperate for them to be true?

Shall I have a guess at what really happened? You met Ford long before my book launch. You thought he was exciting – a change from your boring married life of pub quizzes and feeding the ducks. You didn't tell me you were meeting him because you knew I'd be suspicious.

Then, one day, he invites you to New York for a dirty weekend. You're hesitant. Maybe you haven't slept with him yet. Or maybe you have 'very, very occasionally', but even for you a trip to New York is a bit too much. So he gets his pet hack to plant a story in the newspapers about how I'm sleeping with my patient. This drives you into his arms where you happily stay, fucking your way around the world, until you get pregnant. Suddenly, he loses interest and you realise you're going to be all alone with this child. At this point, the boring husband doesn't seem so bad. So, for the first time in nearly two years, you call him and lead him to believe you miss him. Only he spoils it by turning up earlier than you expected, before the lover's out of the way. Did I get it right?

I'm sorry, but I won't be your fallback husband, and I won't bring up your lover's child.

Goodbye,
Jack

Fuck you! I'm not asking you to bring up my child. I'll do it fine by myself. I was just worried about you. I don't care whether you believe me or not.

You're nowhere near right, by the way. I did go to New York with Julian. I don't know why he had a Paul Smith cardigan – maybe when his wife buys him expensive designer clothes he actually wears them. I may have underplayed my relationship with Zac a little but the essence was true. Besides, admit it, you haven't told me everything about Claudia.

Laura Ferguson
Sent: 17 April 2011 13:15
To: Jack Randall
Subject: Re: Call me!

My dear Jack,

I know you still don't want to speak to me, but I'm not going to give up. I'm going to keep writing and phoning and texting until you let me see you.

I went to the marathon today to cheer on Nina. I was hoping I might see you there, but Mark said he hadn't heard from you since you met him in the pub. I nearly cried seeing all those strangers cheering on strangers. I wonder if there's another marathon in the world where people wear such ill-suited outfits. There's something very British about running twenty-four miles dressed as a giant beer bottle or a camel jockey, don't you think? My favourite was the chicken and egg that ran side by side.

Speaking of which, does it really matter who first left whom, or who slept with whom when? In that letter you never sent me you said the past was everything. It's not. The present is what matters most. And right now, we need each other. If you weren't so damned proud, you'd admit that.

The nurses at the hospital keep asking me who my 'birth partner' will be. It certainly isn't going to be Zac, whom I'm not talking to. I can't ask Andrea, or any of my friends, as I need someone who can be available at a moment's notice. Please, please, please don't make me ask Mum. I want it to be you.

And, whether or not you'll be my birth partner, let me come to your next appointment with the doctor. It doesn't have to mean you've forgiven me, or we're back together or any of that, if you don't want. Just think of it as two old friends side by side, cheering each other on through life's marathon.

Lots of love,
Laura

From: Laura Ferguson
Sent: 29 April 2011 17.03
To: Jack Randall
Subject: Re: Call me!

Jack,

I meant it when I said I wasn't going to give up. If you don't reply, I'm going to start writing something I'll call *The Shepherd's Bush Diaries* full of lurid descriptions of the unsatisfactory sex I had with Zac Ford.

By the way, did you watch the royal wedding today? I kept thinking of that joke in *Private Eye* you used to like, where they tell stories about the Royal Family, but leave out the fact they're royal. You know – 'old man goes to hospital' or 'young man gets drunk in nightclub'. Today it was 'couple who met at university get married'. Take away the silly outfits and the millions of people and that could have been us. Not just your bald spot, but that sweet muffled smile before you said 'I do'.

By the way, I put a stop to the divorce. Did you notice? Please write soon or I may change my mind and start looking around for eligible dentists.

Laura

From: Jack Randall
Sent: 29 April 2011 17.16
To: Laura Randall
Subject: Re: Call me!

Oh, Laura,

Please stop sending me your jokey emails. I hate the way
you laugh at everything. It makes me laugh too and then I
forget that I'm angry with you. And I am very, very angry
– so angry I can't quite remember why. I do remember, in
fact, I do. You cheated on me and lied to me and still you
cover it up with your blurry excuses. And that matters.
It's not just a chicken and egg argument. As you yourself
said, 'There's quite an important difference between
what happened and what didn't.' Your affair happened.
Mine didn't.

But you're right about one thing – I do miss you. And
you may be a liar and you may have broken my heart but
somehow I still think you're pretty cool and I'm still glad
you came knocking on my door twenty years ago.

So that deal you offered, I'm up for it, if you are – just
two old friends cheering each other on. It doesn't mean
I've forgiven you but, no matter how angry I am, I can't
bear the thought of your going through childbirth
with only your mother for company. That would be
too cruel.

And I want you by my side when I see Dr Kumar. I'm not
too proud to admit it.

So meet me at 9 a.m. tomorrow outside the Royal Marsden. I'll be dressed as a camel jockey.

All my love,
Jack

Part 2

Dear Michael,

   You'll have read, by now, some emails Mum and I sent each other before you were born and the diary I wrote in Strasbourg with all her catty comments. I didn't want you to see all of this, as it doesn't show Mum or me in our best light, but she prevailed, as she always does.

   You must be wondering now whether I'm really your dad. Let me finish the story and you'll understand.

   Mum met me, as she'd promised, outside the Royal Marsden. She was paler than I'd ever seen her and her cheeks had filled out. She looked anxious as she smiled and waved at me. A taxi nudged her onto the pavement and we had to wait for the traffic to clear before we could embrace. We talked about the present – how we each looked and where the appointment was and whether we were late – and I wondered if we'd ever be able to talk about the past. I was glad to have her in the room beside me – clenching her fists and leaning forward in her chair, sighing and gulping, smiling and crying and hugging me. It gave meaning to Dr Kumar's lifeless words.

Afterwards, we walked in Hyde Park, among the besuited sandwich eaters and the joggers and the headphoned sunbathers, talking, but not really talking, about you. What Laura wanted to ask, but never did, was whether I could love a child that wasn't mine. What I tried to hint at, but wasn't sure I meant, was that I could.

To be your mother's 'birth partner', I needed a car, a car seat and an empty diary. On eBay I found a Ford Escort Ghia with a 'buy it now' price of £250. I met chris1956 in a petrol station in Uxbridge. His handshake was awkward, as if he'd never done it before. He looked around a lot, as if we were being watched. From a pocket of his half-unzipped bomber jacket he pulled out a thistle of keys. We took the car for a test drive. Chris held onto the armrest and smiled nervously whenever I looked at him.

I paid in cash and drove to John Lewis. The sales assistant told me the baby would need a pushchair and a carrycot, as well as a car seat, so I might as well get a package with all three, on sale for only £800. When I got back to the car, the box was too big for the boot. I took out the car seat, but I couldn't get the buggy in – it didn't want to bend in the ways I wanted it to bend. I leaned on it, walked round and leaned on it again. The instructions bore no relation to the thing I was looking at. I tried pushing harder and it made a straining noise. I looked helplessly at the passers-by, but no one stopped. Stressed and sweating, I made the buggy stoop down low enough to force the boot closed.

I parked outside your grandmother's house, rang Mum and told her to come out as I had a surprise for her. A few minutes later, she was standing on the top step looking in both directions. The handrail to the stairs was wrapped in

Union Jack bunting. The wind tugged at her wispy black maternity dress and she was biting her lips and rubbing herself, with crossed forearms. I honked the horn and she looked towards me and her face fell.

'Is this some kind of joke?' she said, as she walked gingerly down the steps.

'What?' I said.

'Tell me you didn't pay for this car. Tell me they paid you to take it.'

'I paid £200. A bargain. It's so I can drive you to the hospital.'

'I'm not setting foot in that.'

'It's fine. It's got an MOT and everything.'

'This isn't funny, Jack. I'm shit-scared about another miscarriage.' Her voice wavered. 'I put my trust in you and you turn up in some crappy car that looks like it's going to fall apart. Oh, Jack ...' She was beginning to cry.

'I'm sorry,' I said. 'I can't afford a better car. I just spent the last of my savings today.'

'We could have just asked my dad.'

'I'm not taking money off him.'

'Oh come on!' she said. 'What's more important? The baby or your pride?'

'The baby will be fine in this car.'

'I'm not getting in it,' she said.

At 10 a.m., I was sitting on Adam's sofa, staring at the blank TV, when I got a call from Mum.

'It's happening,' she said.

'What? But you're not due for another month.'

'I fucking know that,' she said. 'I'm in a taxi. Meet me at Queen Charlotte's.'

The phone went silent for several seconds, and then the

call died. My car keys weren't in the pockets of my jeans. I dodged around the room, looking in the same places two or three times and cursing myself. I found the keys on the floor of the cupboard and raced out.

The engine whined and tried to go back to sleep. On the third attempt, with a dig of the accelerator, the car lurched forward. The lights turned red just as the car spurted forward. As I screeched round to the right, I found myself leaning against the window, as if I were on a motorbike. I drove past the hospital, further and further, looking for somewhere to park. I was thinking of abandoning the car in the middle of the road when I found a space looking out across a field towards a smudge of buildings.

I ran across the field. The hospital was only a few hundred feet away, but a wire fence blocked my path, so I had to run round the whole building. I was heaving for breath when the sliding doors opened.

'My wife,' I said to the receptionist. 'Laura Randall. She's just come. She's eight months pregnant. Where is she?'

'Slow down, dear,' said an elderly woman with a soothing voice. 'What's your name?'

'Jack Randall.'

'And your partner's name?'

'Laura Randall. Or maybe Ferguson. Laura Ferguson.' She looked at me quizzically. 'Maiden name,' I added.

'I'll just check if she's here.' I closed my eyes and rubbed my brow. I could hear tapping on a keyboard. 'Yes, dear, she's in the delivery ward. Upstairs. Follow the blue arrows on the floor ... Don't run!'

I shuffle-jogged past half-empty waiting rooms, past closed coffee shops, up silver lifts and along white corridors until I reached the delivery ward. A sleepy woman, with one eye that wouldn't move, greeted me in a bored voice.

She responded to my panting explanations by handing me a sheaf of forms and a biro. Only when I'd copied my name and address on three separate pieces of paper, was I told I could go through to her room. It was as empty and bare as a prison cell – just a bed and a mat on the floor, and a large blue ball in a corner. I ran back.

'The nurse will come soon,' she said.

'No, no,' I said. 'That's not it. My wife's not there. She's not in the room you sent me to.' From the other end of the corridor came a cry of pain of lunatic intensity. 'Oh God,' I said. 'Have you seen her? Please tell me where she is.'

'Sorry. Can't help you,' she said. 'My shift's just started. Maybe your partner's gone to the operating theatre.'

'Where's that?'

'I don't think you'd be allowed,' she said.

'I'm her husband, for God's sake!'

'Well, I'll see what I can do. You wait here.'

She left and I was alone. The large plain clock on the wall shuddered its way from minute to minute, but no one came. The door to the delivery rooms was locked so I could only pace around and around the reception. I tried to call Adam but my phone had no signal. I shouted but no one came. The passing of time was agony. I could feel a panic attack rising up within me. I closed my eyes and I prayed – Oh God, please let Laura be all right.

'Mr Randall?' A thin, red-haired woman in a nurse's coat with a silver watch dangling from the pocket was standing in the doorway.

'Yes,' I said.

'Come this way,' she said. 'You'll have to be quick,' she added, and handed me a white coat. 'Put this on.'

'Thank you,' I said. 'Thank you so much. How's Laura? Have you seen her?'

'Yes,' she said. 'I've just come back from them. Don't be surprised if she can't talk to you.'

'Why not?' I said, trying to catch her eye as she paced ahead of me.

'She's been given a lot of medication. The doctor will explain.'

'But is she going to be OK?'

'Oh yes,' she said, stabbing the lift button. 'I'd have thought so.'

'And the baby?'

She waited for the doors to open. 'It's too early to be sure. But birth at thirty-six weeks is not that unusual.'

'You mean the baby's coming out today?'

'Oh yes,' she said, as the doors closed. 'It'll have to.'

As I got out, I saw your mother on a trolley bed at the other end of the corridor outside another lift.

'Don't run, Mr Randall!' the nurse called after me.

I caught up with Mum before the lift opened. Her eyes were closed. She was connected by a corset and wires to a beige machine. Standing next to her was a tall man in a shower cap and pale blue toga and a short Filipina woman who smiled at me.

'What's going on?' I asked.

'We're going into theatre,' the tall man said. 'The waters have broken, there's a risk of infection and the baby's heart rate is low,' the man said. 'It needs to come out.'

My phone rang.

'Turn that off,' the doctor said, before turning to the nurse. 'Heart rate?'

The Filipina woman pointed to the '102' in red digits on the screen of the beige machine. The number changed to 100 and then back to 102.

'What should it be?' I asked.

'At least 110,' he said.

'What's that?' I asked, pointing at the graph paper the machine was producing. A stylus drew a spiking line of peaks and troughs and the machine made a scraping sound, like windscreen wipers.

'That's measuring the contractions.'

'Is it going to be OK?' I asked.

'We're doing everything we can,' the man replied.

In the lift there was a forced, encapsulated calm, but when the door opened they rushed out. Laura's bed crashed into the wall.

'Be careful,' barked the tall man.

I followed a few steps behind as the hulking bed, with its tangle of drips and wires, sledded down the corridor, bumping against the walls and jolting Laura's head from side to side. Swinging double doors let us into the operating theatre – a tense space of spotlights and cold metal. I took a stool near Mum's head and whispered in her ear that everything was going to be OK.

A hushed conversation went on behind me.

'When will it be ready?'

'Fifteen minutes.'

'That's too long.'

'What about forceps?'

'We could try it.'

'It doesn't look good, does it?'

I looked at the machine and the numbers were falling, from 105, to 100, to 95, to 90, to 80. I prayed again – please God, punish me, don't punish Laura or the baby. They haven't done anything wrong. If someone has to die, let it be me.

'I'm going to have to make a cut,' the doctor said. 'Where's the scalpel?' The doctor was looking around the room. The Filipina woman was washing something up in the sink. 'What are you doing there?' he said angrily. 'Leave that. I need a scalpel now!' 60, 57, 55. Then I heard the noise I'd been dreading – a shrill and constant beep from the beige machine, which now produced a flat line on the graph paper.

'Why's it doing that?' I said. 'What does that noise mean?' There was silence, apart from the mechanical cry of the flat-lining machine. 'Someone answer me,' I said, 'please!' I started coughing.

'Why's he in here?' asked the tall man.

'He's the husband,' replied the redhead.

'Get him out of here!'

'I'll go,' I said, 'just tell me what that noise means.'

'Don't worry,' the red-haired nurse said, 'it just means the monitor needs more paper.' 34, 34, 33.

'That baby needs to come out *now!*' shouted the man.

No one said anything. My eyes were shut as I coughed.

'Baby's coming,' said the Filipina woman.

'Quick!' the man said. 'Is the oxygen ready? The baby's going to need oxygen.'

I held my breath. I could feel another cough welling up. I tried to hold it back but it burst out.

'I told you to get him OUT!' shouted the man. 'He might have an infection.'

I followed the redhead out of the room. When my cough settled, I stood by one of the doors, looking in through the small round window. The man had his head bowed and was frowning. He had long plastic gloves up to his elbows. I couldn't see what his hands were doing. There was blood on your mother's legs. And then I saw it – the sticky, black, bloodied, hairy head of a tiny, tiny thing. You.

You were placed, purple and writhing, onto a towel

under a spotlight. A new man in a white coat had appeared from somewhere and he blocked my view.

'Is the baby going to be all right?' I asked the redhead stood beside me.

'I can't say for sure but there's every reason to be hopeful,' she replied. 'It'll have to stay in the Intensive Care Unit for the rest of today, but you'll be able to visit. A lot of babies are born pre-term and grow up fine. Winston Churchill was born far earlier than your child.'

My child. Should I correct her?

'And Laura?' I said.

'Oh, she'll be fine. She'll probably wake up soon.'

You were being rolled out of the room.

'Where are they taking him?' I asked.

'Probably the ICU.'

'We have to watch him. What if they get him muddled with another baby?'

'Don't worry,' she said, smiling. 'There's a white tag round the ankle, see?'

'I want to see where they're taking him.'

You slept in a Perspex box in a room with glass walls. Your head was the size of a fist and the tube that fed into your mouth was as wide as your arm. You were beautiful though – you had tiny shrivelled hands and feet, red round cheeks, pouting lips and long-lashed eyes. The red-haired nurse smiled at me and left. I stayed in the corridor, leaning my forehead against the thick glass – you looked so frail I didn't want to leave. For the first five or ten minutes, your limbs kept twitching, as if you were being electrocuted. Then you stopped moving and lay, still and pale as a corpse. I called out for help. No one came. I ran up and down the corridors until I found a nurse retreating behind a door marked PRIVATE with a mug of tea. I dragged her back to the glass room. She swiped a card down the door lock and beckoned for me to follow. I held back and said I had a chest infection. She put her hand through a hole in the box and, with one wrinkled finger, she prodded you until you wriggled out from under the shell of sleep.

Your mother was bright-eyed and sitting up in bed when I came back. The red-haired nurse was holding her shoulder and adjusting a pillow.

'Jack,' Mum said, 'I've had a baby!'

'I know,' I said. 'I was there.'

'Were you?' she said. 'That's great!'

'Yeah ... How are you feeling?'

'Great!' she said. 'Brilliant. Never better. How's the baby?'

'Cute and very, very small,' I said.

'That's fantastic,' she said, 'I love small things.'

I searched for the usual irony in her voice but there was none.

'Mother's very tired,' the red-haired nurse cut in. 'She needs to rest. Will Father take a step outside with me?'

'Go on, Father,' your mother said with a smile.

The nurse led me by the elbow and closed the door behind us. 'Take a walk with me,' she said.

'But I want to talk to Laura.'

'Your wife needs to rest,' the nurse said. She pulled my arm again but I resisted. 'She's had a lot of medication,' she continued in a slow and careful voice, as if she were reading a story to a child. 'At the moment it's making her happy. But, if she gets excited, or upset, it could all change very quickly. It's best not to disturb her. Leave it five minutes and you'll find she's gone back to sleep.

When she wakes up, she'll be more like normal, but take it easy. Don't be surprised if she doesn't remember the conversation you've just had.'

Your mother slept like you – silent and deathly still. I pulled a chair beside her and whispered her name. She didn't respond. I whispered a little louder and she moaned. I decided to wait. I was still waiting like this an hour later when I heard the door open and I turned to see your grandmother. I stood up and stepped away from the chair. She brushed past me, without catching my eye, grabbed the chair I'd been sitting on and pulled it closer to your mother.

'Laura!' she said. 'Laura!' she repeated loudly. Mum opened a bleary eye. 'Laura, dear,' she said. 'I'm here. I've been so worried. Why didn't you call me? And where's the baby?' she continued. 'Why isn't he here, with you?'

Mum murmured.

'Is it because you didn't have a natural birth?' said your grandmother.

I said I was going for a walk. There was no reply. I walked to the ICU and I stood in the corridor, looking in on you in your Perspex box. No one else was there. I understood something then. You may not have been my son, but you weren't Ford's or Laura's either. None of us could keep your heart beating. You were on your own, behind a glass wall. I tapped the glass and your eyes opened. With smiles and waves and clownish faces I tried to signal encouragement or sympathy or love, or some such emotion that lies beneath words.

Two days later, the tall doctor said you and Mum could leave.

'Already?' she said. 'I thought you needed to watch him.'

'We have,' he said. 'Everything's normal.'

'I'll drive you,' I said.

'It's OK,' she said, 'I'll take a taxi.'

'No,' I said, 'please let me.'

The radio played 'Don't Panic' by Coldplay, as we drove to your grandmother's house. The chorus I'd once thought hackneyed ('We live in a beautiful world, yeah we do, yeah we do') seemed profound and poetic. I drove as slowly as I could, as I knew this might be our only time together as a family, these few minutes in the metal home of my car. The indicator sobbed as we turned into Colville Terrace and I rolled up outside the house and turned off the ignition. You were sleeping and there was no noise in the car at all. Your mother looked earnest. Her mouth opened and I felt sure she was going to say something important.

'I should go now,' she said.

'OK,' I replied with a cheeriness I didn't feel.

Your mother got out and I rushed to open the back door. I untangled you from your web of belts and held you for a few seconds. You weighed no more than a bag of sugar. Your mother took you and paused by the door. You looked like a bundle of rags on her shoulder.

'Thanks, Jack,' she said.

'No problem,' I said. When she turned, I remembered the buggy. 'Wait, Laura ... I've got a present.'

'What is it?' she said.

I ran back to the boot. The Bugaboo sat up eagerly. 'Ta-da!' I said.

'Oh, Jack!' There was a sad lilt to her voice.

I rolled the buggy past her. 'Beep, beep!' I said. 'Make way! Make way for the king of buggies!' I used the

Bugaboo to nudge the door open and stopped. A large black Victorian pram stood in the hallway.

'I'm sorry,' she said. 'I should have told you – Mum's been keeping it in the cellar since I was a child.'

'It doesn't matter.' The Bugaboo rolled up behind the pram. 'Let me hold him again.' I raised you up to eye level. You were awake now. I said, 'Bye-bye Michael.' Your expression didn't change. You just stared at me with your unblinking sky-blue eyes. I held you up, trying to memorise your face. Your mother played with the door latch. I kept holding you till your mouth soured and you twisted in my hands. I handed you back and Mum took you away. And all the noise and colour and beauty of the world was gone in the gust of a closed door.

That was the moment I swore I'd be your father, if Laura would let me. I have never been happier than in the years we've had together since then. Laura was right – it was my calling. What I've given you, you've given me back, many, many times over. When you have a child, as I hope you will, you'll understand the joy of knowing, every time you open the door, that there's someone who'll come running to hug you, someone who wants nothing more in life than just to be with you. You've been the kindest and most loving son a man could ever have. I'm so proud of how you're growing up.

I'm sorry I haven't told you before that I'm not your 'real' father. I've been dreading the day we'd have that conversation. I'm so worried that you'll feel like I've tricked you or let you down. And it felt like, if I put it in words, it'd give it a substance it does not have. For in the days we live in – from the 'cockadoodadoo' you give us each morning, to the final goodnight hug – I'm as real a father as ever there was.

299

So Laura and I decided we'd tell you when you were eighteen, and old enough to understand the difference between words and the realer things they're supposed to stand for. You and Mum are the only real things in my world. I thought when *Freud and Holmes: The Other Oedipus Complex* was published, I'd achieved something – that even when I was gone something of me would survive. But, in truth, it's just a bundle of paper and glue. To be loved by you and Mum, that's been my real achievement.

So happy birthday, darling boy. Don't feel guilty if you're upset with me. Know that I'll always love you, whatever you say, or think, or do.

Lots of love,
Dad

Dear Michael,

Your father (for that is what Jack will always be) died a few months after he wrote that letter. You were only four years old then so it's not your fault but I find it unbearably sad that you can't remember him. The emails and the diary I've given you cover a period of our lives I wouldn't have chosen, but they're all I've got and they give you some idea of what your dad was like. They should also help explain what he meant to me and what I've lost and why I'm not always the best parent. I'm sorry if it's painful for you to read all of this, but for too long I've had no one I can share my grief with. People all around me go about their lives as if the world hasn't changed, as if it makes no difference that he's gone, and it makes me feel so alone.

Let me tell you something about the four years that the three of us lived together. We rented a flat near Gran with a little help from your grandpa. Jack did chemo and it made him thin and pale and bald. He was tired most of the time. I pretended that nothing had changed and it was just Jack being lazy and not wanting to get out of bed. Jack would play along,

301

smiling wanly at my jokes, still pretending he'd woken up at the same time as me.

When he stopped the chemo, he regained some of his strength. We went for a celebratory walk in Hyde Park. I kept glancing across at him, looking for clues. He was panting and drops of sweat ran through his grey stubble. I was frightened by his giddy walk and the strange white curls on the top of his head. I could feel some hideous, cowardly part of me shrinking from him. He stopped by the pond, reached in his pockets and pulled out a plastic bag. I thought he might be about to throw up but instead he showed me the bread inside.

'To feed the ducks,' he said, as I stared at him. 'At last we can be old people with bags. I certainly look the part.'

I laughed and nestled up to him and held my breath so I wouldn't cry.

We waited, you, me and Jack, for Dr Kumar to read from the piece of paper.

'Good news,' he said. 'You're in remission. You're not out of the woods yet but it's a good sign.'

You and Jack kept pace with one another. When you were only able to crawl and sit up, Jack was too tired to leave the house. You used to lie next to each other on the floor, placing little triangles into little triangle holes and playing your baby games together. When you turned one and started to take your first open-mouthed, tottery steps, Jack was strong enough to walk without losing his breath. You each had curly hair about the same length, and everyone used to say you looked just like him. Jack spent more time with you than I did. I had a part-time job, as a script reader, and Jack was too sick to work. In truth, Jack was a better parent than me. The giant Lego blocks, which I could never think of anything to do with apart from build towers, became flowers, and crabs, and giraffes, and castles, and spiders, and ducks (mostly ducks) with the touch of Jack's imagination. When you started at nursery, Jack would pick you up every day and carry you home on his shoulders. Your first sentence was 'This is my daddy.' I was jealous sometimes, but mostly it made me proud.

Zac came for your second birthday. His present was a book in Waterstones wrapping paper. He offered it to you, but you wouldn't take it.

'Go on,' I said. 'Open it!'

You took it and, with help from Jack, tore off the paper. It was *Tintin in America*. You looked up at me, confused.

'Thanks,' I said to Zac. 'That's great. I'm sure he'll really like that in about four years' time when he can read.'

'I thought,' Zac said, 'it might make him excited about America. For when he comes to visit me.'

Jack stood up.

'America?' I said.

'Yeah, I'm moving to LA. I've bought a condo. I leave next week.' Zac bent down and you dropped your eyes to the floor. 'How about a hug for your dad?' You took a step back and curled an arm round Jack's leg. 'Come on,' said Zac, but you only held Jack closer and refused to look up. 'What's wrong with him?' said Zac, looking at me. 'He was really friendly last time.'

'That was six months ago, Zac.'

Zac sent me the odd email but he never asked us to visit him. I can show you some of his works one day. I was probably rather harsh on him – he does have some talent and he's not as bad a person as he may appear from the pages above. I hope one day you'll meet him again.

When you were learning to talk, the visits to Dr Kumar became less frequent. The signs were never all good or all bad.

Good news was always balanced with a warning not to hope for too much. Bad news was softened by reassurance that we'd found the new cells early so there was every chance they could be treated.

Until one day. We were in our usual positions – Dr Kumar behind his desk, with his pieces of paper lined up side by side in plastic wallets; Jack in a grey plastic chair in front of the desk; and you and I in the row behind. Dr Kumar waited a beat longer than usual for us to settle into our seats. You must have sensed something was wrong because you jumped off my lap and ran forward to put your little hand in Jack's.

'I'm sorry,' Dr Kumar said.

You should be proud of what a kind child you were. Jack said you made him happy every day.

Mum

Acknowledgements

I've wanted to be a novelist for as long as I can remember.
I've been writing, in my holidays and spare time, for the
best part of ten years and it is as much a relief as a joy to
be published. I'd like to thank the people without whom
I never would have got this far. First and foremost, that
is my family: Lika, who's been unfailingly supportive and
tried hard to stifle her Laura-like jealousy [Lika: Rory is
the jealous one, not me]; Mary, who's every bit as kind and
loving a child as Michael; Connie, who's only a few months
old now but a very sweet and smiley baby; my dad, on
whose stoicism, patience and good nature I've relied for
many years; and Mum, whom I owe more than words can
say. My only sadness is that it's now too late to try.

Next I'd like to thank Joel Richardson and Claire
Johnson-Creek, the brilliant editorial team at Twenty7,
who've guided the book to where it now is. I'm particularly
grateful to Joel as he had the vision to make me an
offer even when changes still needed to be made. I was
exceptionally lucky to be represented by Clare Conville

of Conville & Walsh. Clare has always been very kind to me, not least when she brought in Rob Dinsdale to help me. Without Rob's smart and insightful suggestions, I doubt this novel would have been published. I'd never have been taken on by Conville & Walsh if it hadn't been for the help of Jill Dawson and her Gold Dust mentoring scheme. And I'd probably have given up long before then if I hadn't been high-fived by Jim Crace in Totleigh Barton many years ago. Jim taught me more about prose in twenty minutes than I've learned from a life of reading novels. It's a great loss, for everyone other than him, that he's given up writing. I only hope he'll continue teaching on Arvon courses, inspiring people like me.

I'm also grateful to the many friends who've read drafts and offered their thoughts, in particular Ellie James (who's been helpful and encouraging right from the start and gone way beyond the call of duty, always responding promptly with sound advice to my insecure emails), James Roycroft (who could be a great editor if he weren't too busy making huge amounts of money), Mike Palmer, Louisa Copeman, Kate Hannay, John Clarke and Kerry Glencourse.

CHAPTER 1

Tuesday, 12 April 1966

Max Mephisto always dressed carefully for a rendezvous with a woman, even if said female was only two days old. Check suit with the new thinner lapels, white shirt, narrow tie. He paused in the hallway to select a trilby. Men were going out without hats now but Max, although he liked to think of himself as a modernist, could not quite bring himself to do this.

He walked briskly down the stairs, ignoring the lift (he wasn't in his dotage yet). In the entrance hall, light was glowing through the stained glass in the front door and Alf, the concierge, was dozing on his chair. He straightened up to a full salute when he heard Max approaching.

'Good morning, Mr Mephisto.'

'Morning, Alf.' Max was grateful that the man didn't know that he was also known by the frankly ridiculous title of Lord Massingham. He had a feeling that Alf would

enjoy that one far too much. As it was he liked to salute and remind people that he'd been in the Royal Army Ordnance Corps ('The Sugar Stick Brigade').

'It's a lovely one,' said Alf. He gave Max an enquiring look as if to say, 'off somewhere nice?' but Max just responded with a vague smile. He liked to keep his life private and, besides, explaining his errand would involve saying the word 'granddaughter'.

Leaving a plainly disappointed Alf behind him, Max stepped out into the sunshine. He was about to walk towards Kensington High Street in search of a cab when someone shouted, 'Max!'

Max turned. Something about the voice seemed to drag him backwards, through velvet curtains, stage doors, vanishing cabinets and digs that smelt of rain and cigarettes. He had to rub his eyes before he could focus on the figure hurrying towards him: grey hair, threadbare suit, anxious expression.

'Max. Thank God I caught you.'

'Ted?' said Max. 'Ted English?'

Max was proud of himself for remembering the man's real name when it was his stage name that was clamouring to be heard. Ted was another magician. The Great Something. With a pang, Max thought of his old friend Stan Parks, also known as The Great Diablo, dead now for two years.

'I've got to talk to you,' said Ted. 'I've just come up from Brighton.'

By the looks of him, he'd run all the way. But Max was intrigued, despite himself. He had a soft spot for Brighton. He often thought that he and the south coast town had a lot in common: both smart on the outside but with something steelier and less charming lurking backstage. Plus, many of his friends lived there.

'I was just on my way out,' said Max. 'My daughter's had a baby.' There, he'd said it. 'I'm on my way to visit her in the maternity hospital.'

'Ruby Magic's had a baby?' Ted seemed temporarily distracted. Ruby would be pleased that he remembered the name of her TV show.

'Yes. A little girl.' No name yet. Ruby said that she and Dex were still arguing over it.

'Please, Max. Just a few minutes. It's . . . it's a matter of life and death.'

Now Max was definitely interested. He steered Ted past the gawping Alf and into the lift. He didn't look as if he'd manage the stairs. As the iron cage creaked upwards, Max suddenly remembered Ted's stage name.

The Great Deceiver.

DI Bob Willis and WDC Meg Connolly stood outside the seafront house and breathed deeply. Sea air is good for you, Meg's mother always said, but today the exercise was more to do with expelling the stench of death.

'You never really get used to it,' said the DI after a few minutes.

Meg was grateful that the DI acknowledged what they'd just seen. She had been involved in violent cases before. Just last year she had investigated the death of a show-business impresario and had nearly got herself murdered for her pains. She had seen a dead body then but it had been recently deceased. She had never before been in a room where a body had lain for two days. The pathologist, Solomon Carter, thought that Cherry Underwood had been stabbed on Sunday night. It was now Tuesday and she hadn't been missed because there was no show on Monday. But fellow lodgers in the boarding house had noticed the smell and, eventually, the landlady had used her skeleton key. She had fainted, right into the arms of Ida Lupin, strongwoman.

'We need to check everyone who was in the house on Sunday night,' said the DI, still expanding his chest like someone in one of those advertisements on the back pages of the newspaper. *Shamed by your poor physique?*

'Yes,' said Meg. It would be a long job because the boarding house was full of people performing at that week's Old Style Music Hall show on the Palace Pier.

'What was her act again?' asked the DI. Meg knew, from station gossip, that the DI's wife had once been part of a troupe that performed naked tableaux. Perhaps this accounted for his embarrassment when discussing anything theatrical now.

'Magician's assistant,' said Meg. 'The act was called The Great Deceiver.'

DI Willis grunted. Meg thought that it was a noise of disgust but, a few minutes later, he said, 'I once knew a magician called The Great Diablo. Lovely chap.'

'Was he a friend of Max Mephisto's?' asked Meg. This might be a gruesome murder case, but she still couldn't get over her fascination with the famous magician.

'They were good friends once,' said DI Willis. 'Served in the war together. With the super too.'

The fact that Max was a friend of their superintendent, Edgar Stephens, only added to his mystique.

'Do you think Max knew Cherry?' asked Meg.

'He wouldn't be bothered with an act like that,' said the DI. 'Max is a Hollywood star now. He's beyond all this.' He waved at the building behind them, which was certainly looking shabby in the spring sunshine, the wrought-iron balconies leaking rusty tears. 'Come on,' he said, as if Meg had been keeping him waiting. 'Let's go and find out who killed Cheryl.'

'Cherry,' said Meg. It seemed very sad that you could be murdered and still people wouldn't get your name right.

CHAPTER 2

'Have you got anything to drink?' asked Ted.

Max glanced at the clock on the mantelpiece. It was only ten a.m. But he opened his drinks cabinet. It occurred to him that Ted must have taken a very early train from Brighton.

He poured a whisky for Ted, who downed it in one gulp. Max refilled the glass, resisting the temptation to have one himself. Nothing says 'devoted grandfather' like turning up at a maternity hospital smelling of alcohol.

'It's Cherry,' said Ted, after a few seconds. 'She's dead.'

Max waited. He wondered if he was meant to know who Cherry was.

Ted drained his glass. The whisky didn't seem to have had much effect and Max thought he remembered rumours about Ted having a drink problem. It happened to lots of old pros but Max was determined that he wouldn't be one of them. He stopped himself from offering Ted another

drink. He didn't want the magician to drink himself into a stupor. Not without telling his story first.

But Ted suddenly seemed to pull himself together. He said, 'Cherry was my assistant. A good one too. I went to see her in her digs on Sunday morning. Just to go through the act. Well, this morning her landlady telephoned. Cherry's been murdered. Stabbed to death in her bedroom. They've just found her body today.'

'My God,' said Max. 'How terrible.'

'Yes,' said Ted. 'She was a lovely girl. And to think . . .'

He produced a large handkerchief with a flourish, as if he was about to perform a trick, but, instead, blew his nose loudly.

'I'm sorry,' said Max. He remembered when Ethel, who had once worked with him, had been brutally murdered. You become close to your assistants. You travel with them, rehearse with them, perform twice nightly. On stage, you need to be able to communicate without words. That was why Max had worked so well with Ruby.

Ted emerged from his handkerchief and his voice changed, became businesslike.

'You know the head of the Brighton police, don't you?'

'I do,' said Max, suddenly wary.

'I want you to go and see him,' said Ted. 'Everyone will think I did it. Tell him I didn't.'

How do I know that you didn't? Max wanted to say. Instead, he tried for a soothing tone: 'I'm sure the police won't jump to any conclusions . . .'

'Please,' said Ted. 'I didn't do it. She was like a daughter to me.' And he started to cry in earnest into the handkerchief.

Meg's first interview was with the owner of the house, Linda Knight. She wasn't anything like Meg's image of a seaside landlady. She was quite young, for one thing, and rather stylish. Linda had dark hair, cut in a chin-length bob with a heavy fringe, and was wearing a skirt that, if not quite a mini, still ended halfway down her thighs. Meg was conscious that her uniform skirt was slightly too short when she was sitting down and that, as usual, she had a run in her tights. But, thank goodness for tights. Meg still remembered the agony of stockings, the annoyance when a suspender broke, the chance that someone would see an inch of goose-pimpled thigh when you sat down.

'Blimey,' said Linda. 'What a morning. That poor girl.' She had a distinct cockney accent, which made Meg like her even more. Meg knew that her own voice betrayed the fact that she was born and brought up in Whitehawk, one of the poorest areas in Brighton.

'Can you take me through what happened?' said Meg. 'I know it's hard. I'm sorry.'

'That's OK, love,' said Linda, 'it's your job. Shall I ask Annie to bring us some tea?'

Meg had no idea who Annie was – the maid, perhaps – but she was all for the idea of tea. Linda went to the door and shouted downstairs, then came back to sit opposite

Meg, knees neatly together. They were in what Linda called 'the lounge', a room with rather startling red walls. It had probably once been a grand drawing room but now the paintwork was peeling and the marble fireplace had been boarded up and replaced by a three-bar electric heater. Two faded sofas faced a large television set. Only the sea view, displayed in the French windows, was unchanging and magnificent.

'When did you suspect something was wrong?' asked Meg.

'I didn't see Cherry on Monday,' said Linda, 'but that wasn't strange in itself. I thought she was probably rehearsing. She didn't come down to supper but I just thought that she might be out with friends or a boyfriend.'

'Did she have a boyfriend that you knew of?'

'No, but I didn't know her that well. She'd only been here a few days. Some of the others – Bigg and Small, Ida – are regulars. But Cherry hadn't been in the business that long.' Linda dabbed her eyes with a small lace hankie.

'Do you know what Cherry did before becoming a magician's assistant?'

'She said something about working in a shop. She was from up north somewhere. Sorry, I'm not being much help. I try to chat to the guests but I don't want to pry.'

'Let's go back to Monday,' said Meg. 'When did you first start to worry?'

'It was the smell,' said Linda apologetically.

The miasma still pervaded the house, even though

11

Cherry's room was, at this very moment, being cleaned by two stalwarts sent from the police station. The sea breeze, which made the velvet curtains rise like sails, couldn't entirely blow it away.

'I smelt something on Monday night,' said Linda. 'But I thought it was the drains. Sorry, I know that's horrible . . .'

'When did you think it might be something else?'

'This morning the smell was still there. It seemed to be worst on the second floor landing and I thought it was coming from Cherry's room. I knocked and there was no answer. I shouted Cherry's name. There were a few of us gathered there by then. Me, Annie, Ida, Bigg and Small – the double act – Mario Fontana, the singer. Eventually I got my key and opened the door. She was on the floor . . .'

Linda stopped and blinked.

'Take your time,' said Meg.

'There was blood on the bed and on the carpet,' said Linda, 'and the smell . . . I almost fainted. Ida caught me. Mario brought me a glass of water. Then I pulled myself together and telephoned the police.'

The call had come in at eight-thirty. Meg and the DI had been on the doorstep at eight-forty-five. Now, according to the clock on the mantelpiece, it was half past ten.

'Did you telephone anyone else?'

'I rang Cherry's partner, Ted. I thought he might know her next of kin but he said he didn't. Then he rang off. Useless article. Probably drunk.'

Ted English was top of Meg's list of suspects. She asked when Linda last saw Cherry.

'It must have been Sunday lunchtime. I always do a roast. Cherry came to the table but she didn't eat much. She said she had a headache and didn't feel well. She went back to her room before dessert.'

'Did you see her again that day?'

'No. I put out sandwiches and cocoa at six but not everyone comes down for that. And, as Cherry said she was ill . . .'

Solomon Carter thought Cherry had been killed on Sunday night, something about blood clots, room temperature and decomposition of the body. The DI had gone quite green listening to him. Meg asked if Linda had seen anyone strange entering the house.

'No, but people are free to come and go. I don't lock the front door until about midnight. It's not like some lodging houses. I mean, we're not in the fifties now. Things have changed. I'm a modern woman. I don't care who my guests have in their rooms.'

Meg was all for being a modern woman but this liberal attitude was going to make the investigation more difficult.

'Can you make me a list of all your lodgers? Everyone who was here on Sunday and Monday?'

'Okey-dokey,' said Linda. Then, without warning, her face crumbled. 'It's just so awful . . . poor Cherry.'

Annie, entering with the tea, looked accusingly at Meg.

*

'She's beautiful,' said Max.

The baby was still crumpled and cross-looking but, even so, Max thought he could see Ruby's perfect features there. He remembered when his son Rocco was born, finally being allowed onto the ward and seeing Lydia holding him like a Madonna. Max had cried then, for almost the first time since adulthood. Of course, he hadn't been there for Ruby's birth, hadn't even known of her existence until she was twenty and applied to be his assistant. Back to magicians' assistants again. Surreptitiously, Max crossed his fingers to ward off the evil eye.

'Has she got a name yet?'

'Poppy,' said Ruby, reaching out to reclaim her daughter.

'Poppy?'

'Yes. It's nice, isn't it? Goes well with Ruby. Dex wanted Marguerite after his mother. Imagine!'

'Imagine,' said Max. He would have preferred Marguerite. 'How is Dex?' he asked.

'Oh, fine. They don't let fathers in until the next day but he stayed here all night, sleeping in the corridor. He whistled our favourite tune so I'd know he was there. When he saw her, he cried.'

Max felt a wave of fellow-feeling for the man who wasn't quite his son-in-law. Dex Dexter might be divorced with two children but he loved Ruby. If it had been up to him, they would be married by now. He wondered how the nurses had treated Ruby, knowing that she was unmarried and that the father of her baby was a black

DISCOVERING DEBUT AUTHORS
PUTTING DIGITAL FIRST

Twenty7 Books is a brand new imprint, publishing exclusively debut novels from the very best new writers. So whether you're a desperate romantic or a crime fiction fiend, discover the bestselling authors of the future by visiting us online.

twenty7